# TURF WAR

GILLIAN GODDEN

# B
Boldwood

First published in Great Britain in 2025 by Boldwood Books Ltd.

Copyright ©Gillian Godden, 2025

Cover Design by Colin Thomas

Cover Images: Colin Thomas

The moral right of Gillian Godden to be identified as the author of this work has been asserted in accordance with the Copyright, Designs and Patents Act 1988.

All rights reserved. No part of this book may be reproduced in any form or by any electronic or mechanical means, including information storage and retrieval systems, without written permission from the author, except for the use of brief quotations in a book review. This book is a work of fiction and, except in the case of historical fact, any resemblance to actual persons, living or dead, is purely coincidental.

Every effort has been made to obtain the necessary permissions with reference to copyright material, both illustrative and quoted. We apologise for any omissions in this respect and will be pleased to make the appropriate acknowledgements in any future edition.

A CIP catalogue record for this book is available from the British Library.

Paperback ISBN 978-1-83561-479-2

Large Print ISBN 978-1-83561-480-8

Hardback ISBN 978-1-83561-478-5

Ebook ISBN 978-1-83561-481-5

Kindle ISBN 978-1-83561-482-2

Audio CD ISBN 978-1-83561-473-0

MP3 CD ISBN 978-1-83561-474-7

Digital audio download ISBN 978-1-83561-476-1

This book is printed on certified sustainable paper. Boldwood Books is dedicated to putting sustainability at the heart of our business. For more information please visit https://www.boldwoodbooks.com/about-us/sustainability/

Boldwood Books Ltd, 23 Bowerdean Street, London, SW6 3TN

www.boldwoodbooks.com

# 1

## REVELATION DAY

Red faced and flustered, Dante Silva ran through the back door of the pub where he lived with his family. 'Mum!' he shouted up the staircase. 'Mum, are you there?' Hearing the noise and laughter from the bar, he walked towards it, puzzled. Everything seemed normal, but Dante had an uneasy feeling. The telephone call he had received earlier from his mum had sounded urgent, but as he stuck his head around the door that led into the pub, everything looked as it normally did. Except his mum was nowhere to be found.

Dan was about to wave Phyllis down, the barmaid who had worked for them since day one, when he felt a hand on his shoulder. He turned sharply. 'Mum! Oh, God, you made me jump. Is everything all right? What's up?' Relieved at seeing her, Dante smiled, until he noticed Maggie Silva wasn't smiling back. She looked different. Stern even.

Maggie shouted through the door. 'Phyllis, we're going into the staff room and are not to be disturbed, okay?' Walking past Dante, she opened the door to the small room, giving him a strange look as she did so.

The uneasy feeling he'd had before returned. As Dan looked inside the staff room, his eyes opened wide and he stood rooted to the spot. 'Dad! You're home.'

Dan looked at his mum and then at his dad, Alex Silva, before making his way forwards to greet him. 'How come you're home?' He smiled, but Dan was puzzled. This wasn't the happy homecoming he would have expected for his father's return and his gut instinct told him something was wrong. Very wrong. No way should his father even be out of prison yet, and his mother had never mentioned anything about an early release. Where were the 'welcome home' banners? Why weren't they smiling? And more to the point, where was Deana, his older sister? If anyone should have been there to greet their father, it should most definitely have been Deana! 'What's wrong? Where's Deana?' Dan asked nervously.

Stubbing his cigarette out into the ashtray, Alex Silva spied his young son. 'I thought you might be able to enlighten us both on that question. After all, she's not stacking bloody shelves, is she?' Alex's voice was low and sombre as he glared at his young son. 'Let's go upstairs. I feel this is going to be a long night.' Standing up, Alex brushed away imaginary dust from his shirt and walked past Dante and Maggie, leading the way upstairs to their living quarters.

A chill ran down Dan's spine. Alex had already hinted that he knew Deana had lied about her part-time job at a supermarket. Their cover was clearly blown and now all their lies were about to bite them on the arse. He followed his mum and dad in silence, his face burning hot with shame and embarrassment. Once upstairs, he half expected to see Deana sitting there, but she wasn't and her eerie absence gave him a sense of foreboding.

Alex held his hand out towards an armchair for Dan to sit

down while he and Maggie sat on the sofa. Tentatively, Dan sat. His mouth was dry. 'Where's Deana, Dad?' he asked again.

Alex rubbed his hands together and sat back in his seat. 'Deana has been kidnapped, Dante.' Alex let his words sink in slowly as he watched Dan's jaw drop and his face pale. The enormity of his words echoed around the room.

'Kidnapped? By who?' Dan's palms felt sweaty and he rubbed them together to dry them. His heart was pounding in his chest and, out of habit, he adjusted his glasses.

'We don't know who has taken her, but we do have an idea why. Well, now we do anyway. Just what have you been up to you lying, thieving, deceitful scumbag?' Alex threw his hands in the air and shook his head angrily. 'You have caused a turf war, Dan! Everyone dealt on their own patch until you two came along thinking the world was your oyster. What are you, the Cartel? This is serious stuff. People have been killed because dealers are turning on each other. And why? Because two stupid school kids think they can outsmart the professionals. For fuck's sake Dan, I thought you at least had a brain. I need every detail from you. Maggie, pour us all a whisky. I don't care if he's underage. He's acted like a man, so let him drink like a man.' Cocking his head to one side, Alex flashed a sarcastic smile. 'I get the feeling he's going to need more than orange juice to oil those vocal chords.'

Maggie got up, not saying a word, but he could see the disappointment in her eyes. Dante remembered warning Deana of this moment, but he hadn't expected to face the firing squad alone. What had happened to her? The last time he'd seen Deana, she had stormed out of the house and slammed the door behind her, going God knows where. And now? Well, only time would tell if they would see her alive again.

Casting a glance at his mother, Dante felt more ashamed about the lies he had told her. She was a good mother, trying to build them a life and they had abused her trust. They had treated their drug dealing like a game when it was real life, and in real life people got hurt. Would their mum ever forgive them? Probably, but she would never forget.

Alex took a gulp of his drink and smacked his lips as the warm liquid moistened his dry throat. He placed the glass on the coffee table before him, in no mood for games. On the surface he felt like a swan, gliding along and trying to accept the situation he was faced with. But underneath he was in a wild panic. He felt sick when he thought about Deana's fate and who was behind her kidnapping. But although his mind was in turmoil, he couldn't let those thoughts swamp his logical thinking. 'I'm waiting, Dan. It's going to be a long night waiting and wondering if Deana's kidnappers are going to call back, so we might as well use the time listening to your story.'

Dante bowed his head before speaking. 'It all started with the cannabis, Dad. You know the plants that you were keeping at Luke's house?'

'Luke?' Alex's brows furrowed. 'You're in this with Luke? So that's three of you...'

'No, four of us. We've been working for his brother Kev as well.'

Shaking his head, Alex reached over to the table and picked up a packet of cigarettes. 'Kev? That arrogant clown who runs a drug den openly? Shit, this just gets worse.'

Nodding his head, Dante swallowed hard. 'I've just been to visit him in hospital. He was beaten up pretty bad, nearly killed. When I went to his flat... well squat, two well-dressed men were about to murder him...' Dante burst into tears and put his head in his hands. 'I'm sorry Dad. Oh my God, I was only trying to help him. They were going to kill him,' Dante sobbed.

Alex's blood ran cold; he had a gut feeling that he wasn't going to like what Dante said next.

'What did you do, Dante?' he asked tentatively. 'How did you help Kev?'

Snot dripped from Dante's nose and he wiped it away with his sleeve. 'Me and Deana had run into some trouble before when we'd dropped off some drugs so we'd started carrying guns... the ones you kept in the golf bag.' Rubbing his face to dry his eyes, Dante looked up at Alex, who sat there stunned as he listened to his son's confession. 'I had it with me, and when I saw they were going to kill Kev, I shot both of them.' A huge sob left Dante's body as the tears rolled down his face.

Alex turned towards Maggie blankly. Neither of them could believe what their young son had just said. He had murdered two men!

Maggie cleared her throat. 'You murdered two men in self-defence? Where are they? What happened to them? Dan! Stop crying! Where are the bodies of these men?' Gripping Alex's hand tightly, Maggie felt sick to the pit of her stomach. She couldn't believe all of this had gone on under her nose and she'd known nothing about it. Had she really been so blind and wrapped up in herself that she had been gullible and accepted everything her children had told her? Inwardly, she felt she had failed them. Neither of them had come to her with their troubles or outlandish ideas. They had snuck around like thieves in the night and led double lives and she had never noticed any difference in their behaviour. Guilt consumed her. Although none of this was her doing, as the parent, she felt she should have noticed something.

Trying to keep her voice steady, she felt she had to ask an important question. 'Before you answer that Dan, are you and Deana taking drugs?' She glanced at Alex.

Dan shook his head. 'Absolutely not, Mum. We've sold drugs and I've made some too, but no, neither of us have dabbled in it. That kind of addiction doesn't interest me or Deana, I swear.'

Alex laughed out loud. 'That kind of addiction?' he queried, not believing his ears. 'What, you think smoking cannabis is worse than killing two men and dealing drugs to other people? You'd better not have sold any to kids, because if you did I will march you up to the police station myself.'

'Not drugs, no, but I have sold some cheap cigarettes to the kids at school. And no, I don't think it's worse than what I've done, Dad. I'm a murderer. I have your blood in my veins, and maybe I'm more like you than we both realised,' Dan snapped out of frustration. 'I shouldn't have been carrying a gun, I know that, but it seemed like a good idea at the time. I'm sorry. I'm sorry, Mum, Dad. But this isn't all bad news. Me and Deana have bought the pub for you; you're the new anonymous owners. We wanted to pay our own university fees without being a drain on you both, but we also wanted to give you some kind of security... I don't deny the money went to our heads a bit, but we didn't realise we would make so much of it. It was crazy.'

Astonished at his revelation, Alex and Maggie looked at Dan with their mouths open. Alex couldn't believe what he was hearing, let alone make sense of it. 'So, you did all of that for us, Dan?' Alex clapped his hands together in a round of applause. 'You and Deana run around dealing drugs, lying, cheating and now murdering people and all of that was to help your mum and dad, was it? So now we're to blame for your shortcomings, are we? How did you buy the pub? And just how much money are you talking about?' It sounded like a horror movie, but this was reality at its worst.

'We made around three hundred thousand pounds each. That's the four of us, not just me and Deana. We've hidden a lot of the money in a unit. We ran out of places to hide it from Mum...' Dan's face burned with shame, as he heard the words leaving his mouth.

Alex let out a low whistle, his eyes wide with amazement. 'Well, that's a lot of money. I can see now why people have got so upset. But you didn't do any of this for us. Buying this place, however you managed it, only eased your conscience. It made you feel you were doing it for a reason, when in actual fact, it was your egos and arrogance that pushed you on. You thought you were outwitting the professionals and it was all a big joke. You stupid, stupid kids. Greedy, spoilt brats. You disgust me and laying the blame at our feet only makes it worse. Well, I think my first port of call should be the hospital. Only Kev can tell us why he was getting beaten to a pulp and who it was that you murdered on his behalf. Maybe he can shed some light on this.'

'He's too drugged up, Dad. He doesn't know what day of the week it is. And that policeman on the door will interrogate you if you go. He lets me in cos he's used to me, but you just being out of prison...'

Alex's eyes narrowed. 'Why has he got some copper on the door of his room, Dan?'

'I don't know. I presume they want to investigate why he took such a brutal beating and need information.'

'Bollocks!' Alex laughed. 'I'll tell you why they have someone there. The truth is, they already know who Kev is and what he is – a dealer. What they want to know is are the very same people who beat him up going to come back and finish the job! They wouldn't waste police time on Kev around the clock. He isn't worth it. But they think that whatever he knows is going to give them a good lead to a major drug dealer who wants his blood badly.' Alex shook his head disbelievingly. What a bloody can of worms.

'Wait! Wait Alex. We said earlier we would listen and not interrupt, but all we've done is fire questions at him. I want to hear the whole sordid story, because all we have at the moment are pieces of a jigsaw puzzle. It seems we have the worst bits out of the way, so at least the shock factor is gone.' Taking a breath, Maggie stood up and poured herself and Alex another whisky. 'Right then, Dante. I want the whole story. The pair of you really have taken me for a fool, haven't you?' Maggie sighed and exhaustion overwhelmed her.

Alex stood up and wrapped his arms around his wife. 'You're right, we need to listen to Dante's story to see if there are any clues about where Deana might be or who has her. We should get Luke around here, too. Let's all put our heads together and try and work out who might have Deana.' Waving a finger in Dante's face, Alex glared at him threateningly. 'I should be beating you to a pulp, Dan but I need your information and contacts. But be warned, this is far from over. So go on, from the beginning and this time, no interruptions from us.' Alex looked at Maggie. 'Agreed?' Seeing Maggie nod her head, they both sat down as Dan started from the very beginning...

Alex's blood boiled as he listened to Dante recount his and Deana's adventures in the criminal world. Of how they had contacted Alex's old friend John to help them launder their ill-gotten gains and how after Dante had murdered the two men, they had been helped by a mysterious woman who had cleaned the flat of any traces that a gruesome beating and murder had taken place. He couldn't believe his ears. Part of him wanted to shake Dante, but he feared if he started, he wouldn't be able to stop. But the business side of him was intrigued by the way they had achieved it. If he hadn't heard it himself from the horse's mouth, he would say it was all a lie.

A knock at the door brought their conversation to a halt.

Maggie opened the lounge door and saw Phyllis standing there. 'Sorry to interrupt Maggie, but I've locked up and here's the keys. I'll drop the latch on my way out.' Maggie was about to take the keys from Phyllis when Alex suddenly spoke.

'Actually Phyllis, I wonder if I might ask a favour of you. Come in.' Alex beckoned Phyllis into the lounge. Frowning, she noticed Dante's red tear-stained face. This was not the happy union she had expected after Alex's sudden return.

'We've got a spot of trouble, Phyllis. I won't go into details, but I know you're a trusted friend of Maggie's and hopefully my own. A friend of sorts, well more a friend of the kids, has been beaten up badly and is in hospital. The police are standing guard because they think the perpetrators may want to finish the job. I'd like to go and see if he's okay, but if I go and tell the copper on the door my name is Alex Silva, it could cast a cloud... if you know what I mean.'

Instantly, Phyllis's hackles went up. Suspiciously, she spied Alex. 'I understand what you mean about your name, but what is it that you want me to find out? What trouble are you in? It all sounds a bit strange to me, Alex.' Phyllis's huge bulk more or less filled the doorway as she folded her arms defensively. 'Why is a policeman on the door and who do they expect to finish the job? How do I know I'm not in danger? Look, Alex, if you want me to go spying for you then I think I'm entitled to know what's going on, don't you?'

As Alex looked at her, he almost smiled. He had forgotten what a huge woman Phyllis was, and how scary she was.

'Sorry Phyllis, I don't want to put you in a difficult position. The kids have got in with the wrong crowd and I just wanted to make sure they were okay as well as their friend. It's maybe nothing, but I shouldn't involve outsiders. Sorry Phyllis, but desperate times call for desperate measures.' Forlornly, Alex looked at her and held out his hand to shake. 'Still friends, eh?'

Phyllis looked at him sternly and took his hand. 'No, Alex. I'm glad to see you're out of prison unscathed but I am involved now, aren't I? You've asked me to do something without explanation, which tells me it's not above board and you don't trust me, and yet you're happy for me to put my neck on the line for it. I deserve better Mr Silva. Don't you think?'

Shaking her hand, Alex felt like biting his tongue. It had been a stupid idea and he sorely regretted even mentioning it. 'Sorry Phyllis. It was a stupid of me, but as for an explanation. Well, this man is a drug dealer and I just wanted to a chance to speak to him. The kids have befriended him and I don't want them involved any more than they already are.'

Phyllis looked over at Dante and his red face and then saw the worried look on Maggie's. Alex could see she was toying with the idea and thinking over his suggestion. 'I ran my own pub for many years Alex, as you know, and came across all sorts, including plenty of drug dealers. What is it you want to know about this man, exactly?'

Seeing that Phyllis had the bit between her teeth, Alex felt comfortable enough to carry on.

'Only, how he is. I hear he's on a lot of medication so very drowsy, so you would possibly learn nothing. I just wanted to know if he's going to mention Dante or Deana as being his friends and whether they will be dragged into his mess.'

'Are you a drug dealer, Dante?' Phyllis barked across the room towards Dan. 'Is that how you've bought all these new gadgets of yours and your designer trainers? I'm not as ignorant to my surroundings as you think.'

Both Maggie and Alex looked across at Dan and stared at his feet. Even they hadn't realised his trainers were designer.

'I've helped him out sometimes,' Dan confessed.

'Well, at least you're not lying to me. I will think on it and let you know in the morning. No promises mind.' Giving Alex a warning look, she nodded to Maggie and put the pub keys in her hand. Turning, she left the room, walked down the stairs and they all stood in silence as they heard the downstairs door shut behind her.

Maggie let out a huge sigh and sat down on the sofa. 'Why did you ask her that, Alex?' Maggie almost whispered.

'Because I have a feeling that whoever called you could be watching the pub. They will want to know if the police are involved. So we all need to keep our heads down for the moment which means none of us going anywhere near that hospital again. But Phyllis can go in our place which means Dante should be safe. I don't need two kidnapped kids. One is hard enough to trace.'

## 2

### THE COLD LIGHT OF DAY

Bleary eyed, Maggie stretched and yawned in bed. It had been a long night for all of them and between herself and Alex, they had taken it in turns to keep watch out of the window and listen for the mobile to ring. Blinking hard, she saw Alex sitting at the bedroom window and felt a sadness wash over her. She had prayed for his homecoming, but not like this. He had come home to nothing but trouble rather than being able to relax and put his feet up after his time in prison.

'Anything to see love?' she yawned and threw back the duvet.

'Nothing. But I know someone is watching us; I can feel it. Although I have been blinded by that monstrosity of a car outside. Just because a pub has a car park, do people think they can use it whenever they like? It must be one of Mark's mechanic jobs, although why someone with an expensive car like this would let him touch it is beyond me. Come and see.'

Maggie stood beside him and looked out of the window. A smile crossed her face as she looked out at the pink car. 'My God, all it needs now is Lady Penelope. It's like something out of the *Thunderbirds*.' She laughed. 'Come on, I'll put the kettle on. You must be shattered. I know I am and you never even slept while I was on watch.'

'I needed to think about the things Dante told us. I can't believe what they've been up to. It beggars belief, Maggie. I have some leads I need to follow and I think we could find some answers, but we need to do something. God knows where Deana is or what's happening to her, but one thing is for sure, she will be frightened. Although, to be honest Maggie, part of me thinks she's getting what she deserves.' Alex held up his hand to stop Maggie's protective protests. 'You play with fire, Maggie, you're going to get your fingers burnt. They have both strutted around like the Godfather without a care in the world. Did they really believe they could just walk away from it all and that would be the end of it? That kind of money is addictive. They didn't need to take drugs, they were already on a high from the adrenalin of the cash they were making. We need to be vigilant in the pub. You never know who might walk in and we're an open target.' Reaching out to her, he pulled her onto his knee. 'Somehow, we will sort this out. But how and when I just don't know...' Putting his arms around her, he gave her a weak smile of reassurance, but inside Alex felt utterly helpless.

'What are these leads you have? Is there something I can do?'

'Firstly, I need to speak to our old friend, John. Why Dante contacted him, I don't know. I can see his reasoning that John could launder their money and buy this place for them, but I wish they had kept him out of it. Secondly, I need to trace the woman who cleaned Kev's flat and let the kids disappear. That doesn't make sense to me. Why should someone be on their side unless they want something? But Dan said they haven't been in touch and made themselves known. But nobody organises something like that without wanting something in return.'

Maggie reached for the cigarette packet that was on the

windowsill and lit one. 'Want to share?' Seeing Alex nod, she held it to his lips. 'Maybe this woman is a friend of John's and he's been keeping an eye on the kids from afar. He's an old friend; he would do that kind of thing.'

'That's one idea, but why didn't he tell me? Why didn't he come to see me? More to the point, why didn't he do more to stop them? He could even have come and told you! I just don't understand. If it was his kids, I'd have wrung their necks and put a stop to their adventure. But no, he buys the pub for them and takes his commission. This is one big mess and Dante is looking at a double murder charge if it ever gets out. Who were the men that beat Kev up and why? My guess is their little adventure was coming to an end and they had been found out. Now they are paying the price. We're *all* paying the price because the fallout from this isn't going to be pretty. Believe me.'

Maggie's face paled as Alex's words about Dan facing a lifetime in prison sunk into her brain. She felt sick at the thought of it.

'But it was self-defence, Alex. Dan didn't go in there to shoot someone.'

'Dan was carrying a gun, Maggie. You don't carry one unless you're going to shoot someone. And where is the gun now? After everything I've taught them, I can't believe he let that gun out of his sight and didn't get rid of it himself. Someone has it with his DNA all over it, which is hard-core evidence, you know that.' Raising his eyebrows, he shrugged. 'All we can do now is wait and let this nightmare unfold.'

A cold chill ran through Maggie, making her shiver, and she rubbed her arms to warm herself. It felt like someone had walked over her grave. Alex was right, she knew that, but she didn't want to face the ramifications of his chilling words. 'I'll put the kettle on.'

Seeing her reaching for her dressing gown, Alex smiled. 'The good old English tradition of a cup of tea. It makes everything better. Doctors should prescribe it.'

Ignoring his comment, Maggie left the room. Alex looked out of the window while finishing his half of the cigarette. 'Where are you, you bastards?' he muttered to himself. 'And where is my daughter?' Running his hands through his black hair, he stood up and let out a huge sigh. Seeing himself in the mirror as he was leaving the bedroom, he realised he hadn't had a shower or changed his clothes since leaving prison yesterday. He was still wearing the suit he had worn in court and it smelt musty and hung oddly on his frame after the weight he had lost. He shook his head as he looked at the vision before him. He might not be able to do much at the moment, but he could make himself look more respectable and smell a bit sweeter!

\* \* \*

Standing in the doorway of the kitchen in his pyjamas, Dante yawned and glanced around expecting to see his father. His eyes were slightly swollen from all the crying he had done the night before and still stung a little. He glanced at Maggie standing at the stove, the smell of bacon wafting around the kitchen. 'Is it safe to come in?'

Turning from the frying pan, Maggie smiled. 'It is, come and sit down, Dan. Your dad's in the shower.'

Giving her a weak smile, Dante walked into the kitchen and sat down at the table. 'I'm sorry Mum. I'm sorry for everything. I'd give anything to turn back the clock.'

'Well, you can't son, and God knows how many times I've heard that in the past,' Alex boomed as he walked into the kitchen, still towel drying his shoulder-length black hair.

Looking down at the table, Dan glanced at his father from under his lashes. 'You hate me, don't you?' he muttered.

'No, I don't. I don't like you very much for all the deceit and the way you have treated your mother, but you're my son and I'm stuck with you. The same as you're stuck with me. I haven't been a good example and people in glass houses shouldn't throw stones, eh? I've dragged you and Deana around the country living in hell holes while trying to clean up my mess and you stuck by me. So who am I to judge anyone?'

Humbled by his father's words, Dante looked up. 'Thanks Dad.'

'Well, get this down you. Bacon sandwiches all around. We're family, Dan. No matter what, we stick together.' Maggie smiled as she watched the two men in her life tuck into their sandwiches. She knew that Alex had done a lot of thinking overnight and possibly laid most of the blame on himself for the mess they were in now. And she knew most people would agree with that, but Alex had never forced them to do anything they didn't want to.

Hearing a loud banging at the door, Alex stood up quickly and wrapped his dressing gown around him. 'I'll go.'

The worried look on Maggie's face dropped as she heard the voice shouting up at the window. 'God, can he smell bacon or what? It's just Mark, Alex.'

Frowning, Alex listened, and then a broad grin crossed his face as he heard the familiar voice of his friend and neighbour boom up at the window. 'Come on you love birds, up and at 'em. Let me in,' Mark shouted and there was more knocking at the door. Alex went down and opened the door and was greeted by a burst of laughter. 'Nice dressing gown, Alex, not quite your colour though.' Smiling, Alex looked down at himself. He had quickly picked up Maggie's pink towelling dressing gown when he'd got out of the shower.

'You don't fancy me then?' Alex laughed.

'Nah mate, legs too hairy for me. Is that bacon I smell?' Marching past Alex, Mark ran upstairs to join them in the kitchen. 'Mine's with brown sauce, Maggie. Come on Dan, pick up the tea pot. A working man needs a builder's tea in the morning.' As usual, Mark had lightened the mood. His brash, funny ways were enough to make anyone laugh. 'I tell you what though Alex, mate, that pink dressing gown of yours is nothing in comparison to that pink car in your car park. I hope the owner comes back for it soon or my Olivia will want one when she sees it.' Mark laughed again, but Dan flashed a glance at Alex and paled.

Not quite understanding Dan's look, Alex frowned. 'I saw that myself, I thought it was one you were fixing.'

'God no. That car's got this year's number plates so will still be under warranty. God knows when it was put there. It certainly wasn't there yesterday.' Mark laughed and put more sugars in his mug of tea before walking to the window with Alex behind him. As they did, Dante pulled on the back of Alex's dressing gown and mouthed, 'It's Deana's car.' Puzzled, Alex looked out of the window while Mark laughed and joked about it.

'It's exactly the kind of car Deana would have picked for herself,' Mark said, oblivious, taking a bite out of his bacon sandwich. 'But she'd have to do a lot of shelf stacking to be able to afford a car like that,' he added, his mouth full.

Alex looked at Maggie and slowly nodded his head. Without thinking, she put her hands to her mouth to stop the gasp escaping and peered closely out of the window.

'Yes, she would, wouldn't she Dan?' said Maggie.

'Most definitely Mum. That's exactly what Deana would buy if she had that kind of money.' Alex, Maggie and Dante all cast furtive glances at each other as they realised just what an innocent bombshell Mark had dropped. Mentally, Alex realised he was right. He couldn't be sure how or when, but that car had been parked there during the night as a message. Someone was definitely watching them. But Alex couldn't understand it; he had sat vigilantly watching for any kind of movement outside. Surely, he would have seen whoever had parked it. If that was Deana's car, as Dante was indicating, then she must have been driving it before her kidnappers had caught up with her.

'Well, if it's joyriders parking it there after stealing it, the pub CCTV cameras will have picked it up, wouldn't they Mum?' Dan piped up.

Puzzled, Alex looked at Maggie. 'You have CCTV cameras installed now? Why didn't you tell me?'

Alex felt he could have strangled Maggie. He had sat awake all night and yet the pub had cameras installed.

'It must have slipped my mind, Alex. And there's only one out the back and the front and it doesn't point directly into the car park. The brewery put them up before they sold this place,' Maggie stammered, realising her oversight. She had been so wrapped up with Dante's confession and thoughts of Deana, she had forgotten all about the cameras.

'So, what are your plans today, Alex?' Mark boomed. 'Olivia is planning a welcome home party for you. Anything for a party, you know us. You can come and see my new summer house, built it myself I did,' said Mark proudly as he stuck out his chest.

Alex looked at him oddly, and cocked his head to one side. 'You've built a summer house?'

'Yes, it's got a kitchen and everything. Gas hob, wired up to a gas bottle, microwave and sink. It's great for outdoor parties. Saves people traipsing through the house with dirty shoes on.'

Instantly Maggie looked down at Mark's filthy work boots. 'What, like you have in mine?' she laughed.

'Let me get dressed and sorted and I'll meet you at yours to admire your carpentry. As for the party, I want to play it low key. No fuss.' Alex was itching to get rid of Mark now that he knew the pub had cameras. He wanted to see what was on them.

'Too late for that Alex, mate. The banners are already being put up outside as we speak. But I've got a few errands to run first.' Turning to Dan, Mark looked at him closely. 'You off to school today, Dante? You look a bit peaky.'

'No, I think he's coming down with something, Mark,' Maggie lied. 'It's best if he stays at home today. I'll ring the school.'

'Yeah, I'd go back to bed if I was you, Dante. You look like shit.'

Giving him a weak smile, Dan nodded. 'Thanks for that. I think I will.'

'Right, I'm off. Thanks for the sandwich and tea. See you later Alex and leave Maggie alone. Give her time to get her breath back, poor cow. She must be saddle sore by now. Months in prison and all that pent-up passion.' Mark laughed and was about to walk out of the door when he turned and wrapped his arms around Alex and patted him on the back. 'It's good to have you back, mate.' Blushing slightly, he quickly turned and left the room, almost running down the stairs to the door.

'Well, he's pleased to see you, but if Olivia is out there putting banners up, that's your cover blown, Alex. There's no turning back, but at least they're doing it with the best of intentions. So don't complain,' Maggie warned.

'Never mind that... Dan, you never said Deana had a pink car. What the fuck is all that about? She's not exactly a low-key dealer, is she? How much did that cost?'

'She hasn't had it long. Her old one was always breaking down. But she always parked her new one at Luke's house... along with my bike.' Dan looked at his mum. He felt with every word that left his mouth, he dug a deeper hole for himself. Half of him wished he'd been kidnapped so that Deana could sit here facing the stern looks of his parents.

Astonished at this new bit of information, Alex let out a huge sigh. 'You know what, I think we should go and see Luke. After all, my short-lived cover is already blown so I might as well go out. So, you've got a fucking motorbike... do you have a licence? Oh shit, scrap that. How fucking old and sensible have I become? So, you and Deana felt you should branch out and spend a shit load of money hoping no one would wonder where you suddenly got your new wheels from. What colour's your bike? Luminous green? For fuck's sake, I can't believe my ears. Why didn't you just put a big flag up saying: drug dealers live here. You two really didn't care or think about what you were doing, did you? Sometimes, I can't believe you're mine.'

Dante had suddenly had enough of taking all the blame and couldn't help snapping back at his father, 'I'm not as stupid as Deana. I warned her about that car. I warned Deana about everything, but she wouldn't listen. Most of it she did just to impress Kev. She's lovestruck and thinks he can do no wrong. I know we both did it, but it wasn't all my doing so why am I taking all the flack, Dad?'

'Because you're the only one here!' Alex shouted, and before he could stop himself he reached out and slapped Dante across the face hard, sending him sprawling on to the kitchen floor. Shocked, Alex instantly regretted doing it. He had never raised a hand to his children, but all of his pent-up anger and frustration had just bubbled over.

'Alex! Stop it!' Maggie screamed and knelt down beside Dante. 'Are you okay, Dan?' she soothed, while he rubbed the red mark which burned on his cheek. Maggie picked the chair up off the floor and held out a hand to help Dante up. Tears fell down his face, as he tried squaring his jaw. His father's slap had felt like a sledgehammer on his face, almost knocking him senseless. He held on to Maggie to steady himself as he got up and sat back in his chair. 'I suppose I deserved that Dad,' he muttered.

'Sorry son, I shouldn't have done that even though you are right – you do deserve it. But I'm sorry.' Excusing himself, Alex walked out and into the bedroom to get dressed. He could have bitten his hand off for striking his son like that.

As Alex sat in the bedroom contemplating his next move, he could hear the staff coming to work downstairs. It felt strange to him. Prison was a strange institution and he realised he'd forgotten the sounds linked to the daily management of the pub. It all seemed very quiet without doors banging and the sound of keys in locks. The men's chatter as they went about their duties for the day. It was the noise, or rather the lack of it that had kept him awake last night. The silence of being home seemed to overwhelm him and he hadn't realised how much. All prison inmates talked about the transition from prison back to civvy street and some found it so difficult that at the first opportunity they did whatever it took to go back. That was why they had probation officers to see them through this time in between.

Looking at his watch, Alex remembered he had to go to the police station and 'check in' too. He only had a week out of prison to sort this mess out and already he dreaded going back. His mind wandered to the chef he had worked alongside and he hoped he was getting on okay. He had been a kind man, although the prison warder had used him like a pawn in his game. When Alex had discovered that the warder was having drugs brought in by way of the kitchen deliveries, he had tipped off the prison governor in a desperate attempt to get out of prison once he'd heard there was trouble at home. Fortunately, it had worked, and the governor had looked upon him favourably and granted him a week's leave, with the possibility of Alex never having to go back. Mentally, Alex didn't want to think that far ahead for fear of disappointment. There was a chance, even if it was a slim one, that he wouldn't have to go back inside and he was clinging onto that for now.

Hearing the coming and goings downstairs brought Alex out of his thoughts. He knew everyone would be busy and that now was the perfect time to look at the CCTV footage. Going downstairs, he saw Maggie and the bar staff stocking up the shelves. 'Morning everyone, don't mind me. I just want a word with Maggie before I go out.'

Maggie walked toward Alex and was surprised to see Phyllis was hot on her heels. 'Could I have a quick word, Alex?'

'Come into the staff room, Phyllis.'

Once in the staff room, the three of them sat down. 'I'll not mess around Alex. That request last night. It occurred to me that this person I would be visiting, I don't even know what they look like.' Suddenly the door burst open and Dante walked in. 'Sorry, I didn't realise you were in here; I was just looking for Mum.'

Alex looked up and beckoned Dan in. 'Come in and shut the door behind you. Phyllis was just saying that she can't do the favour I mentioned last night, because she doesn't know what the person looks like.' Turning towards Phyllis, Alex apologised again. 'Forget it, Phyllis. I shouldn't have put you in that situation – I'm sorry.'

'Yes, she does,' Dante butted in. 'She knows him.' Everyone stared blankly at Dan.

'How do I know him?' Phyllis snapped indignantly and folded her arms in her usual manner.

Excitedly, Dan felt he finally had something positive to add to the conversation. 'Kev came and worked here as the agency chef.

Do you remember, Phyllis, because I know you liked his rhubarb crumble?' Dan grinned.

'The chef!' they all blurted out together. Amazed, Maggie looked around the table. 'Have I been walking around with my eyes closed or something? You always acted like you didn't know each other. I must be a real bloody mug.'

'I remember the young chef. He was good at his job, I must say. Is that the young man in hospital?' Phyllis asked.

Dante nodded.

Phyllis's eyes lit up with this new snippet of news. 'Well, in that case, I don't see a problem with me popping in the hospital and taking him some grapes. After all, we are work colleagues. Why wouldn't I go and see him?' Phyllis winked at Alex.

Alex shook his head. 'Thanks Phyllis, but I don't want to involve you in our mess. It was stupid of me to ask in the first place. I can't apologise enough Phyllis.'

Spying him cautiously, Phyllis took her usual stance and stood with her large feet apart and her arms folded. 'I've had all night to think Alex, and if you're asking me this, then you really are desperate. And Deana's absence hasn't been mentioned, so I can only assume she's involved, too.' Letting out a huge sigh, she nodded her head when no one answered her. 'If I can help, I will, and hearing a young colleague is in hospital and I've just heard about it won't come as any big surprise to the police. I'm just a nosey old woman visiting. I'm not sure what he'll be able to tell me, but I will help if I can. As for the rest, I'd rather not know unless I have to, then if I am ever questioned, I don't have to lie. Is that fair?'

Humbled by Phyllis's show of friendship, which he knew was more for Maggie than himself, Alex felt himself blush. 'That's more than fair.' Alex held out his hand to shake Phyllis's.

'Right, I'd better get back to work before the boss here

deducts my wages for gossiping. And later on, during visiting time I will just disappear, so don't wonder where I am when I'm not about. It will only spark everyone's curiosity. Okay?'

Alex nodded as Phyllis walked away. Sighing, he looked at Maggie. 'You've got a good friend there, Maggie.' Changing the subject, he narrowed his eyes, remembering the job in hand. 'Where are the monitors for these CCTV cameras the brewery put up?'

Shrugging, Maggie shook her head. 'Like I said, they aren't very good. The brewery doesn't expect big trouble around here as it's mainly a quiet area. Well, it was before we moved in!' she laughed. Seeing the smile return to Alex's face, she pointed her finger to the floor. 'They put the monitors in the cellar but follow me love.'

Alex followed Maggie down to the cellar, shaking his head almost disbelievingly. Why would anyone put a CCTV monitor in the cellar? he thought to himself. It was the most ridiculous thing he'd ever heard. 'What are you supposed to do, Maggie? Keep running down to the cellar to see who's outside?'

'I think they only put the cameras up for insurance purposes. It reduced the rate and the insurance company was happy.'

Once down in the cellar, Maggie pointed to what looked like an old black and white television and stood back. 'We'd have better security if we bought a dog.' She grinned.

Alex stepped forward and looked at the fuzzy black and white screen before him and burst out laughing. 'That's supposed to keep you secure? I swear my great grandmother had something like that to watch the queen's coronation on! I can't see anything. I mean, it's not exactly top-notch security, is it?'

Grinning broadly, Maggie stepped forward to the machine below the television monitor and fiddled with the buttons.

'Rewind it back to about midnight. I'll start from there.'

Sitting down on an empty beer barrel, Alex watched the monitor intently. Apart from people walking past, he couldn't make out faces or if they were male or female. The security cameras were indeed a load of crap! Maggie brought them both a mug of tea into the cold cellar and they peered closely at the snowy looking black and white screen.

'Alex, this is useless. Shouldn't we be doing something more to look for Deana? Anything could be happening to her now. Sitting here isn't doing anyone any favours and we're wasting the short time you have out of prison.'

Ignoring her, Alex peered closely at the screen, trying to make sense of it when suddenly something caught his eye. 'Maggie, go back, that bit there.' Maggie picked up the remote control and rewound the tape. 'Stop!' Alex shouted, looking more intensely at the screen. 'Is that a rescue truck?'

Standing up, Alex pointed to the screen. 'Yeah, it's a rescue truck without its flashing yellow lights. Even the headlights aren't on, which isn't right. And surely around here someone would call Mark to come out as he's cheaper and well known.'

'I don't remember seeing that, Alex. Oh my God, was it my shift to be on lookout? Had I fallen asleep?' Downhearted, Maggie sat down again. She felt almost sick at missing such an important clue.

'It could have been either of us, Maggie, and with no lights and no noise it would have been easy to miss if we'd been in the loo. Shit,' Alex cursed. 'I wish this screen was clearer. Is that Deana's car they're unloading from the truck? I think it is. Bastards! I can't see their faces. Rewind it again,' Alex commanded. After she did as she was told, they both watched the screen, trying to make sense of it. 'I think they're wearing balaclavas, Maggie. Everything is pitch black.'

'You're right. For Christ's sake, how did we miss that?' A cold shiver ran down her spine and she shuddered.

Alex shook his head. 'Never mind that, Maggie. Look, only one of them is getting back into the truck. Where's the other one?' Moving closer, Alex nearly had his nose pressed against the monitor. 'Fuck! The other one must have a car parked further away, maybe down a side street or something.' Suddenly, they saw a flash of headlights as a car drove past the camera. 'I bet that's the other guy,' Alex said slowly. 'We would have just thought it was a car driving past. YC6. That's the only part I can make out of the number plate. I can't even make out the model, the headlights are so bright.' Alex took hold of the remote control and switched the monitor off. Trying to stand after kneeling on the cold cement floor, Alex felt pins and needles in his legs and rubbed them, then rubbed his shoulders. 'Bloody hell, it's freezing down here.'

Raising her eyebrows, Maggie smiled. 'Well, it's to keep the beer cold, love. Come on, let's go upstairs. We've fucked up, Alex. I don't know how we missed that, but we did.'

'Those men were just monkeys, Maggie. Street soldiers without a brain cell between them. Probably got a few hundred quid for doing that without knowing why. The biggest clue will be inside Deana's car, but I can't get into it in broad daylight. Everyone's eyes are on that pink monstrosity. Christ, what was Deana thinking?' Alex shook his head. 'She's a bolshy teenager with money to burn. Well, she's burnt now and I hope wherever she is, it's giving her time to think about her actions.' Seeing the angry glare from Maggie, Alex shook his head. 'Oh, I'm worried too. But she's still alive, Maggie. Someone has gone to a lot of trouble already: ringing you, dumping her car outside. So, my gut instinct says she's not dead. They will contact us again soon. All we can do is wait to hear what they want from us. In the meantime, I need to gather as much information as possible. I'm going to the police station to check in and then I'm going to see Luke. Maybe he can shed some light on this.'

'What about John?' Maggie asked hopefully. 'He's a major boss in the mafia world now, Alex. Wouldn't he be able to help? Maybe he could get the men that work for him to put their ears to the ground in case they hear of anything.'

'I don't want to call in favours yet until I know more. There is nothing I can tell him until we know what these people want. I'll ask for his help when I need it.' Alex had a strange nagging feeling about his old friend John. If John knew anything he would have either told Maggie or been to visit Alex by now, knowing he was already home. So why hadn't he called? The obvious answer was that he didn't know anything. Or he knew too much...

# 3

## THE MYSTERY UNFOLDS

Deana wiped the dried blood from her nose, where she had been punched. She could barely see through the slits of her swollen eyes. She had cried so much and felt dirty and dishevelled, as she paced the small room which, in her mind's eye, would be similar to the cell her father was in. The windows were boarded up and there was no air, only a small vent in the wall. The light bulb hung low from its baton and there was a duvet and a pillow in the corner, and much to Deana's distaste a bucket to use as a toilet. The stark bareness made her shudder with cold, and sitting in the corner, she started to weep again. Her mind wandered to her mother and Dante. What were they doing to find her? She felt very afraid and alone.

As the door opened, Deana stood up with the duvet wrapped around her. Her captors always wore balaclavas when they came in the room so she couldn't see their faces. Now, they rolled a large bottle of water towards her and slid across a plastic carton containing cold baked beans with a wooden spoon and a loaf of bread.

'Who are you? What do you want from me, you weirdos?

Where am I?' Deana shouted. 'Does my mother know I've been kidnapped?' Spit dribbled down the side of her mouth and she could once again feel tears pricking her eyes, but she sniffed hard to fight them back. She had no idea where she was or what they wanted, but she wasn't going to let her captors see her fall apart.

'Dogs always bark when they are afraid little girl. Now shut the fuck up.'

'And yes, your mother knows you're not around, and so does your father!' one of the men sneered, nudging his friend as they laughed.

Pausing for a moment, Deana watched the two big burly men, stood in the doorway. She could see their red lips through the holes in the black balaclavas, smiling and then laughing to show a row of teeth. She frowned. 'My father? My father knows I've been kidnapped?'

'Yes, he's out of prison. Now hand over the bucket.'

Stunned, Deana stared at them both, not knowing whether to believe them or not. Her father – out of prison? 'Well, when he comes here to get me, you will be sorry, believe me. You can laugh now but you will be laughing on the other side of your face when he finds me.'

'And just where is here missy? I don't remember sending him a forwarding address when he was released from prison... and he still hasn't come for you. You're nothing but an uppity bitch who's got too big for her boots. It's time you were brought down a peg or two.'

That couldn't be – could it? But why would they say that if it wasn't true? And if it was true, that her father was out of prison, why hadn't her father come for her? None of it made sense, and she wondered if they were just playing cruel mind games with her. Angrily, she cast a glance at the tin bucket full of urine. Bending down, she picked it up and threw it at her captors. The clattering noise of the bucket echoed around the room as the men held up their hands to shield themselves from the contents. One of the men strode forward angrily and cursed at her. Deana could see his balaclava was wet and his T-shirt was stained with piss. Defiantly, she laughed.

'I'll make you sorry for that, you fucking half breed!' He raised his hand.

Deana's head rocked as she felt the harsh blow across her face, making her stumble and fall backwards, banging her head on the wall. Letting out a loud scream, she trembled when she saw him undoing the zipper on his trousers. She'd feared they would rape her and she curled up into a ball to protect herself. Instead, she felt wet, and peering between her hands covering her face, she could see the man holding his penis and laughing as he urinated over her.

'Come on mate, let's give this bitch a warm bath,' he laughed. The other man joined him and did likewise.

Deana could do nothing to protect herself as she felt the urine wet her hair and face. Covering her mouth, she felt sick and started retching as her tormentors laughed, zipped up their trousers and slammed the door behind them.

Tears rolled down her face and deep sobs wracked her body as she sat with her back against the wall rocking back and forth as the urine seeped through her clothes and dripped from her hair. Rubbing her face on a dry part of her sleeve, she felt utterly miserable and alone. Her face burned where the man's hand had slapped her, and as she touched it gently, she could already feel her cheek swelling. Brushing her wet hair back from her face, she cowered in the corner and wrapped the duvet fully around her for warmth and comfort. 'Dad!' she shouted and wailed to herself. 'Help me, Dad. For God's sake if you're out there, help me.' Her head throbbed with pain and her eyes felt heavy as she closed them and cried herself to sleep, her only escape from this prison.

Raising their balaclavas, the men spat on the floor. 'That fucking bitch. Who does she think she is? She's covered me in piss and shit. Well, from now on, we don't empty that bucket. Let her smell her own shit and piss and live in it,' one of them snarled.

'Stop whining, Billy. Your pride is hurt more than you are. I know she's a pain in the arse, but she's a frightened kid. She's just the bait to bring her dad to roost.'

'I don't give a flying fuck about her or her father. My regular was stormed by a gang waving machine guns and eight of my lads were murdered in that shootout and why? Why I ask you?' Poking his finger hard into his friend's shoulder, he glared at him. 'All because of that fucking bitch and her brother. They were selling to customers without my say so or without me knowing. My fucking turf is my turf, and everyone knows it except her. That fat bastard, Punch, sent his men to my drinking hole, accusing me and the lads of selling cheap meth on his turf when it had been that bitch. So, he put two and two together and made five. Now, my head is on the line. I have to deliver that bitch to Punch to clear our names. They slit Kenny's throat because he laughed and denied their accusations. So, his blood is on that bitch's hands too. Two more days and Punch will be back in town. He can have her and good riddance. I hope he orders a public hanging!' he snarled.

Puzzled, and fed up of Andy's ranting, Billy tried changing the subject. 'Why do they call him Punch?'

'Because his fat wife is called Judy. That's her pet name for him. A wooden doll, with a funny hat and a long red nose, who's been banned because of the domestic violent undertones. Fucking says a lot about his marriage, doesn't it?'

Billy stifled his laughter. He had never known why his boss was called that. Initially, he had thought it was because of his fighting ways. He was always throwing a punch, but not in this case apparently. 'Well, I don't know about you, but I'm gonna get out of these stinking clothes, have a shower and a large drink.' Leaning forward, Billy jokingly sniffed Andy. 'You could do with a shower too. Phew! Come on.'

Andy pulled at his shirt and sniffed it as he followed Billy's lead. 'Bitch,' he muttered to himself. If it was the last thing he did, he'd make that bitch and her brother pay.

\* \* \*

'Alex?' Amazed, Luke stood rooted to the spot with the door wide open. 'My God, it's Marley's ghost. How come you're out of prison?' Without thinking, Luke stepped forward and put his arms around Alex. 'It's good to see you mate, it really is.'

'Is it? It might not be after I've said what I have to say.' Alex walked in and stood in the hallway. Remembering Luke's old disabled mum, he looked around. 'Mum in bed?'

'Yeah, she's having a nap.' Feeling a sense of foreboding, Luke felt he knew why Alex had come.

'Come into the kitchen, Alex, and please, if you're going to shout, we will go down into the basement.'

Nodding, Alex walked into the kitchen and sat down at the table watching Luke put the kettle on.

'Do you have anything stronger?'

'Some whisky in the cabinet. Do you want one of those?'

'Yes please. Just a small one though. I need answers, Luke.'

'Let me get you a drink, Alex, then you can ask what you like.'

Alex patiently waited for Luke to return with the whisky before he made himself a cup of tea. Looking around the familiar kitchen, Alex's mind wandered as he tried to imagine his own kids here. Dante cooking drugs on that stove like he'd told himself and Maggie. Deana bossing Luke and Dan around, while holding meetings about her plans. Even Maggie had sat at the table with Luke's mum having dinner.

'Well Alex, what do you want to know?' Luke asked tentatively as he sat opposite him. 'What's Deana told you?'

Hearing Deana's name, Alex put his elbows on the table and rested his head in his hands. 'Deana's been kidnapped, Luke. I don't know where she is or what's happened to her. As for me, I've got one week's leave out of prison to sort my kids' mess out. So where do I begin Luke?'

Wide eyed, Luke instantly stood up. 'Deana's been kidnapped?' Quickly, he put his hands to his mouth to stop himself from shouting out. 'So that's why she hasn't been in touch. When did this happen? And how do you know? Maybe she's just gone away for a few days.' Luke rambled on until Alex held up his hand to stop him.

'If I knew the answer to your questions Luke she wouldn't still be missing, would she? She would be at home, strutting about and slamming doors. But she isn't. So I need you to shed some light on this.'

'How?'

Gulping back his whisky, Alex put the glass down and smacked his lips.

'To start with, why on earth did you go along with Deana and Dante's plans to deal drugs and worse, cook them? You know the risks, Luke. Christ, when I found you, you had been beaten and left for dead. That is what happens in that world. Dog eat dog and people get killed. Why did you encourage them? Why didn't you tell me?'

Rolling his eyes to the ceiling, Luke let out a long sigh. 'I dunno Alex. It sounded small time in the beginning. Deana demanded your share of the cannabis she knew I had stashed away. It was yours Alex after all,' he reasoned. 'And then, well, then I introduced her to Kev.' Lowering his face to the table, Luke wanted to tell Alex that he had warned them many times, but knew how feeble that would sound.

'Kev?' For a moment, Alex frowned. 'Oh, you mean Kev the clown who is currently in hospital having been beaten to a pulp? Your brother Kev who lives in that opium den of druggies with his mirrored sunglasses?'

Pursing his lips together, Luke nodded. 'Yeah, that's the one.'

Spreading his hands wide, Alex urged Luke to continue. 'So, you introduced them to Kev; what happened then?'

'Well, let's just say Deana's attitude changed. She wanted to impress Kev, show him that she was older than her years.'

Alex shook his head from side to side disbelievingly. 'Are you telling me my daughter fancied that clown? Oh, for fuck's sake, this just gets worse.' Lost for words, Alex pushed his empty glass towards Luke.

Taking the hint, Luke filled it again before he carried on talking. 'Yeah, Deana likes Kev – although God knows what she sees in him. Then Dante dropped the bombshell that he was a chemist who could make all the drugs we wanted. And the money became addictive, Alex. It was crazy! The money was just rolling in, and to be fair, Deana and Dan are good business people. I warned them, of course I did, but Deana, well, you know how strong willed she is. She said she was doing it for the family, for when you got out. And to be honest, from my side of things, it was nice to feel part of a family again, especially when Maggie came around with Sunday lunch and met Mum. And me and Dan got along too. He's lonely Alex; he lives at a pub, surrounded by women all the time and he feels like he doesn't fit in anywhere. So he stayed over a few weekends and I taught him to ride a motorbike. And if I'm honest, I enjoyed it as much as him. I'm stuck here with Mum and Kev does fuck all to help apart from the odd few quid he throws in.' Luke stopped talking as he saw Alex trying to take in everything he'd said. 'Do you want to see the bike? It's out the back...' Luke grinned.

Alex nodded as Luke's words settled over him. As he followed Luke to the garage, it dawned on Alex that not only did Luke feel part of a family, but Alex also suspected he had very deep feelings for Deana and had been spurned for Kev.

As they entered the garage, Alex grinned widely. 'My God, that is beautiful.' Walking up to the black motorbike, he ran his hands along the shiny body work. 'Christ, this is really nice and not too big.' Without thinking, Alex straddled the bike and turned the handles. 'I used to have something very similar to this.'

'Why don't you take it for a spin? You know you want to,' Luke urged. He could see the excitement and sparkle in Alex's eyes as he marvelled at the motorbike.

'I'd love to.' Not able to take the broad grin off his face when Luke handed him the keys, Alex waited for the garage doors to roll up and revved up the bike. Luke handed him the black helmet and gave him the thumbs up. As the machine moved beneath him, for a brief moment, Alex felt free. The open road beckoned him and the motorbike seemed to fly on air. He hadn't felt this good in ages. Impulsively, he wanted to take off the helmet and let the wind flow through his black hair, but thought better of it. After half an hour, Alex decided to turn around and go back to Luke's. But this small window of freedom had meant more to him than anyone could imagine.

Taking off the helmet, he shook his shoulder-length black hair. 'Christ that felt good, Luke.'

'Why not take it home? It's Dan's, or rather yours.'

Alex spied the bike but shook his head. 'No. Not yet. If you don't mind, I will leave it here for now. But tell me Luke, why are the coppers guarding Kev in hospital?' Alex asked nonchalantly as they walked through the house back into the kitchen.

'No idea. They want answers I suppose. Maybe they think Kev can give them a name?'

'Personally Luke, I think the police think someone will come back and finish the job...' Clearing his throat, Alex watched Luke and felt something wasn't quite right. 'Who was the woman that cleaned up Kev's flat, Luke? And more to the point, why did she cover your backs? Have you heard from her since?' Alex didn't want it to sound like an interrogation, but he needed answers if he was going to find out who was holding Deana and why.

Shrugging, Luke avoided his gaze. 'Not heard a word from her since that night Alex. No idea who she is but she saved our bacon, especially Dante's as he was the one who shot those two men, wasn't he? Dan shouldn't have even been there that night.'

Alex winced at Luke's words. He seemed very quick to remind Alex that Dan had shot and murdered two people. 'Well, it was to save your brother's life, Luke. Not because he felt like it. Some would claim he acted in self-defence.'

'Mmm and some people would wonder why Dan was carrying a gun in the first place.' For a moment they both stared at each other. Standing up, Alex felt he was being as two faced as Luke when he hugged him and told him how good it was to see him. 'Thanks for being such a good friend to Dan, Luke. Male company, we all need it sometimes no matter how much we all love the ladies eh?'

'Sure thing, Alex. If you need any help regarding Deana, let me know. Sorry, I didn't do more to stop them. I'm as guilty as they are, Alex.' Luke smiled as he waved Alex off. Standing at the gate, Alex stopped and pointed his finger at Luke, his dark eyes glaring at him. 'No Luke. You're worse. You encouraged minors to deal your drugs, to cook them in your house and sell them. You know what happens to dealers and druggies. They get beaten and they get killed. And yet not one word came from you to me – not one bloody word. Considering your age, some people would call it grooming!'

Luke paled as he stood in the doorway, shocked at Alex's outburst as the man walked away. But he knew he'd be back.

# 4

## DEANA

Waking up, Deana blinked and shivered with cold, wrapping the duvet closely around her for warmth. She'd hoped to open her eyes to find herself back in her warm bedroom with the smell of bacon wafting through the air as her mum prepared breakfast. But no, she was still in the dark room and she looked around at the blank walls and the boarded-up window with a mix of anger and fear. She had tried pulling the wood from the window so she could shout outside, but had discovered it had also been boarded up from the outside. Lying there, curled up on the floor, she thought about her family and wondered what they were doing now. Were they missing her? What were they doing to find her? With hindsight, she recalled the last few months and although it had been fun and the money had been good, she would give it all back, every last penny, just to be with her family again. She remembered and regretted her last argument with Dante. The way she had stormed out of the house angrily, because she had known, deep down, that he had been right. Dan was sensible, a thinker who didn't have an impulsive bone in his body. Whereas she never thought about the consequences of her actions, which had led her to this prison cell she was in now. Slowly, the painful memory seeped through her brain.

Throwing his hands up in despair, Dan had looked at his older sister Deana. 'I've had enough Deana. I hate the lies and deceit. It started out as a bit of fun but we've gone too far. How much money is enough for you? We've made money dealing and delivering drugs, but at what cost? If Mum, or rather when Mum finds out how we have betrayed her trust she'll hate us and so will Dad. He's in a prison cell because he wanted to distance himself from people like us! We spent two years on the run in witness protection, isolated from everyone we know and loved. Let's just walk away now unscathed and contemplate how to show our parents the bags of money we have hidden away. It wouldn't surprise me if Dad threw petrol all over it and set it on fire!'

Stubbornly Deana had listened to her brother and stuck her chin out in defiance. 'Oh for God's sake, Dan. We're chips off the old block. Dad will probably shake our hands for making the best of an opportunity!'

'Do you really believe that, Deana? Or is that what you tell yourself to make you feel better and sleep at night?'

'What we've done, Dante, hasn't just been for ourselves. We lost everything and through no fault of our own. It was the Portuguese mafia that turned on Dad. We both want to go to university, and now we can afford to without being a drain on our parents. I want Dad to have a holiday with Mum when he comes out of prison. Don't we deserve some happiness after all the pain and suffering? Okay, people make mistakes, Dad worked with the mafia for years and, although he is paying his dues, we were the ones left behind having parcels of shit put through the letter box. When all of that came out on the news about Dad being a mafia assassin, people hated us! They spat at us in the street!'

A sarcastic smirk appeared on Dan's face. 'Listen to yourself.

You make it sound like the world owes you a living. Just when do you intend telling Mum and Dad all of this? Do you really think they are going to shake our hands and thank us for bringing more shame on the Silva name. Dad has done his best to clear his name and start afresh with Mum and I feel uneasy now that we've potentially dragged them into another mess. And what about that bloody pink car of yours? That's not for Mum and Dad, is it? They don't even know you have it.'

'Like that motorbike of yours, hidden away at someone else's house,' Deana snapped, her face flushed with anger. Turning, she'd slammed the door behind her as she'd left the house and gone to pick up her pink sports car. Driving through London, she'd freed her ponytail from its ribbon and shaken out her blonde hair.

Behind her a black car had flashed its lights, which caught her attention. Puzzled, she'd waited to see if the car wanted to overtake her, but it stayed close behind and flashed its lights again. The traffic wasn't heavy and she looked in her rearview mirror at the car, but it made no attempt to move past her which unnerved her. Looking up she saw a sign for the Rotherhithe tunnel and decided to turn off to get out of this menacing car's way. It was probably just some jokers trying to make fun of her pink car. Even Dan called it the Barbie car. The sunlight disappeared as she entered the tunnel and Dan's harsh words had filled her mind again. Her brain was in turmoil but glimpsing in the mirror again she could see the very same car behind her. The tunnel was more or less deserted and suddenly Deana felt very afraid. The exit of the dark tunnel seemed miles away and her heart was pounding in her chest. Feeling a jolt, and almost losing her grip on the wheel, panic rose in her chest as she realised the car had purposely driven into her. Gripped with fear, she put her foot down, knowing she had to get out of there. Looking for her mobile, she saw that it had fallen off the passenger seat onto the floor, and as hard as she tried, while keeping her eyes on the road, she couldn't reach it. Then she'd felt a huge bang as the car purposely hit her again, making her swerve and bring her car to a halt. Her head had hit the steering wheel and raising her hand, she felt a trickle of blood run down the side of her head and face and now her hand. Dazed and nauseous, she tried focusing as she watched two men approach her car. Suddenly, darkness engulfed her as a blanket or covering was thrown over her head. Her scream was muffled by the thick covering, almost suffocating her. Her head throbbed, and she felt too dazed and disorientated to fight back as she drifted off into unconsciousness while being lifted from the car...

That was all that she remembered, until she'd woken up in this room. So many scenarios ran through her brain of how she could have escaped. A tear escaped, and quickly she brushed it away. It was pointless torturing herself with what she could have done. She hadn't done it and that was that. What tortured her more was how she had treated Dan. All he had done was point out the obvious – they had pushed their luck too far and she had become far too cocky. Although, at this moment in time, she didn't feel very brave or cocky. She felt miserable.

Pricking her ears, she listened for the sound of the men who were her jailers. But the whole place seemed silent. Whoever they were, they seemed to leave around the same time each night. Jumping up, with a new surge of energy, she pulled at the door handle, but the door remained locked shut. It must have been bolted from the outside and her heart sank anew. Walking around the small room, she looked at the window again. Maybe, just maybe, if she could get the wood off from the inside, she could push the wood from the outside off too. Suddenly, she felt excited, but then a fleeting thought crossed her mind. What if she did all of that and there was nothing on the outside? And what about her captors – what would they do to her if they saw the missing wood barring the window? Sitting on the floor again, Deana put her arms around her knees and brought them up to her chin as she stared at the wooden boards and contemplated her escape.

\* \* \*

As he jumped off the bus and walked down the street towards the well-lit pub, Alex's mind was in turmoil. Time was passing and he was no further on than he was since he'd arrived home. There were things he needed to know, but suddenly he felt suffocated by his surroundings and wanted to escape and find the answers to his own problems. He knew the answers were out there somewhere, and he needed to start at the beginning.

Looking up at the pub before he entered, he saw Olivia's welcome home banners plastered all over the outside of the windows. Balloons were tied to anything that would hold them. A wry grin crossed his face as he looked at all of the trouble she had gone to. She and Mark were good friends and always had the best of intentions even if they went about it in a cock-eyed way.

Frowning, Alex suddenly remembered Deana's pink car parked in the car park. Looking around he could see no one around and presumed they would all be in the pub awaiting his return. Walking around the back of the pub, he breathed a sigh of relief when he saw that it was still there untouched. Reaching under his leather jacket, he pulled at the bottom of his shirt until some of the cloth tore off in his hand. 'Old habits die hard,' he muttered to himself and smiled. Using the tail end of the shirt wrapped around his hand, he broke into the car and opened the door. He could smell Deana's perfume and breathed it in. It gave him a sense of comfort, hope even. Not wanting to switch on the inside light for fear of being noticed, he was glad of some street lighting. His eyes quickly scanned the inside of the car, but there was nothing to see and fear gripped him. His heart was in his mouth as he looked at the driver's seat. Taking out his lighter, he peered closer in the dimly lit gloom. True enough there were traces of blood near the head rest and the back of the car. There had clearly been a struggle and knowing Deana she had obviously been taken from her car against her will. He felt sick to the stomach when he thought about his little girl being hurt, cut and bruised. Taking out his mobile, he rang Maggie and told her he had been held up at the police station and that would be home a bit later than planned. Then he got into the car and hot wiring it, he drove off towards Luke's house.

Arriving just a short while later, Alex parked the car outside the garage with the engine still running. Luke opened the front door, clearly surprised to see him again. 'Alex, what are you doing here?'

'Hiding this. Put it in your garage and keep it well hidden. Then give me the keys to that motorbike, I have to go home.' Doing as he was told, Luke got into the car and drove it into the garage then handed Alex the motorbike keys. 'Alex, look, I'm sorry,' Luke muttered, looking down at the floor.

'For what, Luke? Just what part of this hair-brained scheme are you sorry for?' Alex shook his head and put on the motorbike helmet. Pulling up the visor, he looked at Luke's sorrowful demeanour. 'Never mind that now, I have to go.' Revving up the bike, Alex rode off home to his family and his party with his friends. A warm feeling consumed him as he thought about them all. It had been a long time since he'd had somewhere to call home and put down roots, but now they did in this ramshackle pub with this group of misfits. Parking the bike around the corner, he ran to the pub and pushed open the doors. Everyone was wearing party hats and blowing whistles and cheering. 'At last!' Olivia shouted. 'Welcome home, Alex, love.' She gave him a huge, genuine hug that nearly squeezed the life out of him and he looked up at the bar strewn with streamers and banners and saw Maggie standing behind it, her arm around Dan's shoulders. He gave them both a wink and a smile and wished that Deana, his little girl, was here with them. He was more determined than ever to find her and bring her home safe where she belonged.

Just then Mark rushed over. 'Here you go, Alex, get that down your neck.' Reaching out, Alex took the pint of beer Mark offered and took a huge gulp. The cool liquid soothed his throat and made him feel slightly better. As he listened to Mark's loud voice shout over the rest of the crowd with his usual innuendos and bad jokes, a plan hatched in Alex's mind. It was a long shot, but it was worth a try. Anything to get Deana back home.

# 5

## GOOD FRIENDS

Mark waved his empty glass in the air. 'Come on girls, fill them up again. I'm just popping out for a smoke.' Mark walked out towards the beer garden with his ever-present entourage following him. Percy, one of the regulars who never bought a drink himself, sidled up towards the bar. 'Does that mean I'm included in filling those drinks up?' He grinned.

Giving him a look of distaste, Pauline, the barmaid, pulled at the pumps, filling the glasses. 'I suppose it might, you scrounger. Whatever else, Mark wouldn't see you without a drink, would he?'

'Nice one.' Now that his drink was sorted, Percy looked around the bar furtively, eyeing everyone up.

'Oh, for God's sake, Percy. No one in here is going to let you scrounge a cigarette. Go outside and see if Mark will give you one of those as well. What do you do with your pension, because you definitely don't spend it on soap, do you?' Pauline snapped.

Ignoring her barb, Percy picked up his pint of beer and headed off towards the beer garden where Mark and his gang were putting the world to rights.

Phyllis finished serving at the other side of the bar and handed a waitress her tray of drinks. 'Cover me for a minute will you, Pauline. That lot will be outside for a while yet, boasting about their prowess.' Walking towards Alex, who was about to fetch his coat to join Mark outside, Phyllis stopped him. 'Can we have a word in the back room, Alex?'

Puzzled, Alex turned and walked into the little staff room and waited for Phyllis to say whatever was on her mind.

'I can see it slipped your mind with the party and everything, Alex. But, if you remember, I did say I would go and see that Kev in hospital for you.'

Slapping his forehead, Alex sat down on the little two-seater sofa. 'Oh, my God, Phyllis. I've had so much going on today my brain's frazzled.'

'Well, before it gets more frazzled with silly bollocks and the brain-dead morons he hangs around with, let me tell you... he's waking up. That Kev I mean,' she said quietly.

'Kev's waking up. Did you speak to him?' Intrigued, Alex sat back on the sofa and waited. 'Go on Phyllis what happened?'

'There was a policeman there, like you said, but he didn't seem very interested in what was going on. I just waltzed up to the door, and he asked me to sign a visitors' book and after that he seemed satisfied. Anyway, the nurse said they'd taken Kev off the morphine and slowly he was coming round. He'll be a bit groggy and he looks like shit. Christ, whoever did him over, Alex, made a damn good job of it. He was drowsy and not making much sense, so I just asked him how he was. It was pointless really, but I managed to talk to that policeman. He's bored and was glad of the company and an old lady like me doesn't pose a threat.' She laughed. 'It's shit getting old, Alex.'

'I feel like I'm catching you up, Phyllis.' Especially at this moment, he mused to himself, while waiting for her to carry on.

'Well, the police are making investigations into who's committed GBH on Kev, but they also know it has a drug connection and they know Kev is a dealer apparently.' She nodded, all wide eyed and shocked, as though she was dropping some bombshell. 'This copper thinks whoever beat Kev up had good reason and they are expecting other druggies to turn up and finish the job. Let's be honest, Alex, it isn't going to be a dawn raid like on the telly, but a few dealers off the streets I suppose.' She shrugged.

Phyllis hadn't told Alex anything he didn't already know. But, considering how much trouble she had gone to, Alex felt a little enthusiasm was called for. He could see she was waiting for some praise.

'Oh, thanks, Phyllis. I really appreciate you going. I knew drugs would be involved somewhere. You're a diamond, Phyllis. Thank you.' Standing up, he kissed her on the cheek for good measure, but he could see she wasn't impressed.

'Don't bullshit me, Alex. Why do I get the feeling your kids are up to their necks in this? If you're wondering if he's mentioning names, he isn't. I doubt at the moment if he can remember his own name.' Alex stepped back a little as a snarl crossed Phyllis's face. 'Just answer me one thing, Alex, and I want the truth now.'

Shocked at the change in her attitude, Alex spread his hands wide open. 'What? What's with the violence, Phyllis?'

'Did you or your kids do that to that young man? Is that why you're so interested in him? Did you arrange that?' She glared at him, all fired up, ready for an argument.

Alex let out a huge sigh and sat down. Smiling, he looked up at her. 'No Phyllis, that isn't the reason I'm interested. They didn't do it and neither did I. None of us have arranged that kid's beating. Sit down and I'll tell you a story. It's not pretty, but I think you deserve the truth.'

Now it was Phyllis's turn to look puzzled, and she did as she was told.

'Deana has been kidnapped. Her, Dan and this Kev have been up to no good selling cannabis.' Alex felt this was enough truth for Phyllis right now and didn't want to tell her too much. 'They have trodden on someone's toes and I don't know who, which is why I think Kev might be the answer. No one apart from the immediate family know this, and I'm trying to sort it out.' Despairingly, Alex rubbed his hands through his black, tousled hair and rested his head back on the sofa, exhausted. 'Don't ask me what I'm going to do, Phyllis, because I don't bloody know. There hasn't been a word about Deana apart from a phone call with her screaming in the background.' Alex omitted the car business, because suddenly he felt he had said far too much. He had expected Phyllis to panic, but instead she sat beside him poker faced before speaking.

'Well, at least that's the truth. As for Deana, I'm sure you would have heard something if they'd murdered her, whoever these kidnappers are. Are you sure she hasn't just gone for a jaunt and thinks this is a game? God knows, she's stupid enough to do something like that. Have you called the police?' Phyllis tapped her fingers on her chin. 'But then maybe, just maybe, that is what these kidnappers are expecting. Let's be honest Alex, they might be expecting you to spill the beans – you're a known grass after all.' Holding her hands up in defence, Phyllis shook her head. 'Don't bite my head off. This is what the world thinks, whether you like it or not. But if you need anything lad, I will do what I can, and I will keep my ears to the ground. It's surprising what you hear over that bar. Now, I'd better get back. But, if you need anything, well' – she smiled and patted his knee comfortingly – 'you know lad, I don't have to say it.'

For a brief moment Alex felt like a young kid again with his mother soothing his cares away. Blushing slightly, he gave Phyllis a weak smile as she left the room. He didn't know what to think, but his talk with Phyllis had given him an idea. It had crossed his mind earlier and he had dismissed it, but the more he thought about it the more sense it made. He needed to know if Deana's kidnapping was anything to do with him. What if he had been barking up the wrong tree all this time and it was himself who was to blame for this. Maybe, he reasoned to himself, whoever had taken Deana had taken the next best thing if they couldn't have him. He needed more time. A week wasn't enough and he had to do something about that first. Remembering that Mark and the boys would be outside waiting for him, he picked up his jacket and walked through the bar towards the beer garden, spying Maggie as he did.

'Alex, take this tray of drinks outside to Mark will you. I'm run off my feet,' she laughed.

Impulsively, Alex pulled Maggie forward and kissed her. He could feel a stirring within him that only she could satisfy. 'You rascal,' she laughed. 'Taking advantage of a woman with her hands full.'

Taking the tray off her, Alex put it on the bar and put his arms around her and kissed her more ardently, much to the cheers of the customers. 'Get a room you two,' someone shouted as Alex pulled away smiling. 'That, Mrs Silva, is a promise of things to come later.' He winked.

Surprised by this sudden passion, Maggie grinned. 'Then don't have too many of those, eh?' she said nodding at the glasses of whisky and beers on the tray.

'Don't worry about me Maggie. It puts fire in my veins when I think of you.' Picking up the tray, he wrestled his way out of the bar and followed the sound of Mark's voice outside.

'Cor blimey, Alex, when you said you were going for your coat, I didn't think you meant to the high street!' Mark laughed.

'I've brought supplies mate,' Alex laughed.

'Come on, Alex, you need to catch up mate. It's your party after all. Pete here was just telling us that he hasn't seen his girlfriend for three weeks and he can feel his passion boiling up inside him. Bloody hell, in this light, I think he fancies me. Mind you with the moustache she's got, she's not far off,' said Mark, rubbing his long bushy beard. Everyone roared with laughter at Pete's expense.

Raising his eyebrows in mock surprise, Alex couldn't help laughing. 'You've got a girlfriend, Pete? I thought you were chasing that nurse from number seventy-five?'

Pete, with his low parting and thin comb-over to hide his bald patch, shook his head. 'Nah, I think she must be a lesbian. I gave her a chance, even took a bottle of sherry around to her house. But she's bloody frigid. I like my women willing and passionate.'

'You mean,' Mark butted in, 'you like your women with a pulse and not one you have to blow up with your bicycle pump first.' Everyone roared with laughter.

Dante seemed to bring out tray after tray of drinks as the evening wore on, and the crowd in the beer garden grew larger than what was in the pub, giving Maggie and the bar staff a chance to take a breather. The kitchen staff had cleaned up and gone and it was just the bar area that needed tidying. 'Go on you two, you've done enough, and I've got a feeling that bunch out there will be there for some time.'

Both Phyllis and Pauline, still holding their bar towels in their hands, stopped. 'Are you sure, Maggie?'

'Yes, go on, you've had a busy night. I'll call your taxis to see if they can come sooner.'

Within no time at all, the taxis were beeping their horns outside. Maggie bolted the front doors and poured herself a glass of wine and wandered out towards the beer garden to join the stragglers still there. It was breezy but not cold and walking towards Olivia, Maggie sat down to join her. 'I think they've enjoyed their evening, don't you, Olivia?'

'Yeah, but I always have to be the bad guy, don't I? Good fun Mark, pouring drinks down everyone's throat is the life and soul of the party, but it's me that's got to call time. It's a work day tomorrow. I can't see Mark doing much, can you?'

Surprised at Olivia's outburst, Maggie inwardly empathised. Seeing it from Olivia's side, she could see her point, but she could tell there was more to her grumblings.

'What's up love?' asked Maggie.

'I was hoping to have another baby. Oh, I know George is a grown up, but lately I feel broody. The thing is Maggie, I'm going through an early menopause. I've not been feeling well and I went to the doctors for blood tests, and that's the answer. So, now, it's not going to happen is it?' Tears brimmed on Olivia's lashes as she took another sip of her wine.

'People do conceive during the menopause, Olivia, especially as your periods are so messed up. It does happen. And anyway, you're happy and you're lucky you've had George. He's a lovely lad.'

Olivia put her arms around Maggie. 'I love you, Maggie,' she said, the worse for wear. 'I've never really had any friends, and I know I can be a bit dippy at times, but you're like family to Mark and me.'

'And you're family to us, Olivia. So, I will call time on this lock-in, or lock-out as it's outside and you won't be the bad guy, eh?'

Slurring and nudging Alex in the ribs, Mark grinned. 'You alright, Alex? Have you had a good night?'

'I have mate. It's good to be with mates again, although...' Alex paused. He felt now was the time to drop the seed that might help his problems.

'Although what, mate?' Mark asked defensively and glared around at the others. 'Has someone said something to you about being inside?'

'No, nothing like that. I've just heard my mother in Portugal is ill. I haven't seen her for a while, what with being in witness protection and stuff. Couldn't make contact as well you know. I can't go and see her now either.'

Mark's brows crossed, and a puzzled look crossed his face. 'Why not? You have to go and see your mum now that you can. You're a free man. If you're worried about this place, I will step up, if you need me to.'

'I know you would, mate.' Alex let out a huge sigh and prepared to drop his bombshell. He didn't know if he was barking up the wrong tree but felt it was worth a try. 'The thing is, I don't have a passport any more.' Pausing, he let his words sink into Mark's tipsy brain.

Putting his arm around Alex's shoulders, Mark laughed. 'Is that all? No one looks like their passport photos, Alex.'

Alex's hopes rose, waiting for Mark's next sentence, 'What do you mean?' he asked innocently.

'Use mine for fuck's sake. You can't not go and see your mother if she's dying. It's about eight years old and I barely use it. To be honest, I don't like flying.'

'I couldn't use yours. We look so different.'

'Like I said mate, no one looks like their passport photos,

especially years on. People dye their hair, shave their heads and put on weight in that time. It's been good for identification, but, if you can use it be my guest.'

Alex felt like punching the air. This was the answer he wanted. To sort things out, his gut instinct told him he had to go back to the beginning. Were the Portuguese mafia behind this? Was it him they really wanted? If so, then he felt it would be a fair trade, and he would hand himself over to them and get Deana home.

'Oh, I couldn't do that Mark. We could both get into trouble if we were found out.'

'Trouble's my middle name.' Mark winked. 'Go on, you go and see your mother. Will Maggie be going with you?'

'No, she'll want to stay with Dante and to be fair, she didn't really get on with my family. I would just like to go before it's too late, if you know what I mean.'

'Done deal then Alex mate. I will pop around tomorrow. You organise your flight and stuff.' Looking over to where Olivia was sat, Mark gulped back the last dregs of his pint. 'Looks like we'd better call it a night.' As though by magic, Maggie walked over and clapped her hands together.

'Come on you lot, haven't you got homes to go to? I've got work in the morning even if you haven't.' She laughed and started gathering their glasses together on a tray. Everyone finished their drinks and slowly departed, while Alex began clearing away with Maggie.

'Crikey, it's cold out here. Do you all wear asbestos vests or something?'

As Alex looked at Maggie, a naughty smile crossed his face, and that familiar twinkle Maggie knew so well sparkled in his eyes. Looking at his slim, blonde wife wearing a thin T-shirt and jeans, with just a cardigan over her shoulders, he couldn't help but notice her protruding nipples, enhanced by the cold night air. Impulsively, he reached out and tweaked one.

'Well, there's no need to ask what's on your mind, you randy devil. Did you have a good night love?' Maggie asked, grinning back.

Pulling her closer, Alex kissed her. 'It's getting better every minute, and it's not over yet, Mrs Silva.' He grinned. Breathing in her perfume as he nuzzled her neck, he felt himself harden and pulled her even closer as his hands roamed under her T-shirt.

Their kisses became more ardent and passionate while Maggie let her hand fall to Alex's crotch and stroked the erection forming in his jeans. As passion consumed them both, suddenly nothing else mattered, just each other as they clung to each other. Alex pulled at Maggie's jeans as she felt herself being lifted and placed on the picnic bench, while Alex brushed away empty glasses on to the grass. Still kissing her, as their hands roamed over each other, Alex quickly undid the belt on his trousers as his manhood throbbed. Maggie moaned out loud and lay back, wrapping her legs around him. With each thrust, they both felt themselves reaching the peak of their passion. Face flushed, Maggie felt the firework explosion inside her body. Shuddering, she cried out, clinging to Alex as he threw his head back with one last thrust, which left them both panting for breath. Kissing her gently on the lips, Alex stood up and fastened his clothes, then held his hand out to help Maggie off the table.

'Phew,' she breathed, straightening herself up. 'Where the hell did that come from, Alex?'

'God knows, but I'm bloody glad it did. Christ, you're a sexy woman, Maggie, and you seem to be getting younger every day. Look at your figure and those pert tits. How could anyone resist, eh?'

'And what about you, Alex? You look so much like your old

self again. We just have one more mountain to climb and things would be perfect,' she sighed. 'I suppose we'd better clean up.' Maggie looked at the broken glass on the floor and the discarded glasses on the other tables.

'I have something in mind regarding Deana, Maggie, I don't want you to worry. We will get her home.' He slipped his arm around her slim waist and together they walked back inside the pub, leaving the glasses to be tidied up tomorrow.

Maggie was intrigued by Alex's words. 'What do you mean you have something in mind regarding Deana?'

'Before I raise your hopes or dash them, I need to find something out. But wait until the morning and all will be revealed. It's just an idea, love, but I promise we will have our girl home soon.' Lovingly, he brushed a wisp of blonde hair from her face. 'Do you trust me?' he asked, already knowing the answer.

'I trust you with my life, Alex. You know that. And I know if you have something forming in your mind, you'll tell me when you're ready.' She smiled. 'But I do feel there is something else on your mind at the moment...' Looking down, Maggie stroked the front of his trousers and saw the outline of his erection bulging. Raising her eyebrows, she couldn't help smiling at his insatiable appetite and saw Alex grin in return. Turning off all the lights, they walked upstairs together.

# 6

## A SEARCH FOR THE TRUTH

After their night of passionate sex, Maggie felt like she was walking on air as she fried bacon and eggs for the two men in her life. Hearing the hammering at the door, she put another couple of rashers of bacon in the pan and made her way downstairs. 'Mark! You're early.' She laughed. She stood aside as he walked in and ran up the stairs into the kitchen.

'Cor Maggie, is that bacon frying?' He sniffed the air and looked in the pan as Maggie joined him.

'You know full well it is, Mark and yes, there is enough for you. Don't you think it's time you told Olivia you're no longer on her diet?' She laughed.

'Nah, she's convinced herself that I'm losing weight and that's good enough for me. I'll go down the gym later and burn some calories. She likes me hot and sweaty.' He laughed. Maggie rolled her eyes at him before turning towards the cooker. As much as she liked Mark, there was definitely nothing about him she fancied, nor ever would. As though on cue Alex came through, dressed but still rubbing his hair with a towel. 'I thought I could hear those velvet tones of yours, Mark. I take it you're after breakfast again.'

'I am mate, but I've also popped round to give you this, though how you're going to get away from your temporary parole is the big question. Brown sauce on mine, Maggie,' he shouted while reaching in his back pocket and taking out his passport. Opening it, he handed it over to Alex. 'Fuck, I don't even look like me these days. I can't believe I've changed that much. But people do, don't they? That passport is nearly ten years old. Its only got another year left on it.'

Hearing the word 'passport', Maggie turned slowly and looked at Alex, who caught her gaze. Her gut instinct told her this was what Alex had been hinting at last night. But, why would Alex want a passport, she thought to herself while making a bacon sandwich for Mark.

Mark and Alex were huddled together looking at Mark's passport and laughing at the old photo. Dan entered and peered over Alex's shoulders and burst out laughing, too. 'Did you really wear small hoop earrings, Mark?'

'I did mate. It was a cool look when I worked as a bouncer on the pub doors and stuff. Everyone did it. Not now though. I would look like a real tit, wouldn't I?'

Alex looked closer at the photo while encouraging Mark to laugh about his looks. He also had his ear pierced and so when he used this passport, he would make a point of wearing an earring too.

As Maggie put the breakfast on the plates, she was itching for Mark to leave. She wanted to know what Alex was up to and why Mark had brought his passport. Faking a smile, she poured the tea and let them get on with it. Suddenly she had lost her appetite and her mind was in turmoil. 'It's nearly nine, I'd better start clearing up outside before the staff come in. It's not fair leaving it to them.'

'Oh, aye.' Mark winked. 'Early night after we left, was it?' With a mouth full of bread, he stood up and playfully put his hands over Dante's ears. 'Is that why Alex gets a hearty breakfast, Maggie?' Bursting out laughing, Mark looked at Alex. 'Fuck mate, that's why I'm only getting porridge sachets. Olivia isn't getting enough!' Again, he laughed at his own joke and picked up the other half of his sandwich. 'I'm off anyway. Cars to fix, people to please.' With a wave and a smile, Mark ran downstairs.

As the smile dropped from Maggie's face, she sat down and absent mindedly picked up her cold tea and sipped it. 'Well? Spill the beans, Alex. Why do you need Mark's passport? Are you going to make a run for it and leave us all – is that it?' A cold shiver ran down her spine. When she thought how loving he had been last night and all the time he had been planning his escape. She felt sick to her stomach.

Alex reached out and held her hand. 'Nobody is deserting anyone, Maggie. How could you think such a thing?' His face flushed and he glared at her. His soft brown eyes were now full of anger. 'For fuck's sake Maggie, no. No way can you think that of me.' He stood up from the table, almost knocking over the cups. 'I told you last night I had something up my sleeve and I was waiting for Mark. Well, he's come good. How the hell can you think I would desert my family when my family is in deep shit?'

'Sorry Alex.' Tears rolled down Maggie's face. 'I'm sorry, I just thought, well, I don't know what I thought,' she stammered. 'But why do you need a passport?'

'Mum, Dad!' Dante shouted. 'Will you both just calm down? Christ, no wonder me and Deana went off the rails. Why don't you just talk to each other?'

Taken aback, they both stared at Dan in amazement.

'Dad, why do you want Mark's passport? You can apply for your own now. So, what's the rush? Are we going on holiday? Just the three of us without Deana?'

Alex suddenly looked at his son through different eyes. Dante had grown up and he hadn't seen it happening. Sitting down calmly, Alex motioned to Maggie to do likewise. Taking a breath, Alex looked at them both before speaking. 'I need to go back to Portugal, to the beginning of my story. It has occurred to me that Deana has been kidnapped not because of your drug dealing, Dante, but because of me and my old mafia friends. My only problem is that I only have a few days left and I can't extend my parole, but there is one man in Portugal that I knew as a kid who I think will be able to give me answers. I worked for him when he was boss of all the families. I know he is still alive, but he's as old as Moses now. But he will tell me what I want to know. He may even have the lead as to where Deana is and why. But I need to report to the police daily. So I will need to catch a flight early in the morning and come back the same day.'

'And what if you never come back?' Maggie snapped.

'I told you I'm not leaving you, for God's sake. We've been through too much. But to solve this problem I need to start again.'

'I might know a way to extend your leave from prison,' Dan butted in. 'It's a long shot, but it's better than nothing.'

'How?' both Maggie and Alex asked.

'I haven't thought through the details yet, but let's say if you had measles or chicken pox, you know, something contagious, they wouldn't want you in prison and you wouldn't be well enough to go out.'

'Yeah, but then the police would come here, Dante. Even to just peek around the door.'

'Not if you had solid proof they wouldn't. If you had a doctor's note for instance.'

'But then I would need to see a doctor, Dan...' Alex was intrigued and pushed him further for answers.

'Not necessarily, Dad. To start with you're a special case and the doctors wouldn't want you going to the surgery with all those vulnerable patients who are ill, not to mention pregnant women and children. These days, you can send photos to the doctors if it's something contagious or you can't get an appointment and need medication. You don't always need to see a doctor face to face these days,' Dan emphasised.

Maggie listened patiently as the two men hatched their plan, but she felt there was one crucial thing missing. 'So Dante, we call the doctors and tell them your dad has the plague and want to send pictures... of what? Where are these spots, Dan? Have you thought of that?'

'We find them online. There are a million photos of all kinds of things online. We send one of those,' he said triumphantly and sat back in his chair.

Disbelieving, Alex stared at Dan and then at Maggie. 'I'm old school, Dan. How do I find a photo of the plague as your mum puts it?' He smiled awkwardly. 'And send it to a doctor to get a sick note?'

'I can do that. You will possibly have to speak to the doctor. No doubt you will get a call from them and so you will have to put on your best sick voice. But you would be surprised how many people use the internet to lie, Dad. Scammers do it all the time.'

'I'm not that stupid, Dan, but I don't want you involved any more than you already are.'

'I am involved. Someone has kidnapped my sister. I am a Silva and we stick together. That's what you always say. All I'm doing is giving you a photo after I've brushed it up a little. What you do with it is your business.'

Alex looked at Maggie for approval. It seemed like a good plan – if it worked, he thought to himself.

'You do realise, Alex, once you step on to Portuguese soil, you're a dead man walking. You might never come back and I don't think I can cope with that.'

'Twenty-four hours Maggie, that's all I'll need and I will be careful. That's if I pass Mark's passport scrutiny.'

'You will, Dad. Look at women who dye their hair all the time. You will look like you've just grown yours, which is a possibility. Mark would look so different if he grew his and chopped off that beard, wouldn't he?' Dan encouraged.

Alex nodded, deep in thought. It was a good plan and it sounded feasible. It was just Maggie he needed to convince, and he could see she wasn't sure.

Maggie's stomach felt twisted in turmoil. She knew the mafia boss Alex was talking about; she had met him. He had also once fought Alex's corner when the other bosses had been against Alex. He had wanted justice for Alex, but by then his voice had meant little. The other bosses had wanted Alex's blood and had bonded together, leaving Alex no option but to go into witness protection. 'How do you know he's still alive?' Maggie asked.

'John mentioned him in our last conversation. He's very ill and dying by all accounts. That's why I need to act fast. He may be dead now, I don't know. But, if he is alive, I bet he has some answers for me.'

Maggie rolled her eyes to the ceiling. 'Well, let's see what happens first. Your plan might not work.' Mentally, she felt guilty because she hoped dearly it wouldn't work and then she couldn't be blamed for opposing it. Letting out a huge sigh, she threw her hands in the air. 'I give in. You have obviously already made up your minds to do this against my protests. So, if you want to try it – go ahead.'

Instantly, Dan jumped up and got his laptop and got to work. 'Mum, you will have to make the call to the doctors explaining the situation.' With a heavy heart, she was surprised she got through to the doctor's receptionist so quickly. Alex and Dan stood beside her while she made the call and lied. She went through all the details about his release from prison and that he would need a note to confirm it was measles and that he would be contagious. As predicted by Dan, they asked for a photo of the rash. As many as possible so that he could be diagnosed. Her throat felt dry; it felt like she had been talking for hours, although it was barely ten minutes.

'Okay Mum, wait on your phone, they will send you a link to upload the photos.'

As her phone bleeped to indicate a message, Maggie opened it. 'What now?'

Waving his fingers in the air like a pianist warming up, Dan transferred professional photos of measles on someone's arm and chest to her phone. He had blurred them a little and had taken out the background to make it look more authentic and also amateur. 'That should do it. Now send them, Mum.' Her heart was thumping in her chest as she did as she was told. 'I could be done for fraud for this you know.'

'Now all we do is wait. It will be passed to the doctor and it's up to him,' Dan shrugged.

Maggie went down to the bar and started clearing up to keep busy. She had no idea how long this situation would take and wanted to keep busy. The day seemed to pass in a daze and eventually the long-awaited phone call from the doctor came. Alex put on his weak voice as the doctor spoke to him and informed him that he would write him a sick note for the police and prison informing them it was measles and that he was infectious. Alex nearly punched the air and had to hide his exuberance by feigning illness, but once off the phone, he gave Dan a high five. 'For Christ's sake Dante it worked. It bloody worked!'

'The only thing that has worked Alex, is that your son is now a criminal fraudster and scammer,' Maggie snapped.

'For God's sake, Maggie. The doctor has given me a week's extension. That's not major fraud, is it? You know I need to do this, and I will be back, I promise.'

'Is that in a box or in person?' Frightened, angry tears rolled down Maggie's face. 'I love you, Alex and we have all faced so much together but you're willing to walk into the lion's den and get yourself killed. All in the name of pride.'

Alex's tone softened, and he put his arms around her waist and pulled her closer to him. 'Don't, Maggie love. It's not pride, it's my gut instinct. I feel the answers about what's happened to Deana are over there. You know I wouldn't go back if I didn't feel so strongly about getting our girl home and putting all this behind us once and for all. I love you too, Maggie and I need you to support me on this. I can't do it without you; you're my rock. One more phone call to the police station who will inform the prison. If you don't want me to do this, I won't. I won't do it without your support, Maggie.'

Looking at his face for a moment, Maggie felt hesitant but found herself nodding her head. 'Okay, I will make the call, and you had better buy yourself a return ticket.' She smiled, although inwardly, she felt like crying.

'Dad, we have work to do,' Dan butted in. 'We need to go through all of Mark's details so that you know them off by heart. We need to cover everything, Dad, just in case you're asked.'

Alex had to admire Dante's prowess for detail. 'Okay, let's start the Spanish inquisition, Dan, while your mum calls the police.' He glanced at Maggie and watched as she picked up the phone and lied for him again. He felt guilty about it, but if they wanted answers and to understand who had Deana and why then they needed to do this. And Alex also felt as though fate was on their side. If it was the wrong thing to do then things wouldn't have gone so smoothly, would they? No, he reasoned with himself, it was as though it was meant to be.

* * *

Everything was in place. All Alex had to do now was buy his ticket in Mark's name. Dan had drilled him like a sergeant major and even in the privacy of their own home had called him Mark to see if he responded. Maggie had accepted the situation but was adamant she wasn't going to call Alex Mark in the bedroom, claiming that would be her worst nightmare. Before Alex made his flight arrangements, he wanted to make a visit to Kev in hospital. Phyllis had said they were waking him up, and he had only a short window to get some answers from him.

'Hey, Alex,' Mark shouted through from the bar. 'Come out here and have a drink. I need to speak to you.' While Alex felt he was too busy to put up with another one of Mark's drinking sessions, he needed to appease him for his generosity. That passport was gold dust. 'What is it, Mark? Come through to the back.' Alex needed to keep out of sight in case the police popped in to see Maggie and check on him.

Pushing his way through the bar, Mark went in the back room. 'Did I bring my wrenches with me this morning, Alex? I don't remember doing so, but I can't find them anywhere. Shit, if I don't have those I can't work.'

Puzzled by the unexpected question, Alex shook his head. 'Well, I didn't open the door to you this morning, so I didn't see what you had in your hand when you arrived. Maggie will know though.'

'I'll ask her. I've searched everywhere and I can't find them.' Shouting through for Maggie, Alex explained what Mark was so worried about and both Mark and Alex were confused when Maggie burst out laughing. 'Oh my God Mark, where did you have them last?'

Thinking to himself, he stroked his bushy beard. 'I was working on that old Range Rover on my drive, and they were in my tool box then with the wheel keys. Can't change a bloody tyre without the wheel keys.'

'Well, when myself, Olivia and Emma do our nightly frisk we will get them back for you. Don't worry, they are safe.'

Both men stared at her open mouthed, waiting for an explanation.

'It's Larry, he can't help it. He steals everything like a magpie. We get it back once he's been put to bed. Hasn't Olivia told you about Larry?' Maggie laughed.

Mark paled. 'Get me a drink, I think I need one. And while you're at it, Maggie love, get yourself and Alex one too. Has Olivia got another man?'

Maggie disappeared and returned moments later with a pint of beer for both of them. Mark looked ashen as he waited for her to speak. 'Tell me the truth now Maggie, I won't shout or create havoc. I just need to know.'

'Calm down Mark, she hasn't got another man. You know the nurse that Pete used to chase around, hoping for a relationship?' Maggie waited for them both to nod their heads before she carried on. 'Well, her old grandad has outlived both of her parents and is now ninety-eight years old. He has dementia, but he still has a great sense of humour. Oh my God, some of the things he comes out with are hilarious. He's quite independent, and can still dress himself, but he puts on about three shirts because he's forgotten he's put the first one on. His granddaughter, the nurse, is caring for him single handedly, but we all chip in to help. The thing is, Larry is a bit of a magpie and shoves everything up his jumper. Believe me, we have all had stuff go missing. He stole my coat once and when I asked for it back, he swore he'd had it for years and to stop trying to steal it or he would call the FBI!' Maggie burst out laughing. 'It's a funny story, but a sad one too.'

For the first time that day, Maggie felt herself relax and took a sip of Alex's beer. 'Apparently, he used to be in the RAF and in later years flew planes for Pan Am. Can you believe it? Some days, I can't remember what I came downstairs for and I'm a third of his age.'

Alex shook his head and remembered his own mother. 'That is sad though, to think he's done and seen so much and come to this ending.'

'That's not the sad part. It's Les, his husband...' Maggie tailed off, pausing for effect.

'I thought you said he was the nurse's grandfather. That means he was married, doesn't it?' Mark asked, scratching his head as he waited for an explanation.

'That's the sad part. Don't forget Larry is ninety-eight and in his day gay men were frowned upon and imprisoned. He had to marry and live a double life. In later years, once his wife had died, he met Les and they were happy. Les still visits him every day but he can't look after Larry any more, he has his own health problems. So, we all keep him safe and he's no bother, just a magpie. Jen, his granddaughter, always goes in his bedroom and frisks his clothing before he goes to bed. He has stuff stashed everywhere and she brings it here. Christ, some days the back tables look like a bring-and-buy sale. Jen was embarrassed at first, but we're used to it now and at least we know where the stuff is. In fact, she will be here soon,' said Maggie, looking at her watch. 'So have your drink, Mark, and in future don't leave shiny things lying about.' Maggie laughed.

Alex laughed. 'Well, I've got to pop out for a while, but I'll be back later.'

'Have you got your ticket yet so that you can go to Portugal?' asked Mark innocently.

'I told Mark I needed to go back to Portugal before it was too late. That's why he's lending me his passport.' Alex stammered and looked at Maggie.

'You've got to go Alex. Nothing worse than a parent dying and you not being there.'

Maggie winced inside when she thought of the web of lies they were creating. A death of a parent in Portugal? What next?

'Thanks Mark, well, like I say I have to go. Excuse me.' Standing up, Alex avoided Maggie's glare and left. Once outside, he breathed in the fresh air and quickly ran around the corner to the parked motorbike. This way, with the helmet on, no one would see him, and to be honest, he loved the freedom it gave him. Whizzing in and out of the traffic, he could leave the lies and worries behind. For just a short time, he felt free!

7

LOOSE ENDS

At the hospital, the policeman who was supposed to be keeping an eye on Kev, was nowhere to be seen. Walking into the room surrounded by windows, Alex half closed the blinds and walked over to Kev's bedside. He was asleep, and inwardly Alex felt his visit had been a waste of time.

Gently, he shook his arm. 'Are you awake, Kev? Are you okay?' Stirring from his slumber, Alex waited patiently as Kev's blinked hard and stared at him. Seeing Kev's injuries had come as a bit of a shock to Alex. He'd expected him to look a bit battered and bruised, but this was unbelievable. Both of his legs were in plaster, including one of his arms. Half of his head had been shaved and was wrapped with a bandage and his face was all the different colours of the rainbow, although the changing colour meant the bruises were fading and what looked like swelling seemed to be disappearing. 'Your Deana's dad, aren't you?' Kev mumbled. As he half smiled, Alex noticed he had a couple of teeth missing at the front, too. He could see now why the police usually had someone on standby outside. This was more than GBH, it was attempted murder. Alex doubted very much that there was a part of Kev without a bruise on him. Looking around the room full of machines bleeping, Alex sighed. He could suddenly understand why Dan had shot the bastards who had done this to Kev, although he didn't agree with his methods. But squaring up to these men with a punch would have only got Dan killed in the process.

'Yes, I am Deana's dad. We have met, I don't know if you recognise me?'

'Yeah, I do. Luke's mate.' Kev's eyes were dropping closed and Alex knew he needed to get to the point before he fell asleep again.

'Listen, Deana has been kidnapped, and I wonder if it's because of your drug exploits. People are angry and waging war about you undercutting everyone. Who were these men that did this to you? Did you know them? You can tell the police whatever you like, but you need to tell me the truth.'

Kev seemed to stir more as Alex blurted out everything at once.

'Deana has been kidnapped?' he queried. 'Oh fuck, well, if it's the same blokes that did this to me, she's probably dead.'

Alex sighed and rubbed his face in frustration. 'Thanks for that. Nothing like a cheerful conversation. I don't believe she is dead, yet. But why were you beaten, Kev? Where were you and how did you meet the men who did this? Were you at your flat? Was it one of the crackheads you have in there?'

Slowly, Kev shook his head. 'No, I met them at a club. They were smart looking blokes, suited and booted. One of them was really nice, but when he followed me to the toilets I must have been pissed, because I passed out. I didn't see them again until the night they both turned up at my flat. They wanted some gear, some special gear... if you know what I mean.'

'You mean the meth you've had Dante cooking? Yeah, I know

all about that. So, are you telling me they asked specifically for that?'

'Yes. I'd given them the address of my place when they'd bought gear off me in the bar. You know my flat's like a drop-in centre.' Kev began coughing, and Alex reached over and picked up his beaker with a straw inside so that he could drink.

Tentatively, Alex felt he had to ask the ultimate question. 'Do you remember Dan being there, at your flat, when those men were beating you up?'

'Vaguely, I remember hearing the shots from a gun and to be honest, I thought I'd been shot. But I was in and out of consciousness when Deana and Luke arrived and then that fat Scottish woman.' A weak smile crossed Kev's face. 'I was dying, and they were having a tea party, eh?'

'What have you told the police? Have you mentioned Dante and what he did?'

'So that's why you're here. I wondered why you hadn't brought any grapes. No, I haven't told the police about Dante. Apparently, there aren't any dead bodies in my flat, anyway, according to Luke. I wouldn't grass, you know that. Anyway, Dan saved my life. Okay, I don't look so good now, but I'm alive and will live to fight another day...'

Alex sighed with relief. The last thing he wanted was a half-conscious Kev confessing everything to the police and putting Dan in the spotlight. 'That copper has come in and questioned me a few times. He knows I've done a bit of dealing, but nothing major. He keeps going on about gang wars in London and thinks it could all be related. He doesn't say much but sometimes his tongue runs away with him out of boredom. What are you going to do about Deana?'

'Whatever I can.' As an afterthought, Alex looked at Kev

closely. 'Actually, I hear you've been flirting with her and messing around with her. Is that true?'

'No Alex, I've no interest in Deana. It's been her chasing me. She's always fluttering her eyelashes and buying me things. I have absolutely no interest in your daughter, she's not my type.'

Anger boiled up inside of Alex, and impulsively he grabbed hold of the front of Kev's surgical gown. 'Good, because she's far too good for you, you little bastard. She's a beautiful girl and you have taken advantage of her with your stupid clothes and loud mouth. What do you mean she's not your type?'

Kev did his best with his bandaged hand to free himself from Alex's grasp. 'You don't understand, Alex. She is beautiful and I hope she meets her Prince Charming. But it's not me and she won't take no for an answer. She even told everyone at her birthday party that I was her boyfriend, which was embarrassing.'

'Embarrassing? You should be pleased she would give you a second look. I should finish you off, you cheeky bastard.'

'No, no Alex, you don't understand. If Deana was the last woman on earth, I wouldn't fancy her... in fact' – Kev swallowed hard – 'you're more my type than she is...'

A puzzled frown crossed Alex's face as he tried to comprehend what Kev was saying. 'Are you saying you're... well,' Alex stammered, 'that you prefer men?'

Slowly, Kev nodded his head. 'Ask Luke. He's the one madly in love with Deana, but she hasn't given him a second look. Not my fault.'

Stunned at Kev's confession, Alex didn't know what to say and was actually pleased when the policeman opened the door.

'Everything okay in here?' he asked inquisitively. 'I didn't see you come in.'

'Well, you weren't on the door watching anything were you!'

Alex snapped. Wanting to make a hasty retreat, he patted Kev on the hand. 'I will see you soon, Kev and get well soon. Sorry about the grapes.' He smiled as he walked past the policeman. Already putting on his motorbike helmet and avoiding his stare, Alex walked out of the hospital.

Riding along, the more Alex tried piecing everything together, the more loose ends there seemed to be. The easy way Kev had given out his address to those two guys bothered him, especially as they were strangers to him. Or maybe Kev had had something else in mind. Now he knew the truth about Kev's sexuality, his comments about how one of them was smart and handsome made sense. Poor bastard, Alex mused to himself, he didn't deserve that beating. And thankfully, he had said nothing about Dan. But who was this fat Scottish woman they all mentioned being there? Alex's mind was in turmoil. It was blatant that Kev didn't know who she was, or he would have said so. So, it wasn't a client of his. Alex knew that finding her would give him the answers he needed.

* * *

'I leave first thing in the morning. They had a cancellation, and the ticket was even cheaper.'

Maggie wrung her hands with worry. 'What time, Alex?'

Seeing the concern on her face, he tried to make light of it. 'Around 5 a.m. so I will be leaving early hours. Come on Maggie, I might be following a false lead here, but the bottom line is, I just don't know what else to do. We've heard nothing about Deana and I can only hope she's safe. Whoever her kidnappers are, it seems they are waiting for something, and I can't hang around waiting for them to make the first move. This is our best chance at finding out where she is and who has taken her.'

'I can't lose a daughter and my husband too, Alex. What have you done with her car? I see it's not in the car park any more.'

'I've hidden it in Luke's garage for the time being. They sent their message and we received it. I'm not going to lie to you but there was blood inside, not much, but signs of a struggle.'

Tears brimmed on Maggie's lashes and she choked them back. 'I give you my blessing, Alex, but I will not lie and say that I am happy about you going back there. You're a hated man. People have long memories and are bitter about what you've done to their families. Please keep safe Alex and come home safely my love.' Maggie almost threw herself at Alex, wrapping her arms tightly around his neck and kissing him passionately.

'Oy, oy, am I interrupting the love birds?' Startled, they parted to see Mark standing before them. 'I just wondered if you've got your ticket yet Alex and needed a lift to the airport? I also wanted a word with Maggie about Olivia.'

'Olivia? Why, what's wrong?' Maggie remembered her conversation with Olivia and had an idea what it would be about.

Mark closed the downstairs staff room door, so that no one in the bar could hear him. 'She's been to see the doctor and he's given her some happy pills.'

Maggie sat down and smiled at Mark's off-hand comments about anti-depressants. 'I know she's been a bit down lately and I think I know why Mark. What can I do to help?'

Confused, Alex asked if they wanted him to leave so they could talk in private.

'No mate, Olivia got it into her head that she wanted another baby. After all these years, can you believe it? But she's going through the menopause apparently and the doc says it's not going to happen. I want to cheer her up a bit, but I don't know what to do and I'm so ham-fisted about these things I don't know what to say or do to make her feel better.'

Maggie smiled. 'You're worried about your wife because you love her, that's not ham-fisted, Mark, it's just love. Why don't you take her away for a few days, in your camper van? She likes that, doesn't she? She just needs time to come to terms with it all so why don't you spend time together, just you two? Look after your wife, put her first.' Alex looked down at the floor as he saw the emotional turmoil in Mark's face. 'Am I a bad husband, Maggie?'

'Christ, Mark, you're a big softy and she knows it. No one could ever say you were a bad husband. We all know how much you love her, but she's just feeling a little fragile now. Do something to take her mind off it and give her something else to do. You know she likes a project. Why doesn't she have one of her Avon parties? She could organise one here in the side room, ladies only night. Find things for her to do that she likes and that you can do together or with George. Her little boy is no longer a little boy; he's growing up, becoming independent, and doesn't need her as much. It's hard for us mums, you know.'

'You seem to manage, Maggie.'

'Do I? Well, maybe I just don't show it. Or I'm not as sensitive as Olivia is. But, believe me, I feel it when my little ones don't need me as much. When they are not in and the house is tidy, the silence is deafening so I just try and keep myself busy. What else can I do? Children are a gift, but they are not ours to keep. They have to make their own way.' Maggie looked at Alex with tears in her eyes. He knew she was thinking about Deana and where in the world she might be. Or if she was safe or even alive.

Awkwardly, Alex stood still, hoping to make himself invisible during this heartfelt conversation. It seemed strange watching a burly, loud man like Mark almost crumble before Maggie with helplessness. Even more so when Mark stepped forward and wrapped his arms around her. 'Thanks, Maggie. I knew you would come up with something. I'll sort it; you've given me an idea.'

'I tell you what, Mark, George is upstairs with Dan playing on the PlayStation. They are fed and watered so why don't you take two plates of roast dinners and puddings with you and have dinner tonight with Olivia alone, without her having to cook. Take some wine, make an evening of it, make her feel special.' Maggie smiled.

In a choked voice, Mark looked at Alex. 'You've got a good one there, Alex.' And without another word Mark left.

'I thought he was going to cry, Maggie. And he's right, I do have a good wife in you.' Alex walked over to Maggie and took her in his arms. Maggie had said to put your family first and that was exactly what Alex was going to do. Next stop Portugal and the past he hoped he had left behind.

# 8

## PORTUGAL AND FRENEMIES

Stepping off the aeroplane, Alex felt the warm sunshine warm his bones instantly. Home, he thought to himself. He hadn't been back in years, and yet already old memories floated through his mind. He had crept out of his bed like a thief in the night and left Maggie asleep. She'd done her best to stay awake but eventually sleep had taken over. He knew that would probably be the last good night's sleep she would have until his return. Pensively, he looked at his watch. He knew where he needed to be, but it was still early and he needed to kill time. By his reckoning, it would take about three hours to get to Faro, which was one of the richest parts of Portugal. But first, for old time's sake, Alex wanted to visit the mainland Algarve, which was a very poor area and one he knew intimately. Inwardly, he felt he may never see this place again.

His stomach churned as he travelled to the poorer side of the mainland. Suddenly, he felt homesick for this place. As he reached his destination, he looked down the familiar dusty, cobbled street where he had been brought up. Seeing a familiar looking house, he realised that he and his family had once lived in the attic. It had been painted and modernised slightly, but not much. White sheets still billowed outside of the houses on washing lines, drying in the sun, and kids, much like he had once been, were playing football in the street while the sun shone brightly.

Feeling the sweat on his brow, Alex took off his jacket and held it over his shoulder as he walked down memory lane. Suddenly, the young boys, noticing his well-dressed manner, held out their hands and asked for money. They seemed surprised when he spoke to them in their own language and handed over some cash. As their football came flying towards him, Alex put down his jacket and kicked it around with them until his age and the heat of the sun exhausted him. Not much had changed since he'd last been here, he mused.

But Alex didn't have time to waste here; he had another bus to catch and another objective in mind before he made the trip to Faro. After the long ride, he alighted the bus outside some cemetery gates. Outside was a small flower stall that had been there for years, and Alex bought a small bouquet from the old woman on the stall. Entering the cemetery, Alex walked along the many headstones until he found what he was looking for. *Mrs Beatriz Silva*, he read on the headstone and fell to his knees. Without realising it, tears fell down Alex's face.

'I've come home Mama,' he said aloud. 'I hope you've found peace wherever you are.' His mother's life had been a hard one, and his alcoholic, violent father hadn't helped. His father hadn't always been an alcoholic, but when he'd lost his job as a fisherman because of a hand injury, he'd started drinking and his whole persona changed. His mother, Beatriz, had been the only wage earner and only once his father had drunk away what he needed of her wages would they then be allowed to buy food to eat. Alex had vowed that he would never live like that again so he had turned to crime. Skipping the catholic church, that had also doubled up as a school for poor kids, he'd met the man who had once saved his life. And the man he intended to see tonight.

Mr Pereira Senior had run a taxi firm that had a few rusty cars and a coffee shop with tables on the pavement outside. But it also served as a gambler's paradise and illegal drinking hole and drug den. Everything was black market with Mr Pereira – if you wanted it, he could get it. And if you needed a loan, he would give you one, but with the expected interest. Locals turned a blind eye to his dodgy dealings because he enriched their lives with employment.

As a kid, Alex had hung around the taxi firm and voluntarily cleared the coffee cups from the tables outside. Mr Pereira had given him a job as the coffee boy and cleaner. Mr Pereira had liked Alex's sharp brain and eagerness; he had also liked the fact that Alex hardly spoke but took in everything. Eventually, Alex had earned Pereira's trust and began dropping off parcels for him, which were usually drugs, and picking up money for Pereira from his debtors.

But Pereira had rewarded Alex well and handing over money to his mother had made Alex feel good. Knowing that she could pay the rent and not buy scraps of food pleased her enormously, even though she was worried about the company he kept.

Smiling to himself as he pulled at the grass and arranged the flowers on the overgrown grave, Alex remembered how his mother had gone to church and prayed for him and his sins relentlessly but had taken his money anyway. As time had passed and he'd become more solvent, Alex had become the main breadwinner for his family and had slowly watched his father drink himself to death, which he'd secretly been glad about. He'd hated him and hated the way he would take off his buckled belt and either hit Alex or his mother with it. Many times, he had been playing outside and had heard the screams of his mother from the attic window.

As he'd got older, he had bought her a house, but by then she was unwell. She kept forgetting things and wandered around aimlessly in her underwear. Eventually, Alex had made the heartbreaking decision to put her in residential care. Although he made sure she was comfortable, she died not knowing who Alex was. She didn't recognise him but talked about her son, Alex, when he visited her. He had felt death was a release for her.

Sadness overwhelmed him and he wondered how different things might have been, in different circumstances. All these years later and there were times when Alex still felt like that helpless boy who came from nothing. Scolding himself, he shook his head. He was a very lucky man. He had a wife who loved him and two children whom he loved very much. Tidying the grave up as much as possible, he kissed his finger and laid it on the headstone. 'I love you mum,' he whispered and walked away. Now it was time to focus on the job he'd come here to do.

\* \* \*

From a distance, Alex took in the huge manor house with its huge iron gates. He looked up at the sky; the sun was going down and it was getting cooler now. His vague memory of the house helped him know where the danger points might be that he'd need to look out for. He could see men milling around inside the gates near the large, landscaped gardens. The smell of the orange trees wafted in the breeze.

Stubbing out his cigarette, Alex walked around the far side of the house. The wall wasn't so high around the sides, because there was so much greenery and bushes there. No one would ever think of breaking into a house like this that was guarded by soldiers. And they weren't the army type, but mafia men with rifles hung over their shoulders.

Alex opened the small black rucksack he had brought with him and took out a large iron hook he'd bought from the hardware shop. Then he attached it to a rope he'd also bought and knotted it securely. It would hopefully wrap around the trees or bushes to help him climb over the wall. His hands felt sweaty and his heart was pounding in his chest. His first attempt to climb the wall ended in disaster and he fell. Finding another spot in the wall with more bushes and trees, he threw the rope up again, and this time it hooked onto a tree's large branch. Pulling at it to make sure it was secure, he felt satisfied and attempted once more to climb the wall. This time he was successful and he threw himself over the wall, landing in a prickly overgrown area. His fingers stung and were bleeding, and he cursed himself for not being able to buy gloves.

Looking up at the balconies, he could see lights on inside the house and a pair of French windows were slightly open, letting in the evening breeze. Alex knew from memory that the room was the main bedroom where Mr Pereira, or Mr P as he was known locally, would be residing. Alex was sure of it.

Stealthily, he kept in the darkness, near the shadows of the bushes away from the lights of the house and ran across the manicured lawn. Alex knew this was what Maggie was afraid of; that he was walking back into the Pereira home, and he didn't know what the consequences would be for him. Watching, Alex saw a few men lighting cigarettes and standing together on the balcony laughing and talking. Everything seemed very relaxed, which usually meant the boss wasn't home. It sickened him to think he'd come all this way, been scratched to fuck and nearly broken his neck for nothing!

Hearing voices, he started to climb up the side of the house to a side balcony. This was easier because there were many places to place his feet to give him a leg up. Hiding behind a low wall, he could still see the men smoking and as he waited, they finished their conversation and departed to their usual posts. With his heart in his mouth, Alex waited, not daring to breathe, as one man walked towards the wall he was hiding behind. As he drew closer, Alex knew he couldn't risk this man sounding the alarm and swiftly stepping forward, he plunged the knife he had bought into the man's stomach, and then again into his chest. Seeing him fall backwards onto the stone railing, Alex kicked him over the balcony. 'Old habits die hard,' he mused to himself.

Slightly bloodstained himself, he looked down at the giveaway signs of blood on the floor. Sooner or later, someone would see it or miss the man and sound the alarm so he had to act fast. His heart pounding in his chest, he crept along to the open window which had long voile curtains blowing in the breeze. Craning his neck, Alex tried to see inside but couldn't. Rubbing the blood on his hands onto his black shirt, Alex put the knife back into his pocket as he thought about his next move. He could hear someone talking inside the room and then heard the door shut as whoever it was left.

'Come in, Alex, the coast is clear.' The rasping voice startled him and Alex stood rooted to the spot, unable to move. 'Come in, I said.'

Summoning up all of his courage and expecting to be shot dead, Alex closed his eyes and parted the curtain and entered the room. Surprised, he stood looking at the unexpected scene before him. In the middle of the very expensive bedroom with white marbled floors and subtle lighting stood a large bed. In the middle of the bed lay the man Alex had come to see – Mr Pereira. The old man had an oxygen mask on his old and withered face and Alex thought how small he looked, surrounded by hospital machinery in the giant bed. The old man's hand raised and weakly he beckoned Alex towards him. This was not how Alex remembered him, but then many years had passed since they had last seen each other.

Raising his mask slightly, Pereira smiled. 'I still have the ears of a rat, Alex, and I'd know your scent anywhere. After all, I trained you. I knew you would come; I've been expecting it and I'm glad you have. That's why I leave the windows open. I knew your visit wouldn't be a conventional one.' Coughing slightly, he put the mask back to his face and breathed in the oxygen.

Alex looked nervously at the doors, before looking back towards Mr Pereira.

'No one will come and disturb us unless I press my buzzer. So, speak Alex, but do it quietly.' Pereira started coughing, and Alex spied a drink beside the bed and reached over, holding the beaker with a straw to the old man's lips. He waited while he took a sip, then put his oxygen mask back on him. Grateful, the old man nodded his head and lay back on his mountain of pillows.

'I need to find my daughter... Deana,' Alex blurted out suddenly. 'She has been kidnapped, is possibly dead by now... it's been days and we've heard nothing.' Alex hated saying the words out loud, but he knew there was a chance Deana could already be dead. 'Is it the bounty on my head? Has someone decided to kill my family instead of me? Have you given the order?' Without realising it, Alex found himself holding the old man's hand, fondly. Pereira had always treated Alex fairly and had once been a father figure in his life.

Removing the mask, and with laboured breaths, Pereira shook his head weakly. 'I am a dying old man, Alex. I am nothing now and they speak in front of me as though I am invisible. Have you spoken to John about your concerns? I believe he is enjoying his new celebrity status as mafia boss that you handed to him on a plate. You're the one who gave him his freedom in court. You're the one who grassed everyone up, while he walked freely claiming his crown as head of the families.'

Alex sat on the edge of the bed and leaned closer. Pereira's voice was almost a whisper now and Alex was having trouble hearing his words. 'Keep your friends close, Alex, and your enemies closer. I don't believe your daughter is dead yet... at least she wasn't a day ago.'

Alex ran his hands through his hair and let out a huge sigh of relief.

Pereira patted Alex's hand. 'I hear you have friends in high and low places these days?' He smiled.

Puzzled, Alex looked at him, not knowing who he meant.

'The Diamond woman. Queen of the Milieu? She is firm but fair and she has her own agenda. But that's for you to work out.'

'You know her?'

Patsy Diamond was a woman many feared and ran her own gangland empire in the north. Alex had met her only once and was intrigued by just how much the old man knew. There was more to all of this, he was sure of it, but time was short.

'Everyone in this business knows everyone else, Alex. I have had dealings with Mrs Diamond and she is a fair business woman. Keep her onside if you can. She has weighed up the odds and chosen you.'

Confused, Alex didn't want to press the subject further. He just wanted to get Deana back home safely. He would deal with the rest later.

'Do you know where my daughter is?'

'Look closer to home, Alex. I don't know where she is. I wish I did, but the answers you need lie under your nose.' The old man burst into a fit of coughing and waved his hand at Alex to get out of sight. Taking the hint, Alex ran and hid in the en-suite bathroom. Hearing a woman's voice, his ears pricked up and he could tell by her chatter that she was a nurse. She was soothing Pereira and giving him medication to help him sleep. As soon as she had left, Alex stepped out of his hiding place and approached Pereira again. 'Is there any more I should know Pereira?'

'Only that I am sorry. Sorry that my son ruined your life. I couldn't help you then, no one would listen to me. But you were justified in killing my grandson for attempting to rape your wife. If it had been me, I would have done the same thing. Now I need you to do me a favour, Alex.'

'Anything, Pereira. You know that. And there is no need to apologise. What's done is done.'

'Then end my misery, Alex. If I were a dog, they would put me down. Help me, Alex. I'm a burden and no one else has the guts to do it, even though they wished they could. I trust you, Alex.'

A sick feeling overwhelmed Alex when he heard what the old man was asking of him, but he understood it. This was no life for this once great man. Leaning forward, Alex kissed Pereira on the forehead and reached for the pillow beside him and held it down over his face. There was a weak struggle, but then Alex felt the life drain from Pereira and the man was at peace. Removing the pillow, Alex stood there for a moment staring at his old friend and then placed the buzzer in his hand and replaced the oxygen mask. 'Rest in peace old man.'

Without a backward glance, Alex retraced his steps as he made his way out of the house and back over the wall onto the dark streets. Tears fell down his face. Alex had killed many people, but this was the worst thing he had ever been asked to do. As he thought of the old man lying there, he felt guilty and his mind was in turmoil, but he knew that Pereira had literally taken their meeting to his grave. But to everyone else, it would look like the old man had died peacefully in his sleep.

# 9

## ENLIGHTENMENT

Making his way directly to the airport, Alex decided to wait there even though his flight wasn't for another few hours. On reaching the airport, hot and sweaty, he went directly to the toilets, washed up and changed into the clean clothes he had in his rucksack. He dumped the ones he'd used, which were dirty, torn and bloodstained, in the bins. Alex was exhausted and couldn't remember the last time he'd eaten anything. Now, he felt hungry. The airport was crowded and looking around, Alex decided to go for the easy option and bought a burger and a coffee from a fast-food place. Finding a seat, Alex settled down to eat. Some people around him were sleeping while waiting for their flights, and Alex wished he could join them in a moment's peace. The hot coffee soothed his throat and his meal seemed to go down in one bite. Dawn was slowly breaking outside, and he watched the sun come up as he tried to process everything that had happened since he'd been here.

As he looked around the busy airport, Alex was suddenly distracted by someone he thought he knew. Craning his neck, Alex blinked hard as he watched the man walking to the check-in desk. Alex wasn't sure if he was dreaming, or if the person he was seeing was really there. Because Alex was sure the man he was looking at was his old friend John!

John, dressed in his best navy suit and tie, looked very much the gentleman with his hair slicked back and his briefcase. A fleeting thought crossed Alex's mind. Had he been in Pereira's house at the same time as himself? Presumably, he would have gone there if he was in Portugal. And now, it seemed they were going to be on the same aeroplane home, although John would be flying business class no doubt and Alex flying normal, standard tourist class. Alex couldn't take his eyes off John, as he smiled and charmed the young woman on the check-in desk. Impulsively, Alex was about to jump out of his seat and confront him, there and then, when he saw two henchmen approach John. He wasn't alone. His blood boiled, but he thought better of it. The airport was no place for a confrontation, and he knew he would come off the worse for it. So, for now, Alex would watch and wait.

\* \* \*

Deana had only seen her kidnappers once today. They had opened the door and thrown a bottle of water at her and a loaf of bread and then quickly shut the door behind them. She had sat on her duvet in the corner expecting some kind of torment, but it hadn't come. She listened as she heard the bolt slide across the outside of the door and their footsteps disappear into the distance. Tearing open the wrapper from the bread, she ate some dry slices. Then opening the bottle of water she almost downed it in one.

All night, she had pushed and pushed at the boards on the window and her fingers were scratched and torn with splinters. Finally, she had eased a plank off from the inside. She had noted that the nails were still embedded in it, which would make it easier for her to put back into the holes in the walls before her kidnappers came in and noticed them missing. The hardest part had been pushing through the window with her trainer to try to move the boarding away from the outside. Deana couldn't believe how hard it had been to break glass. No matter how hard she had pushed and banged the glass, it hadn't given way.

Now, with some dry bread in her stomach, Deana was ready to give it another go. Taking the loose plank in her hands, she held her breath and pushed with all her might against the glass. As if by magic it had instantly cracked and shattered. The noise seemed deafening to her in the silence, and she was sure that if anyone was in the house they would have heard the noise. Holding her breath for a moment, she waited. Her ears pricked for the sound of footsteps returning and the door opening. Her heart was pounding, and she trembled with fear. God knows what would happen to her if she was found trying to escape. For what seemed like forever she stood in silence waiting... but nothing happened and no one came.

Going back to the broken window, she was careful not to cut her hands on the shattered remnants of glass. Using the plank again she pushed at the boards on the outside of the window. Now, she had better access, her adrenalin surged in her veins and blow after blow she could see one of the planks outside coming loose, until she heard it drop, making a clanging noise as it fell to the floor. Doing her best to avoid the broken glass, Deana poked her head through the hole to see outside. Gulping in the fresh air and filling her lungs, she blinked hard to adjust her eyes to the gloomy light outside.

From what she could make out, she was in the middle of an industrial business unit surrounded by scaffolding, but she had no idea where she was exactly. She felt desolate and alone and as exhaustion swept over her, she sat on the floor with her legs crossed. She ached and she was tired, but most of all she missed home and her family. Feeling utterly miserable, tears ran down her face once more. She didn't know what else to do. Her hands were bleeding from the scratches, but she didn't want to waste her water washing them. Attaching the inside plank and its nails back into the holes in the walls, she stared at it. It didn't look right, but she wondered if her kidnappers would even notice. They would definitely notice the plank of wood that had fallen to the ground outside, but she would deal with the consequences of that another time. Giving up all hope of ever seeing her family again, she lay on her soiled duvet and cried herself to sleep.

* * *

Sitting on the aeroplane, Alex longed to sleep for just a few hours. His mind was in turmoil, as he thought over everything that Pereira had said and tried to fit pieces together. Who was it that he needed to look at closer to home? Did this point back to the kids and what had happened to Kev in that flat? Suddenly, Alex opened his eyes wide as a thought occurred to him. Why had Luke said that Dante shouldn't have been at Kev's that night? He had dismissed it at the time, but now it made him wonder. Tossing it over in his mind, he felt Luke knew more about this whole situation than he had admitted.

Alex also realised that Luke was the last person to see Deana when she had gone to his house to pick up her car. Dan had told him and Maggie that they had argued, and Alex thought Luke would have known about that too. If he hadn't seen the argument first-hand, Deana would have still been ranting about it to him. And yet Luke had let her get into her car upset and drive off that day. Slowly things were unravelling in Alex's brain and he didn't like the sound of it.

As the plane landed, Alex's eyes darted everywhere and he felt on high alert. He desperately didn't want John spotting him. He knew John would have a car come to meet him, and Alex felt nervous and twitchy as he passed through customs. It seemed to take forever, but once Alex was through he ran to the first toilets he could spot and decided to stay there out of sight for half an hour.

Eventually, Alex felt the coast was clear and left the airport. As he found his motorbike, he felt safer as he put his helmet on, covering his face, but he felt drained. He wanted a hot shower, food and most of all sleep, although he knew his mind wouldn't let him and neither would Maggie. He would omit to tell her that he had murdered two people while he was away. As he started up the motorbike, he made his way home, his mind buzzing still.

\* \* \*

'Alex! You're home!' Maggie shouted as she squeezed him so tight he could barely breathe. Maggie was elated to see him. Dante was next to hug him tightly and between the three of them they had a huge family hug together.

'Well, what's the news?' Maggie asked excitedly. 'Did you find out what you needed to know? What about Deana... do you know where she is? Is she safe?'

'Whoa, please. Maggie, I'm tired. I'm hungry and I smell. Let me have a shower and a rest first, eh? I'm pretty sure Deana is still alive, but I need to think through what I've discovered before I share it with you, okay?'

'But you're okay otherwise?' Taking his hands in hers, she saw the tell-tale scratches and a worried look crossed her face.

'I fell in some bushes, but I'm okay. I will tell you later, but I think we're closer to the truth now. Just give me an hour, eh, love?' Patting Dan on the head, Alex walked to the bathroom and let the hot water from the shower rain down on his head. Only now, could he see just how badly he had scratched himself and the bruises that were forming on his body.

As he walked into the bedroom, Maggie was putting a mug of coffee and a bacon sandwich on the bedside table. 'Eat and drink before you sleep, love.' She smiled. Seeing the dark rings under his eyes, she kissed him. 'Give me a shout when you're ready, you look shattered.'

Pulling back the duvet, Alex crawled into bed. No sooner had his head hit the pillow than he was fast asleep.

* * *

Seeing the relief at his father's return, Dante felt it was time to bring up the subject on his mind that had been bothering him. 'Mum, I'm fed up of this home learning and being cooped up in here all day. Can't I go back to school?'

A worried look crossed Maggie's face. 'I don't know, Dante. Look what's happened to Deana. What if someone kidnapped you, too? And you're not cooped up behind closed doors. We live in a pub! Lots of people come in here that you know.'

'Yeah, but I could still be kidnapped while picking up empty beer glasses from outside. I'm just so bored, Mum!'

'Maybe you could go and see your friend Luke? You haven't seen him for a few days. And I'll have a word with your father about school. You might be cooped up in a pub, but you're surrounded by family and friends and freedom. Your father was cooped up in a ten-by-ten cell, deprived of all that. And Deana, well, God knows where she is. I shudder when I think about it. It feels like she's been gone for months and yet it's only been days. I smell her clothes in the laundry basket just to get the scent of her.' Maggie sniffed as tears filled her eyes.

Dan grimaced when he thought about Deana and where she might be. He hoped his mum would relent and let him go back to school but he knew she needed to run it past his dad first. So, he would spend another day filling the dishwasher and rinsing the bloody cutlery under the red-hot spray, almost burning his hands. His mind wandered back to Deana, and he wondered what she was doing – if anything. Strangely enough, he missed her bossy ways, her banter, even her insults! He didn't like being an only child. Crossing his fingers as he made his way to the kitchen, he silently prayed for her safety.

\* \* \*

Much later, Alex woke up and yawning, he threw back the duvet. His whole body ached and although he was still shattered, he couldn't sleep any more. His stomach was making gurgling noises and as he jumped into the shower again, he began to feel revived. As he'd slept, his brain had begun to work out his next plan of action – Luke or John. Deep down, his gut instinct told him they were both as guilty as hell in this matter and they knew more than they were letting on. Luke could wait; John was the bigger fish. And the nagging question in all of this was, why? Why hadn't John told him what his kids were up to?

Following the smells of different foods coming from the downstairs restaurant, Alex found Maggie sat on the other side of the bar having a coffee with Olivia, but still on hand if needed. 'Is there a spare one of whatever that chef is cooking up, love?'

Maggie's face lit up instantly. 'He's cooking whatever you

fancy, love. How about a big juicy steak with all of the trimmings?'

Giving her the thumbs up, Alex followed Maggie as she stood up and found him a table in the restaurant. 'I'll go and tell chef. In fact, why don't you ask Mark to join you?' she asked him.

'I tell you what, why don't we make it a foursome and you and Olivia can join us too. Or six of us if George and Dante are around. As long as you remember, no shop talk and no Deana talk. That's off limits until were alone, okay?'

'Okay, that will be nice, but I do want to hear about your trip sooner or later.'

Seeing him nod his head, Maggie first went to inform Olivia that they were having dinner together and to tell Mark to come straight to the pub, then she gave Dan and George a shout. Maggie felt happier inside, although she wasn't sure why with Deana still missing. She supposed it was because Alex was home. Going back to Portugal could have been a death sentence if he'd been spotted and she hadn't had a moment's peace until she saw him back home alive.

Mark arrived wearing his dirty work boots and oily sweater and as they all gathered at the table, Alex opened a bottle of red wine, and they all chatted amiably. Just then a very flustered middle-aged woman came into the pub and smiled weakly at them.

'Oh God, what's he done now?' Olivia whispered.

'Who?' Looking around, Alex spotted the woman standing in the middle of the restaurant holding a carrier bag. The woman came over to join them.

With her face full of apology and embarrassment, she shook her head. 'I'm so sorry, Maggie. Here, take these back.'

Curiously, Alex craned his neck to look in the carrier bag, frowning as he looked up at Maggie and then the woman. Maggie was full of assurance for the woman, and on seeing Alex's confused look, introduced them. 'Alex, this is Jen, the nurse I was telling you about. She popped in earlier with Larry and it seems while her back was turned, he pocketed our salt and pepper pots!' Maggie laughed.

Alex burst out laughing. It was the first time he had felt like laughing in a long time. 'Is this the resident pickpocket you were mentioning?' Standing up, Alex pulled out a chair for Jen. 'You look like you need a glass of wine. Sit down, Jen.' Alex still couldn't help smiling while he poured her a glass of wine. 'Tell me more about your grandfather, is it?'

Seeing Alex's warm, welcoming grin, Jen couldn't help smiling back and sipped at the wine Alex had poured for her. 'There's nothing to say really. He just can't help himself.' She shrugged. 'I won't join you if you don't mind. I've got to get back. Les is coming to sit with him and watch a musical while I do a night shift at the hospital. At least he's asleep at night. And anyway, I've just noticed Pete walk into the bar. He hasn't spoken to me for weeks since the penny dropped and I told him I had no interest in going to bingo with him.' Jen smiled, then broke out into a laugh. Finishing her drink, she got up and left.

'I do like her,' Maggie commented. 'She takes everything in her stride, but she's got a lot on her plate.'

'So does Pete by the sound of it. He's got a girlfriend now, but he hasn't seen her for weeks either.' Laughed Mark.

'Well, I've got a job,' exclaimed Olivia, changing the subject and silencing everyone. 'I'm working as a cleaner for the local school. It's a job on their banking rota, with the council.'

'Since when?' asked Mark, looking as though the wind had just been knocked out of his sails. 'Where did that come from? I thought we were talking about Pete?'

'Since yesterday. I'm not going to be a mum again, so I might as well do something else with my time.' It was obvious Olivia had been trying to find the right time to make her announcement, and that this dinner had helped, but it was clear that Mark wasn't happy about Olivia being a cleaner.

'That's great, Olivia,' encouraged Alex, trying not to spoil her moment. 'Getting a job with the council is no mean feat. That really is something to celebrate, isn't it, Mark?'

'Yeah, yeah,' Mark stammered, taking Alex's lead. 'Alex is right, they must like the sound of you.'

Alex grinned, trying to make light of a tense moment. 'That means you can sit back, Mark and let your wife keep you. Imagine all those extra days you can take off!'

'What? Like you, you mean,' Mark snapped, still trying to take in Olivia's announcement. Seeing the shocked look on Alex's face, he quickly apologised. 'Sorry mate, I didn't mean it like that. You haven't really had a lot of time to sort yourself out, have you?'

Feeling the sting of the truth, Alex wondered if that was what everyone thought. Looking at Maggie, he realised just how many hours she worked, and she never once moaned about it. She had built this pub up from a run-down shithole into a thriving restaurant and pub and apart from helping out here and there, he could take no credit for it. He suddenly felt ashamed.

'You're right, Mark. Maggie has done the hard work and I've been a liability most of the time.' Maggie shook her head and kissed Alex on the cheek, but he carried on. 'It's time to sort myself out.' Alex raised his glass to make a toast. 'To the future!'

They all smiled and chinked their glasses together, but Alex felt this was a wake-up call. Mark's comment had certainly given him something to think about. He needed to find his own way. But where to begin? What was he good at? All he had ever done had been illegal. Now reality dawned. He wanted a fresh start and he had hopefully been given one, but he had to find his own way in life.

Interrupting his thoughts, Mark tried again to make amends. 'Well, aren't you just going to run the pub with Maggie, Alex? Most couples run a pub together.'

'The pub is Maggie's baby. Her name is above the door, and she has put all the hours in to make it thrive. I'll have to consider my options.' Again, Maggie tried butting in, raising her objections. 'No love, Mark is right. I need to find something for myself, and I will.' He kissed Maggie and then picked up his glass again. 'Now enough of all that. Tonight is for family and friends and to celebrate Olivia's new job. Well done, love. Cheers!' Everyone raised their glasses again, but a dark cloud had settled over Alex. The future was a blank page in front of him but would he ever be able to shake off his past?

# 10

## DECISIONS

The next morning, Alex lay on the bed and watched Maggie put her make-up on and get dressed. He loved admiring her body and pert breasts and each time he saw her, he still felt something stir within him. Trying to think of something else, and not his libido, he thought he would discuss his daily plans with her. 'I'm going to see John today. I've already called him and it seems you need an appointment to see the lord and master these days,' Alex laughed. 'I feel he might have some answers for me. Especially about why he was in Portugal. And I would have also thought he would have come and told me, or you that Pereira had died, but he hasn't. We all knew him and surely, it's just good manners to come and inform us?'

'Maybe we don't count any more, Alex? And you haven't really said why you want to see him, although I agree, he may be able to help.'

'He's involved in all of this, Maggie, I know it. But to be certain, I need to ask him one question. And his answer will determine if he is our friend or not.'

'Ooh, Mr Mystery. I like that.' Maggie smiled while putting on her lipstick. 'By the way, I've said Dante can go back to school today. We can't keep him at home forever... what do you think?'

'I think it's safe enough. I don't think whoever has Deana wants both kids, otherwise, they would have done it by now. On the other hand, I still don't know what they're waiting for. We've heard nothing, but today I'm going to change all of that.'

Hearing the seriousness in his voice, Maggie sighed heavily. She finished her make-up, had one last spray of perfume and left the bedroom to start another day of work.

Alex looked through his wardrobe and at the back found his old suits that Maggie must have salvaged from the old days. They had been dry cleaned and kept in plastic covers and were just what Alex needed. Fight fire with fire, he thought to himself. Taking a couple out, he liked the look of the grey one that shone like silk. As he tried it on, the memories came flooding back. He had worn it when he had been an important figure among the mafia families. And now, he was going to go to war in it. He had lost a few pounds since he had worn it last, and it fitted better, not so snug around the waist. Slicking his black, wavy hair back into a ponytail, Alex looked at himself in the mirror. Mafia man, Alex Silva, aka the Silva Bullet, stared back at him. He hadn't seen him for a long time, but it was like looking at an old friend.

Once his taxi stopped outside of John's block of flats and offices in Chelsea, Alex felt mentally prepared for what he was going to say, but still the nerves ran through his body.

Met by the men inside John's house, Alex was frisked.

'Stop it, for goodness' sake. Come in Alex. Old habits die hard with this lot.' John strode forward down the well-polished, wooden floors of the immaculately decorated apartment, his hand stretched out to greet Alex. 'Come inside and have a drink. I must say, I prefer these clothes to the last uniform I saw you wearing.' John laughed and steered Alex towards his study.

Spying him closely, Alex hugged John, which was their usual greeting. John's new suave and charming ways exuded authority. John's office resembled a boardroom, and crystal decanters sat on a silver tray in the middle of the table. As Alex looked around, he could see what Pereira had meant by his new celebrity status. On the walls of the office were framed photos of John with famous rock stars and actors – all adding to his new status being accepted by one and all.

After pouring them both a drink, John sat down. 'Well, as there isn't a rope over the wall, I can see you have broken out of prison, or have they let you out early?' John asked. He was dressed in a light grey suit and silk tie, and the tanned glow of his face made him look more handsome than Alex remembered.

Surprised slightly, Alex ignored the question. Surely, John knew he was out of prison. 'Have you been away John, on holiday I mean?' Alex asked calmly as he sipped whisky from the thick-cut crystal square glass. He knew he had been away, because he had seen him at the airport, but would John admit to it? Alex felt this pomp and ceremony was to prove something or make a point, but he wasn't sure what. Why did John feel the need to impress him?

Stretching out his arms, John yawned. 'Unfortunately not, Alex. I haven't had time. Most of this tan is off a sun bed.'

Alex nodded and took another sip of his drink as he leaned back in his chair. 'Do you never feel like going back to the old country and relaxing with your friends and family out there?'

'Portugal? No, I haven't been there in ages. Why do you ask?' John asked defensively.

Alex's heart sank. He'd wanted John to tell him the truth, but he had lied to him. A sadness settled over Alex. 'No reason, I just saw your sun tan and looked at my arms that look like a bottle of milk.' Alex laughed.

'Rubbish! You have always had that swarthy, Portuguese look, Alex. So, you said it was important to see me. What can I do for you?' John spread his hands open wide. 'Anything you want, Alex.'

As Alex looked at his old friend, he wanted to spit at him, or worse. Suddenly, his blood boiled as he faced this liar in front of him. 'My daughter, Deana, has been kidnapped, John,' he said, matter-of-factly. 'I'm sure you've heard about it, and the bottom line is I want her back – unscathed.' In a low monotone voice, Alex spelt out the reason for his visit. As silence fell in the room, Alex picked up his glass again and took another sip of whisky while watching John over the top of his glass.

Under the sun tan, John paled. 'Well, I see you still don't mince your words, Alex. But you haven't called Deana by her real name, have you?' John snapped. 'Which as you know by now is also that of drug dealer!'

Alex slammed his glass onto table and John raised his hand to stop him.

'Don't. There are two armed men out there who would blow your head off. And I am only saying what everyone else knows.'

Ignoring the threats, Alex carried on. He hadn't come for an argument, he had come for answers. 'If you knew that, why didn't you tell me, John? I've been in prison, behind bars. If you knew what the kids were up to, why didn't you tell me as my friend?'

Sitting upright, and straightening his tie, somewhat nervously under Alex's watchful eye, John spoke more calmly. 'Because I *didn't* know, Alex.' John held his hands up in submission. 'Truly, I didn't know it was your kids that were causing street wars... at least not straight away. They were loose cannons, yes, but every street soldier and known troublemaker was getting the blame for their actions. Insider dealing, creaming off the top and stealing from their bosses, you name it. Gang against gang, all tearing each other apart and all because of your two teenagers. Christ, if it wasn't so serious, it would be laughable!' he exclaimed.

'So how did you find out?' Anger dripped from Alex's mouth as he watched his friend squirm before him.

'They told me... No, they boasted to me what they were doing. I couldn't believe my fucking ears. At least Dante has respect. But Deana has a bad attitude. She feels she has a right to do as she pleases. Maybe she is more like you than you think.'

'So, confession time, John. When they told you, why didn't you tell me or Maggie?'

'Confession time for you, Alex. Why have you waited this long before coming to see me? You've been out of prison for days. Why not come sooner, when you first knew she was missing?'

'Now we're getting to the truth, John. Do you know where she is?'

'No, I don't. I am paid protection money, Alex, to look after people's turf. I make sure that no one steps on anyone's toes and that things run smoothly. And it wasn't until my office turned into Piccadilly Circus with gangsters and dealers banging on my door at all times of night and day asking about rival gangs moving in on their turf and selling on their doorstep and what did I know about it? And the truth was, Alex, I knew fuck all!' John shouted. 'I knew fuck all about it, but I couldn't say that, could I? Me, the boss of the organisation, hasn't got a clue about what is going on under his nose. Everyone is raving about this new drug that hits the spot and what's more, it's cheaper than the shit everyone else is selling. But who is cooking it? Where does it come from? Rival gangs were blaming and shooting each other... and why?' Red faced and angry, John couldn't stop himself from shouting his frustrations. 'Well, the fucking reason is your kids! The fucking Silva kids think they are on some kind of school outing but they don't realise the trail of havoc they are leaving in their wake!' Angrily, John stood up and started to pace the room.

'What was I to do, Alex? I had no idea who was behind all of this and yet constantly, people were coming to me for answers. I was drowning, until one day Dante called me and wanted to meet up. He and Deana both got willingly into the back of my car and confessed everything to me. They wanted my help to buy the pub for Maggie so that they didn't feel like dealers. They were doing it all for the right reasons, to help their family, but a dealer is a dealer, Alex. Between them, they have been driving around, here there and everywhere undercutting people's prices. They have made hundreds of thousands of pounds, which means they have stolen off other dealers, doesn't it? It was a death wish, and you know it.' John wagged his finger in Alex's calm face.

'And then what? What did you do next, John?' Alex remained poker faced. He could see how agitated John was and the angrier John got, the calmer he felt.

'They were losing faith in me. Don't you understand? I had to throw them a bone. So, when it came to it, the choice was between myself, my reputation and my life or two stupid kids who have watched too many gangster movies and think they can impersonate them. So, in answer to the question you want, I gave the dealers your kids' names. They were collateral damage, Alex. I had no choice.' John sighed as the emotion and anger left. He ran a hand over his face before speaking again. 'But I also kept my word to them. I told them I would arrange the sale of the pub and have the deeds sent on to them and I kept my word, Alex.' John stressed.

Alex watched John's face redden as he tried to defend what

he had done. 'I believe you also took your commission too. You forgot to mention that.' Alex's calm demeanour seemed to irritate John even more. 'And yet whilst I appreciate the pressure was on, especially for a man in your position' – Alex slowly looked him up and down – 'you still didn't tip me off in any way about what was going on. I could have tried to put a stop to it all without it getting out of hand. But now it is too late. So, where is Deana? Who took this information and kidnapped her? Is she already dead?' Alex asked as his hatred for John intensified.

'I'm not sure, Alex...'

Alex stood up. 'I think you are sure, John. And I want her home, in one piece, alive and well. No dead bodies left on my doorstep, eh?'

Angrily and with one swoop of his hand, John cleared the table, knocking the crystal decanters to the floor. The loud noise brought John's minders running into the room with their guns ready in their hands. Breathing heavily, John waved his hand for them to leave. 'It's okay. It's nothing, just an accident. You can leave.' After one last glance at Alex, the men left.

'Do not give me orders, Alex. You're a nobody now! It's me people look up to. So, let's just call this a friendly argument and I won't take it any further.'

Alex laughed at how pathetic John sounded. 'One more question, John, if I may. You knew I was out of prison and I am sure you will be glad when I go back inside, but why didn't you contact me? A friendly hello might have been nice.'

Looking down at the floor, John shook his head. 'You ruined a very good lucrative drug injection into the prisons.'

Incredulously, Alex looked at his one-time friend. 'You were helping supply the drugs inside? You know the shit time they gave me in prison – they nearly had me killed, John, and for what? For fuck's sake, just how low have you sunk with all of your power?'

'At least I have respect, Alex! No one respects you!' John shouted at Alex again but Alex shook his head sadly.

'Firstly John, no one respects you. Not me, not any of your new minions and definitely none of the old families we used to work for. And especially not Pereira who I just visited before he sadly met his end. I have to say, your doppelganger looked very well dressed at the airport!'

John's face dropped and his jaw almost fell onto his chest. Clearly taken aback at Alex's news, he pulled out a chair and sat down. 'You saw Pereira? You know he's dead?'

Alex stood up and walked towards the door. 'Yes, John, I know Pereira is dead.' Alex grinned. 'I killed him.' With that, Alex left John gobsmacked with his latest bombshell.

Once outside, Alex loosened his tie and lit a cigarette. He wanted to walk a while to clear his head before going home. As he acknowledged that his gut instinct hadn't deserted him, he felt sick when he realised that John had betrayed his children. They had been kids together, had worked together and it had been John who had sat at the back of the courtroom as Alex had pointed the finger at every one of the mafia bosses. It was John who had assured him that the bounty would be taken off Alex's head, but he had lied time and time again. For now, he couldn't kill John, which was his ultimate intention. He had to bide his time because he knew John was the key to finding Deana.

Already Alex could mentally see John hastily making phone calls to the people that mattered. Wherever they had Deana, they would move her, but he felt sure they wouldn't kill her. Not now. For the time being, his hands were tied, but he also knew John wouldn't have admitted anything to him if Deana was already dead because he would have nothing left to bargain with.

Finishing his cigarette, Alex hailed a taxi. He didn't care how much it would cost all the way to Kent. It would give him time to think and get everything in order so he could relay it all to Maggie. How stupid and innocent his kids had been walking into the lion's den and telling him everything. Christ, they were naive. No one is your friend when it comes to money – Alex had learnt that the hard way.

## 11

### LOVE, JEALOUSY AND HATE

Walking back into the pub, Alex was about to go straight upstairs but could hear more than the usual chatter coming from the small staff room. Curiously, he put his ear to the door, but didn't recognise any of the voices. Suddenly, a hand touched his shoulder, making him jump out of his skin. 'What the...?'

'Shush.' Dan put his finger to his lips. 'It's a private wake and Mum said they could have it in the back room.' Dan winked and beckoned Alex upstairs. Intrigued, Alex followed him and, once out of ear shot, looked at his son questioningly.

'It's Joanie.' Dan grinned. 'Mad as a box of frogs she is and a right miserable cow! But she goes to bingo club and one of those old lady coffee mornings...'

Frowning, Alex couldn't make the connection. 'So, what has that got to do with our back room?'

Dan burst out laughing. 'Well, she makes a point of reading the obituaries, looking for people who have died and then turns up at the funeral hoping they lay on a good spread. Christ, she's like the grim reaper.'

'Are you telling me that old bag makes a habit of visiting

funerals for the wake? Don't people realise that she's not one of the family or something?'

Dan's face was almost red with laughter as he nodded his head. 'People are too polite to ask an old lady what she is doing at the funeral. After all, most of the family that turn up don't know each other that much. And distant families just turn up out of duty and hope for something left in the will.'

'Bloody hell, this place gets worse! A professional mourner!' After his tense meeting with John, Alex felt himself laugh and relax. 'So, whose wake is it this time? It sounds like quite a bunch.' For a wake, there didn't sound like much mourning going on. If anything, there was nothing but laughter.

'It was some Scottish bloke. They called him the "tartan jockstrap". Apparently, he used to do a drag act at women's hen parties in his younger days.' Dan was laughing so much he had to sit down on the sofa, while watching his dad's confused face.

Popping her head around the door, Maggie smiled. 'Oh Alex, you're back. I didn't hear you come in.'

'Well, you wouldn't, would you. Not with that noise downstairs. Dan said it was a wake?'

Maggie grinned. 'Oh, it is love. He used to be a—'

'Yeah, I know,' Alex butted in. 'A stripper, a drag act, whatever!' Alex laughed.

'Hey, don't knock it love. It's lightened the mood and we're giving him a good send off. Everyone is enjoying themselves.' Maggie laughed. 'And Christ, they're drinking like fish!'

'The Tartan Jockstrap though. What kind of a name is that?'

'Catchy, I'd say.' Maggie winked. 'Anyway, how did your meeting go?'

'I'll tell you later; you'd better get back to the flying Scotsman.'

'Oh, God, I hope not. They cremated him an hour ago.' Maggie laughed as she made her way back downstairs.

As Alex thought about his meeting with John, he also remembered one vital key to his puzzle he needed to speak to Dante about. 'Put the kettle on, Dan. Anyway, I wanted to have a word with you about Luke.'

'Luke? What about him? Oh Dad, we're not going to argue again, are we?'

'No, son. There are just some things I want to go over to get straight in my mind.'

Dan busied himself making coffee and then carrying two mugs into the lounge, he sat down and waited for his dad's interrogation.

'Don't look so worried,' Alex said, as he took a mug from Dante. 'Now, I believe Deana had a crush on Kev, is that right? And given what I know now, he didn't feel the same way.'

Dan looked at Alex confused, and waited for Alex to fill in the blanks.

'It seems that Kev has omitted to tell Deana and you by all accounts, that he's gay and never had any intentions of being more than just a good friend.'

Dan's jaw dropped. 'I had absolutely no idea, Dad.' Seeing the funny side of things, Dante burst out laughing, 'So Kev is gay and Deana has been throwing herself at him and buying him presents to sweeten him up!' Dan laughed again. 'Oh my God, she would cringe in her boots if she knew! I wonder if any of her college mates had their gaydar on that night and knew?'

'Well, you certainly didn't,' Alex joked. 'But seriously, Luke never told you about Kev?' Seeing Dan shake his head, Alex took a sip of his drink before continuing. 'And how does Luke feel about Deana? I get the feeling that he's keen. How did he feel about Deana mooning over his brother, did he ever say?'

'No, he never mentioned it. Luke did try stopping Deana spending money on Kev, but you know Deana, she doesn't take advice easy. But he never asked her out or anything, if that's what you mean?'

Alex felt he had his answer. Luke liked, possibly even loved, Deana and she hadn't given him the time of day, apart from friendship and their partnership in crime. He'd kept Kev's secret because he knew Deana hanging around Kev kept her close and in his company, didn't it? Fucking jealousy, Alex cursed inwardly. What exactly had Luke done to his brother and to Deana? That was the question Alex still needed answers to.

'Who I am interested in, is this Scottish woman who cleaned up Kev's flat. Who was she and more to the point why did she help you? It doesn't make any sense, Dan. Fairy godmothers don't turn up out of the blue and cover your tracks for you, especially with two dead bodies lying there. Did she take the gun? Or was it someone else? Any idea?'

Forlornly, Dan shook his head. 'Don't know, Dad. It was a bit manic that night. It never entered my mind about the gun. We just did what she told us, dumped Kev and left.'

Thinking to himself, Alex wondered if John had the gun. It was a possibility and was definite insurance should he need it. Alex knew he would need to ask him but thought better of it for now. He still had questions about Luke.

'Yeah, I understand that and you must have been in shock, but I still don't understand what was she doing there? And she arrived just in the nick of time, eh?' Alex's mind was spinning. So many questions left unanswered spun around his brain. There were so many loose ends and yet he felt sure the answers were under his nose – just as Pereira had said. Alex just couldn't think clearly. He just needed some space to figure it all out.

\* \* \*

Two men walked into the derelict building where Deana was being held. Neither of them wanted to be there, this wasn't part of their job description. 'Fuck, this place is disgusting. I'll need to wipe my feet on the way out. What is this place?' Throwing his cigarette butt on the floor, Nick the Prick, as he was known for his constant womanising, opened the shutter on the door of a unit, surrounded by scaffolding. The place was falling apart and slates were missing off the roof. Looking up, he could see there was a flat above it, which was where he presumed he'd find his target.

Shrugging, the other man grimaced. 'It used to be an industrial estate for business, by the look of it. Thank God for Google, cos I would never have found it otherwise.'

Pulling up the shutter, they both stood back for a moment and looked down at their black, well-fitted suits. 'If I'd have known we were coming to a shithole I wouldn't have worn one of my best suits. Christ, how come we have to do a spot of babysitting? I've got better things to do.'

'Look, Sparky, I'm no babysitter either. But John wants us to do this, and as Punch and those two morons working for him have fucked up, we don't have a choice. Personally, I just feel like looking in on her and accidentally leaving the door open...'

'I can't believe they've left a woman in here.' For a moment, they both stopped at the bottom of the bare wooden stairs and looked at each other. 'Do you think she's dead, already, Sparky?'

'Only one way to find out. Let's get this over with.' Sparky marched ahead, stomping his feet on every step. Looking around at the many doors on the landing, he tried each of the handles. One by one they turned and opened and they checked each room to see if there was anyone inside. As they reached the first locked door, Sparky nodded to Nick and held out his hands for the keys.

Opening the door, they both took a step back and held their noses. 'What the fuck is that stink?'

Spotting a rolled-up duvet cover on the floor, Nick cautiously pulled at it and was shocked when he saw a young blonde girl underneath it who was dirty, dishevelled and bruised.

'Who are you?' The girl blinked hard and glared at them.

For a moment, Sparky and Nick stared at each other. 'We're moving you today. It seems you've upset a lot of people, love.'

'Where's the other two?' Deana croaked, half asleep. 'They didn't come yesterday.'

'That's because they are otherwise detained by the local constabulary. How long have you been here?' Nick looked at the dishevelled young girl and cringed inside. Both himself and Sparky had been told that it was a sensitive subject they were being asked to look after and that it was a woman drug dealer, but she was just a kid. Taking out his wallet, he took out some money. 'Sparky, find a takeaway around here and get some food and drinks, eh?'

Holding up his hands and refusing the money, Sparky left the room. He felt sickened by the sight and the smell of the room – he wouldn't leave a dog like that, he thought to himself.

'Can you stand?' asked Nick, holding out a hand to steady her. Deana nodded and did as she was told. 'How old are you, love?'

'Eighteen.' She yawned and stood up straight. Looking around, Nick found a wooden chair and brought it over for her to sit on. Her hands were scratched and torn, and her first instincts were to look at the boarded-up window.

'Been trying to escape, love?'

'Wouldn't you, from this place? Are you going to hit me for trying to escape, because I don't give a shit any more. I'm tired of being cooped up in here. You lot kidnapped me and have just left me to rot!' Deana snapped.

'I don't hit women, especially girls. But I've got my orders and that's to move you somewhere else. Do you smoke?' Nick held out his cigarette packet and lighter. Deana shook her head, and then changed her mind. 'Might as well, nothing else to do.' Licking her lips to moisten them, she took the cigarette from Nick, coughing as he lit it and they both smiled at each other. 'Like I said, I don't smoke usually, but then I'm not usually kidnapped either. Are you going to let me go home?' Deana asked hopefully. This man seemed a lot friendlier than the other two she had dealt with. He looked around the same age as her father, his suit was better fitting than his predecessors, and he looked more professional than those evil clowns that had kidnapped her. 'You could you know. I won't say anything,' she pleaded.

'What's your name?' Nick asked. 'And how come you're a drug dealer? Shouldn't you be at gigs or shopping with other girls your age?'

'My name's Deana. Me and my brother sold some cannabis and meth. It seems we've offended people by doing it. But we never meant to hurt anyone. Surely, I don't deserve this? Just let me go home please. My mum will be out of her mind. You could just say you got here and I wasn't here,' she pleaded. As tears rolled down her face, she repeated herself again and again.

Nick was in turmoil; he couldn't do what she was asking, even though he was tempted. His own life was at stake. John knew she was still at the unit, and there was no way he could say she wasn't there. And he wasn't 100 per cent about Sparky. He was a great electrician and enjoyed using his skills on victims during torture, but if someone decided to turn the tables on him, he would surely crumble and confess.

'No can do, love. I'm here to do a job. You're safe, alive... just. I'm going to feed and water you and take you to a better place. I don't know what is planned for you Deana, but I have orders to follow.'

Interrupting them, Sparky walked in. 'There was a McDonald's up the road. Here, take this.' He placed a bag and a drink on the floor and then stood back as though he was going to catch something.

Deana sat down and opened the bag. The cola he had brought her didn't touch the sides. Grabbing a bunch of French fries, she crammed them into her mouth and chewed quickly. Watching her, Nick felt sick. She was like a wounded, starving animal and he hated it.

'Where are you taking me?' Deana asked with her mouth still full of food.

Looking around, Nick grimaced. 'Somewhere better than this place.' Waiting until she had nearly finished, Nick let out a sigh. 'Now, we're going to take you to the car. I need to cover your head, and I want you to behave. I may be acting reasonable now, but scream, shout or make waves, Deana, and I could change the habit of a lifetime... have you got that?'

Still licking her lips from her food, she nodded, accepting her fate. 'When my dad finds out about this, he will go crazy whether I'm alive or not.'

'Well, where's your dad now, eh? If that's a threat blondie, don't bother. I've heard them all before,' Sparky spat out. He hated this grim place and couldn't wait to leave.

'My father is Alex Silva. And believe me, he won't take this lying down.'

Nick cast a glance at Sparky but played ignorant. He knew who she was talking about; only someone from the planet Mars wouldn't. That name had been all over the tabloids.

Taking off his jacket, he put it over Deana's head, much to her annoyance. 'Do as I say, Deana. It won't be for long.' Relaxing a little, Deana bowed her head while Nick wrapped his coat around her.

'You know, we should have done this in the dark. It's fucking broad daylight,' Sparky snapped.

'Do you see anyone around? Even you couldn't find it without Google!'

Annoyed, Nick walked Deana out of the room and down the stairs.

'Why are we covering her head inside, Nick?'

'So, big mouth, shouting my name all over the place, she can't recognise this place and point it out in case the police investigate it.'

'Well, they are going to shoot her anyway. Don't know why we don't just do it now and save ourselves a whole lot of bother...'

Fear consumed Deana as she was led, under Nick's guidance, down the wooden staircase. The other man, she felt sure, wanted to kill her. She was a burden to him and he had better things to do, but Nick wanted to follow his orders and leave with a clear conscience. Good cop, bad cop. Either way, she was afraid, very afraid. Suddenly, the fresh air hit her, and she gulped it in. Her legs felt weak and looking down, she saw the men's polished black shoes, the pavement and the wheels of a car. As she waited to get in, she felt herself being pushed forward, and let out a scream. Then she was surrounded by darkness as the boot of the car shut upon her. Deana could barely move and nausea overwhelmed her as she felt the car drive off.

Sparky lit two cigarettes and handed one to Nick, who was driving. 'I see now why they call you Nick the Prick. One look at a young, blonde and you're as sweet as pie. Bet that prick of yours lit up when it saw her,' Sparky laughed.

'Are you calling me a kiddy fiddler? Have you seen the age of her for fuck's sake. Shut your filthy mouth.'

Holding his hands up in submission, Sparky let out a nervous laugh. 'Okay, it was just a joke. Not a bad looking bird though. Do you really believe her dad is Alex Silva?'

'Dunno. But if he is and he finds out we've moved his daughter we're dead meat. I know John said she was a drug dealer, but doesn't John know Alex Silva? How come he never mentioned that? Seems like there's more to this than we know.'

'Are you losing your balls and afraid of an old mafia man who means nothing these days? He's got no protection; they fucking hate him. Last I heard on the news, him and his missus were running some pub in Kent.' Sparky let out a low whistle, full of sarcasm. 'Really done well for himself, hasn't he? Not exactly the costa del crime, is it?'

'No, I'm not losing my balls, but I ain't fucking stupid either. Let's just drop her to that flat and leave her be. I want nothing more to do with it. Ex-mafia man or not, it's our hands that are dirty and I am not taking a bullet over a kid.'

Slyly, Sparky cast Nick a glance. 'You could just drop her off somewhere and leave her there,' he said slowly, almost teasingly.

'Yeah, I could and so could you, you rattle snake. Don't fuck with me to earn brownie points with the boss. The inside of a body bag has no appeal for me. Now, shut up and let's finish what we started.' Throwing his cigarette out of the car window, Nick turned up the radio and put his foot down. He had a feeling this was a very bad idea.

* * *

John stood up once he was informed that Sparky and Nick were there to see him. 'I will see them in my small study,' he said to one of his men.

Charming and smiling, John strode forward to greet them

both. 'Come in boys and tell me about your day.' Offering them a drink, John sat at his desk, while Sparky and Nick stood before him.

'The parcel was delivered to another safe place, sir,' said Nick. 'Just as requested.'

John looked at them both over his glass of whisky. 'I take it she was alive then and everything was okay?'

Moistening his lips, Nick was about to ask about Deana, but Sparky beat him to it. 'She said her dad is Alex Silva and that we had better watch out. Christ, she was full of shit and so was that room boss.' He laughed, almost making light of the situation.

Turning his head towards Sparky, Nick could see he had said the wrong thing. John's eyes flashed like daggers.

'You know who she is then?' John asked calmly.

Sparky altered his stance and stood cockily in front of John, adjusting his tie. 'Well, we know who she says she is, but it's probably bullshit. Everyone has heard the stories about the Silvas. She was just mouthing off!' he laughed, trying to make light of it and to impress John again.

'Thank you for doing a good job. I have a bonus for you as it was such a sensitive project.'

'Any time boss. You want it, you got it, eh Nick?'

John smiled and nodded his head, while opening his desk drawer. Taking his gun out of the drawer, he saw Sparky pale before him.

'No boss, no. I ain't done nothing wrong, boss.'

John fired one shot into Sparky's forehead and watched him fall to the ground. Nick stood there rooted to the spot in shock. He knew he would be next and closed his eyes tightly shut, not daring to move.

'Did you hear her mention the Silva name Nick?' John asked, ignoring Sparky's dead body on the floor. Glancing down, Nick looked at the hole in Sparky's forehead. Slowly, he shook his head. 'Who?' he asked, half dazed... then he looked up at John. 'No, I don't remember anyone mentioning that name, boss.'

'That's good. Maybe you were in another room or something.' John smiled, almost charmingly.

Nick couldn't take his eyes off Sparky. Only a few minutes ago, he was alive joking and being his usual cocky self. Now he was dead with a hole in his forehead on the wooden floor of John's office. No one liked John; he was a cold hearted, selfish bastard, but it was better to be in the circle looking out instead of being out of the circle looking in.

Swallowing hard and clenching his sweaty fists together by his side, Nick nodded. His throat felt dry. 'I don't remember hearing anything, boss. I just did what you asked and left.'

'That's good to hear. I would hate to lose two men in one day. Now, I suggest you leave, I have to get the cleaner to take out the rubbish. Just as well my small study has a wooden floor, I would hate to ruin the carpets.' John smiled and lifting his glass, he took a sip of his whisky, then picked up the telephone and started dialling a number, ignoring Nick completely. Realising he was dismissed, Nick forced one leg in front of the other and walked towards the door. Opening it, he took one last glance at Sparky's dead body and left.

## 12

### A FRIEND IN NEED

Sparky's death played on Nick's mind. It could so easily have been himself and then his own kids would have been left without a father and his wife would have been left a widow. It had been the flick of a coin, although Sparky's cocky mannerisms hadn't ingratiated him much with their boss. Although he had worked for the firm for twenty years, the new regime with a new boss didn't hold much of a future. The loan shark business was booming, but only because John had increased the interest rates, almost doubling them. People who had paid for years were now even deeper in debt and it was causing ripples in what was once calm waters.

Now other gangs were muscling in, offering cheaper rates and shooting John's street soldiers when they went to collect. Scoffing at his own nickname, Nick the Prick, he felt it was now very apt, because now he felt like a real prick for working for a man like John, even though he hadn't really had a choice in the matter. The money was addictive and it gave you a certain status. You never had to wait for a table in a restaurant or pay for a drink at a bar and the women liked the idea of being with a naughty gangster. That had been his downfall, flashing the cash, wearing expensive suits and having women fall at his feet.

Nick's mind was in turmoil. He remembered his old friend, Titch, and his mate who hadn't been seen or heard of for ages and yet no one questioned their absence. Nick took a drink of his well-earned pint of beer and looked at his surroundings. It had been Nick's job to inform Sparky's wife, Julie, that he was dead and apparently John had already sent a wreath. Christ! The man hadn't been dead more than a few hours and yet, Julie had already had her card marked. She wasn't to report him missing, and if asked by the police, he had run off with another woman. By the time he had arrived at her house she had been scared witless. John had sent fifty grand to grease the path and had called it Sparky's redundancy money.

Looking up, Nick looked at the barmaid who'd served him. She was an overweight hefty woman with very badly blonde permed hair to her shoulders. Finishing his pint of lager, he took out the twenty-pound note that he had scribbled on earlier in black marker pen, and folding it in half, he beckoned her over. 'Thanks love, get yourself a drink.' Surprised, the barmaid held out her hand and took the note. She was about to gush her gratitude when Nick turned and hastily left the pub. Once outside, he took a deep breath and hoped to God he had done the right thing. Getting into his car, he lit a cigarette and looked up at the pub with its lights shining in the darkness. Above the door a sign read, 'Proprietor, Margaret Silva.' Nick walked quickly to his car and drove off into the night.

\* \* \*

Taking a pint up to Alex, Maggie smiled and gave him a kiss on the cheek. 'I thought you might like a drink with your movie. Are you okay being cooped up here?'

Yawning, Alex looked at the time. 'Yeah, Dan's on that PlayStation thing with George and I've just got off the phone with the police. I could win an Oscar with my best poorly voice.' He grinned. 'Is Mark in the bar tonight? I thought he might have come up to see me.'

'No, apparently Olivia isn't feeling well so they are having a few drinks at home. He did ask if you wanted to join them.'

'No, I've taken too many chances being out and about over the last few days. I think it's all finally catching up with me. Once the adrenalin is gone, you go into melt down, love.'

'I know.' Sitting on the sofa beside him, Maggie cuddled up to him as he put his arm around her. 'We're no further on in finding Deana though, Alex, and now I'm going to lose you too when you have to go back to prison again.'

'I don't think we're that far off. There are still some loose ends to follow up, but somehow, I feel I already know the answers... not that Deana's dead,' he added quickly. 'I think something has gone wrong with the plan and they, whoever they are, don't know what to do with her, otherwise they would have been in touch before now. Plus, they are enjoying tormenting and torturing me in the process. Deana is made of strong stuff and she's a survivor. We will find her, Maggie, and when we do, God help whoever did this.'

The cosiness of them sitting in the lamp lit lounge alone for once was suddenly interrupted. 'Maggie, you might want to see this.' Phyllis stood in the doorway waving a piece of paper in her hand. Leaning closer, Maggie saw that it was a twenty-pound note.

'Oh God,' Maggie moaned, as her heart sank. 'Is it a forgery?'

Crossly, Phyllis stood there giving her a look full of sarcasm.

'You think I don't know the difference between a real note and a fake by now?'

Correcting herself, Maggie stood up. 'What's the matter then?'

'I don't know, but it's not often well-dressed strangers come into this pub and tip the barmaid after being served one pint of beer. Look at it, Maggie.'

On closer inspection, Maggie saw the black marker pen scrawled all over the note. 'Alex, take a look at this,' she said, handing it to him.

Taking it off her, Alex read the writing on the note. It was a London address on an estate he was vaguely familiar with. Staring at it again, he looked up at Maggie and Phyllis. 'Deana!' Maggie began to tremble and sat down on the sofa, her legs unable to hold her up any longer. 'Do you think that's where she is, Alex?' Tears ran down her face; be it happiness or fear, she wasn't sure.

For a moment, Alex stared at the note. 'Have you seen the person who handed you this before, Phyllis? Were they male or female?' For a fleeting moment, the woman who had come to visit him before, and the name Pereira had mentioned went through Alex's mind. Could it have been Patsy Diamond who had handed this over?

'He was male, around forty. Very handsome and suited and booted. Didn't say anything, just ordered his drink, drank it and then told me to get myself one before he left. The way he ran out of the door you would think his arse was on fire! It could be nothing, people sometimes write on money, but it's a bit weird, which is why I brought it straight up. In all of my years, Alex, no one and I mean no one has ever given me a twenty-pound tip!'

As he listened to Phyllis, Alex's heart was pounding in his chest. 'It could be a trap, Maggie. They are going to expect me to go racing around there, aren't they?'

Phyllis scoffed. 'If it was a trap they would have made it clear that this was meant for you, surely? Who's to say I would even hand the note over to you. I could have pocketed that and you would be no wiser. Surely, whoever wanted you to have that address would make damn sure you got it if it was a trap?'

Although Alex's mind spun, he listened to Phyllis's reasoning. She was right, whoever had done this had done it hastily and without thinking about it fully.

'If you're going, Alex, I'm going too. You're not facing this alone. She is my daughter and God knows what we're going to find,' Maggie stressed. Deana was now within touching distance and her maternal instinct took over.

'We're not getting her back tonight, Maggie. I'm sorry, but we need to stake the place out first and see who comes and goes. If we go rushing in then we could all be killed – Deana too.' Trying to think logically, Alex battled against his own urges to go straight in there and get Deana back. 'Twenty minutes ago, Maggie, we didn't know where she was and now we do. Let's not go barging in to a host of gun fire. Someone will be watching her; they are not going to leave her alone in a flat, are they?'

Knowing that Alex made sense, Maggie nodded her head. 'But when are we going to see this place? Couldn't we drive past it or something?'

'Yes, we'll go and take a look now. Phyllis, can you keep an eye on Dan and George for us?'

'Course I will and I'll wait until you get back. I'm not leaving this place until I know you're home safe and sound – no arguments now.' Sticking her chin out stubbornly, she wagged her finger at Alex and Maggie to stop them butting in.

'Thanks Phyllis.' Alex stepped forward and kissed her on the cheek. 'I'll make sure you get your twenty-pound tip back!'

'Now go on, bugger off.' Alex thought she nearly smiled,

although it could have been wind. Phyllis never smiled, but she was 100 per cent diamond and a loyal friend.

Alex couldn't contain himself any longer. 'Come on, Maggie, let's go and see this place and see if we can get our girl back. If we are lucky we might see whoever is holding her leave for the night. They won't want people seeing them coming and going during the day. It's worth a try.'

As they left the pub, Maggie looked oddly at Alex as he held her hand and walked her past their car that was parked in the street outside the pub. 'Come on, I know a quicker way.'

Maggie walked around the corner and couldn't understand what was happening. Suddenly, Alex stopped next to a jet-black motorbike and opened the box on the back. 'Two helmets,' he said, holding them up in his hand. 'Put one on. We will get through the traffic quicker with this.'

Stunned, Maggie looked at the bike and automatically took the helmet. 'Where did you get this from?'

'Long story, Maggie.' Alex was quite pleased when Maggie put the helmet on with no more questions and he helped her fasten it properly. He was glad they weren't using the car because Maggie would talk all the way there. This way, he had silence and he'd be able to think.

The journey seemed to go on forever, but as Alex wove in and out of the traffic, he felt satisfied that he had made the right choice. As always, in London, the traffic was nose to nose, but eventually they stopped outside three high-rise tower blocks. Parking, Alex turned off the engine and lights. 'What was the name of the tower block, Maggie?' he whispered.

'Aquarius House,' Maggie replied as she pointed to the far left. 'I think it's that one there. This one is called Capricorn House.'

'For fuck's sake, I wish the council would come up with something original. They are all called after birth signs!'

'Are you sure this is right, Alex? This place looks clean and tidy, the flats do, too.'

Alex had to agree, he was expecting some shithole somewhere, especially when he thought about Kev's block of flats. But this place looked like people cared for their homes.

'Let's take the bull by the horns, Maggie, and see if that lift works.' Looking around, Alex could see people coming and going, so only lifted his helmet slightly so that Maggie could hear him. Nervously, they walked to the lift and got in, along with another man and a woman. Alex cast a furtive glance at Maggie, his heart pounding in his chest. Looking down at the buttons showing all of the different floors, he pressed number ten and turned his head to the couple beside him.

'Five please,' said the man, indicating what floor he wanted. Looking at him, Alex could see that he was some sort of painter or decorator, given the paint splashes on his blue overalls. The man was grumbling about the cold to the woman. It was obvious they were together, and once the lift doors opened, they both got out. As the doors closed again, they carried on to the tenth floor.

'Oh Alex. My baby, I mean our baby is yards away from us. Can't we just burst in there and get her? For God's sake, Alex, she could be home with us tonight, safe in her own bed,' Maggie pleaded. Tears brimmed on her lashes, but Alex shook his head.

'No Maggie. We could make this situation a whole lot worse. We don't know if she's actually here and this could be a trap. John wasn't exactly happy when I visited him. He knows Deana's missing and that we would go to any lengths to get her back. Don't raise your hopes until we know something for sure. Patience Maggie. I'm as eager as you, but let's do it with minimal chaos. Deana could end up getting hurt if we barge in there all guns blazing. Just a little longer, eh?'

Alex felt his stomach somersault. He also felt sick at the

thought that Deana was in touching distance. But he was worried that this all seemed so simple. Suddenly, out of the blue, the address of Deana's whereabouts had landed in their lap. It was suspicious to say the least, but seeing Maggie's pain hurt his heart. He felt guilty that he was standing in her path. He knew Maggie's feisty side and knew she would most certainly hammer on that door to get Deana back, but he had to make her see sense. Neither of them knew what was on the other side of that door waiting for them.

As the lift doors opened, they both stepped outside into a corridor containing twenty or more doors. Quickly, they scanned the numbers and then spotted the one they were looking for. Alex suddenly wished he'd brought a gun and could shoot the bloody door down, but that wouldn't solve anything. There could be four or more men in there all armed. Their first aim would be Deana, he knew that, because that was what he would do. Not let them get the booty they came for. Fleetingly, he remembered once throwing a rucksack containing fifty thousand pounds onto a log burner so a rival gun wouldn't get it and they had ended up with nothing. And his own gut instinct told him that was what could happen here.

The pair of them stood staring at a front door. Maggie looked around the corridor. Seeing no one around, she kissed her fingers and touched the door. 'I love you Deana darling. I'm here; I wish you knew I was here.' Maggie couldn't stop the tears rolling down her face. 'Oh Alex,' she croaked. 'Do something.' There was nothing worse for a parent than feeling helpless when their child was in pain.

'I will.' Turning, Alex pressed the button for the lift and grabbed Maggie by the arm. No sooner had the doors opened than he pulled her inside the lift. 'I should never have let you come. This is only making your pain worse. At least we've seen the place though and at least we know it exists...' As the lift descended, Alex held Maggie tightly as she sniffed away her tears. 'I'm sorry Maggie, I shouldn't have shouted at you. But, if you're still feeling brave, I have an idea.'

Confused, Maggie nodded. Sniffing and rubbing her eyes dry, she followed Alex. Alex walked to a local Chinese takeaway and ordered a standard curry, paid for it and left. The determined look on his face made Maggie decide not to ask questions; she could see Alex was angry and didn't want an argument. Arriving back at the tower block, they both went back up to the flat in silence.

'Right, this is your moment. You're a takeaway delivery driver. Keep your helmet on and lift only the visor. When someone opens the door, you hand them the bag and tell them the price. I'm going to stay in the lift with the door open waiting for you in case you have to run for it. No one will be looking for a woman, they will be looking for me. But if you need to – run for it.'

Maggie's heart was in her mouth, and for all of her bravado, her courage was leaving her. She felt nervous and sweaty as she walked to the flat door and knocked on it. She couldn't hear footsteps inside and no one answered the door. Turning towards Alex, who had the door of the lift half open, she shrugged. Miming, Alex urged Maggie to knock harder and Maggie banged on the door again and shouted through the letter box, 'Takeaway!' Turning towards Alex, she saw the smile on his face, and he gave her the thumbs up. They both waited with bated breath, but nothing happened. After working herself up, Maggie felt flat. There was no sound coming from inside the flat and there was nothing left to do but leave. Then suddenly, as Maggie was about to join Alex in the lift, they heard a chain being taken off from inside a door and the flat next door opened. A woman came out and shouted for them to hold the lift. Doing as they were told,

Alex stood in silence as the woman spoke to Maggie. 'Mmm that smells nice, what is it?'

'Chinese, it's for the flat next door to yours, but they aren't answering,' Maggie stammered.

'Sounds like a joke to me. The bloke who lives there hasn't been seen for a week. I think he's on holiday or something. Are you sure you've got the right address and block of flats? I would ring your boss, I bet he's written the address down wrong and someone is waiting for their dinner.' She smiled. Getting out of the lift, the woman waved them off and made her way to her car as Maggie and Alex walked slowly back to the motorbike.

'That's weird,' Alex whispered. 'Do you think this whole thing has been a hoax?'

'I don't know.'

'The plot thickens Maggie and now I am more confused than ever. All I know is, someone meant for us to have this address, but why?' Puzzled, Alex started up the bike and rode on. Now, his mind was in deeper turmoil. He'd already decided that tomorrow he would go back alone and pick the lock. It wouldn't be bolted from the inside if someone had locked the door as they'd left the flat. Yes, tomorrow, he would go and get his daughter back... to hell with the consequences.

* * *

Frantically, Deana banged on the bedroom door of her new prison. She had heard a voice through the letter box, but no matter how much she'd shouted they couldn't hear her. She looked at her surroundings. The room was at least more comfortable, but there was still no escape. Although there was a window, she saw that she was so high up, everyone walking around looked like ants. There was no point in breaking a window; all she would do would be letting the cold in. She had asked how long she was going to be there but both men had shrugged. She had nearly suffocated in the boot of that car and then one of them had pointed a gun at her and warned her not to scream or he was on orders to shoot her. Nick had brought a couple of shopping bags with bottles of water and food inside. 'I don't know what's coming to you, but I've tried my best. My conscience is clear.'

Muttering under her breath, Deana had thanked him. He'd been kind, but she felt desperate as she looked out of the window and banged on the door again. Her small taste of freedom had given her hope, but now she felt nothing. Nick had said that her original kidnappers had been arrested, which meant their plans had gone awry. So what now? Would she rot away in here without anyone ever knowing or finding her dead body? What if something else happened to her captors and no one ever knew she was here? The very thought of it terrified her and brought tears to her eyes. She felt very alone and full of despair. Throwing herself on the bed, she cried herself to sleep.

## 13

### ODDS AND EVENS

'Dad, do you think it would be okay if I go and see Kev after school?' Dante asked over breakfast. 'I thought it might cheer him up. Luke called yesterday and said that the copper is no longer watching him. I think they've given up there.'

'Yeah, I thought they would. Presumably the trail is cold on their investigations.'

Dan looked down at his toast and then back up at his father. 'Well, Kev will remember that night for sure. It will haunt him.'

'You know, son. For every ten bad decisions you make in life, make sure you do one good one people will remember you for. Kev will be eternally grateful you turned up that night. Otherwise, we'd all be going to his funeral. What's done is done, Dan, you can't turn back the clock.' Alex put down his newspaper, and changing the subject, asked, 'The deeds to this place. Do you have them?'

A big grin spread across Dante's face. 'Sure, Dad, I'll go and get them.' Nearly knocking over his chair as he stood up with excitement, Dan dashed from the room. Alex had wondered about the deeds and had wanted to make sure they were real, and that John hadn't conned the kids out of their money. Yawning, he now felt he could sleep for a year. He'd had a restless night and so had Maggie. The clock was ticking for him until he had to go back to prison and now was the time for action. He would go and visit Luke today and then later on he would go back to that flat. Evening would be better; Alex felt sure all the flats would be busy during the day. Kids coming and going to school, people going to work or the shops; it all added up to too many witnesses for what he had in mind.

Dan rushed back into the room waving an envelope in the air. 'Here you go. The deeds to this place.' The beaming smile on his face was almost infectious and Alex smiled back as he opened the envelope. The paperwork looked in order with all of the official stamps, but Alex decided he would find his own solicitor and get it checked out so that he could be sure. He also wanted to visit Luke today and tie up those last loose ends and he felt Luke, and his love for Deana, could be the key.

'Alex, phone for you. I think you need to answer this.' Flush-faced Maggie beckoned him to the landline. Alex looked up. 'Who is it? Is it the police?'

Maggie put her finger to her lips to stop him talking. 'John,' she mouthed.

Bemused, Alex frowned and took the phone from Maggie. 'John, how nice to hear from you,' Alex lied. Keeping his voice chirpy, he asked how he was.

'I know you were bullshitting me the other day about killing Pereira and I hope we can put our differences behind us. Could you come and see me sometime today? I don't really like talking on the phone.' John laughed and Alex could tell John was lying as much as he was.

'Well, could you give me some idea about what you would like to talk about?' Alex asked.

'I've been doing some digging about Deana, and I have something for you. After all, I did say we were friends and I would always have your back. Now it's my chance to prove it. Come about 5 p.m. I should be done with business about then.' As Alex listened, a plan formed in his brain. 'Could I bring Maggie, too? I'm sure your news is good and I would like her to hear it and to thank you herself.'

'Yes, sure. It would be good for us all to have a catch up. See you then.'

Maggie had her head close to the phone so she could hear the conversation. Horrified, she looked at Alex as he put the phone down. 'Why did you say I'd go?' she snapped.

'Because John will think he's on safer ground if I take you with me. We're not going to argue in front of you and I wouldn't cause any trouble in front of you, would I?' Alex grinned.

'Fair enough. I'm sure you have a plan up your sleeve, though God knows what.'

'Well, I've got a full day ahead of me. Lots of things to do, but I'll make sure I'm back in good time to pick you up.'

'Where are you going?' Maggie asked, intrigued about Alex's plans. 'Have you forgot about Deana?'

'No, of course not, but I'm not doing anything until I hear what information John has for me.' Alex waved an envelope in her face. 'I also want to get this checked out.'

'What is it?'

'The deeds or so-called deeds to this place. I'm going to call a solicitor and see if I can have an appointment this morning. Then I want to go and see Luke. There is more to him than meets the eye, I just know it.'

'My God, you really do have the bit between your teeth today.' She laughed. 'Do you think the pub really is ours, Alex?' Maggie looked wide eyed at the deeds to the pub. Alex thought she looked like a little girl who had got her favourite doll for Christmas.

'If it is, you're secure for life, even if you wanted to sell, you'd get a good price.' Seeing Maggie shake her head, he grinned. He knew she loved this place and wouldn't part with it. This was her baby and she loved everything about it... including the regulars, who were odd to say the least!

'I'm going to shower now that you and Dante have finished with the bathroom. Why am I always last?' He laughed.

Giving him a peck on the lips, she smiled. 'You always save the best until last, Alex. You know that.' Maggie's loud cackle echoed around the room as she walked downstairs to the pub. As Alex saw Maggie skip down the stairs, he felt her happiness was for all the wrong reasons. Their kids had committed crimes to buy this place, but Maggie seemed to have put all that to the back of her mind. Sighing and rolling his eyes to the ceiling, Alex walked to the bathroom. He had other things on his mind and now it was time to get them sorted out. He was sick of waiting and sick of treading on eggshells.

While he showered, he was mentally forming a plan in his mind. John was in for a big surprise today. He had exploited his kids, and he had been underhand in not telling him about the situation. He could have helped more, if he'd wanted to, but instead he had taken a commission from the kids to buy this place. John had thrown his kids under a bus to save his own skin. And Alex was going to make him pay for that.

'Alex! Alex!' Maggie shouted from the bottom of the stairs. 'That appointment you wanted. They have a cancellation at ten if you want it?'

Realising she meant the solicitors, Alex smiled to himself. With all his might, he hoped those papers were legal, because Maggie seemed to have set her heart on it. This was her empire now and the very thought of it seemed to wipe away the last few years they had spent in hiding. She was happy and for now, that was all that mattered.

While Alex was still wearing his dressing gown after his shower, Maggie popped her head around the bedroom door. 'There's someone to see you, Alex. Are you decent?'

Frowning, he tried to make out what she was miming to him, but then he saw the policeman's cap coming through the door. 'Morning Mr Silva, we were passing and thought we would just check on you. They say you're not infectious now or shouldn't be. So, we won't waste any of your valuable time.'

Alex feigned a cough and sat down on the bed. 'Thanks for coming; sorry, I just feel a bit dizzy. You don't mind if I sit down, do you?'

'We're not the army, Mr Silva. Sit down by all means. As we say, just checking in on you, making sure you haven't fled the country.'

'Not much chance of that without a passport.' Alex smiled.

'Would you two like a bacon butty while you're here? On the house, of course. You must be famished,' Maggie butted in. She could see the appreciation in their eyes and they nodded eagerly.

'Well, we're due for a break, so we could take them with us.'

'No sooner said than done. I'll go and organise it. Come downstairs when you're ready. And you, Alex, get back into bed. You've had your shower but get some rest.'

Taking the hint and glad of her interruption, he nodded. 'I think I will have a lie down if you don't mind.'

Maggie went downstairs to organise sandwiches and coffee, and the two policemen started to make their way out of the bedroom. 'Well, Mr Silva, everything seems to be in order here. We'll just pop down and see your wife. Very worthwhile visiting this morning. Hope you're feeling better soon.'

Alex watched them leave and thought how different Kent police officers were to London ones. Taking Maggie's heed, he lay back on the bed for a moment just in case the police came back up to say goodbye. Hearing steps on the stairs, Alex waited, but it was Maggie who popped her head around the door. 'It's okay, they've gone. It was lucky you were here.' Maggie breathed a sigh of relief.

'Well, it's done now and they seemed satisfied, although I get the feeling they might pop in again for a free breakfast.'

'Me too. They seemed more than happy. Let them come. I dropped the hint that breakfast finished at 10.30 a.m. so at least we'll know what time to expect them. Anyway, I really do have to go this time. Got a pile of orders to get through.'

'What, no wake and funeral send-offs today?' Alex laughed.

'No, that's next Wednesday for your information.' Maggie stuck her tongue out at him and left. And Alex got ready to face the day ahead of him.

**14**

SUMMING UP

The trip to the solicitors was as Alex expected. Short and sweet. He showed the solicitors the paperwork and they said they would look into it and be in touch. It wasn't much of a consultation for 150 pounds.

As he mounted his motorbike, he gave a sigh as he put his helmet on. Now, it was time for the next hurdle of the day... Luke.

Arriving at Luke's house, Alex felt a tad nervous about what he was going to hear, but more determined than ever to find out exactly what Luke knew.

Opening the door and seeing Alex standing there, Luke paled and seemed a little surprised to see his old acquaintance. 'Alex, what brings you here? I see you're making good use of the motorbike. Look, come in but the carer is here so be careful what you say, you know where the kitchen is.' As Luke opened the door wide, Alex nodded as he followed him inside the house.

'How is your mum, Luke?' Alex asked, more out of politeness than anything else. He was champing at the bit to say his piece but couldn't just yet.

'Not good. They want mum to go into a care home, but she

doesn't want to. District nurses come regularly now too. She's in a lot of pain and they're trying to make her comfortable. She might as well die at home than anywhere else.'

Seeing the sadness in Luke's face, Alex felt the paternal side of him rise. 'It's going to seem strange not having your mum to look after, if and when she goes.'

'She's going, Alex. Let's face it. There's no need to beat around the bush, eh? But, yeah, it will be weird, won't know what to do with myself. Maybe I'll get a job.' He smiled, trying to make light of the situation, but both of them sensed the tension in the room.

Giving him a weak smile, Alex nodded in agreement. 'Maybe you will.'

They were interrupted by the carer rushing downstairs. 'I'll be going now, Luke, but I'll be back around five if that's okay? The district nurse is coming in the meantime.'

'Erm, I might have to pop out later,' said Luke. 'Visit my brother Kev. You know, I told you about him.'

'Well, the key safe is outside; she can let herself in. Give Kev my best. Your mum's sleeping now anyway. She won't need anything.' Nodding to Alex, although they hadn't been introduced, she waved her goodbyes and left.

Luke stood up and switched the kettle on. 'They're always rushing. They don't get much time between visits and they have a lot of patients to get around. Well, Alex, you've waited patiently, so what is it you want? I get the feeling this isn't a social call,' Luke asked nervously.

'The night Kev got battered. There was a Scottish woman. Who is she and why do I have a feeling you know?' Alex watched Luke closely as his face reddened and he looked down at his mug.

'What makes you say that, Alex?' Luke stammered.

'Because I think you knew those men were going to be there that night, didn't you? Why did she turn up and disappear without a bye your leave? Who tipped her off? And don't lie to me Luke. I am sick of people lying to me. Deana and I once saved your life; now it's time for you to save hers.'

Raising his voice, Luke said, 'I don't know where Deana is Alex, if that's what you're implying. Fuck! No way do I know who did that to Deana!'

'Now that I believe, but the rest...' Alex's calm demeanour made Luke uneasy. Turning, he looked out of the window as though deep in thought, then looked back at Alex.

'I kind of know of the Scottish woman. She has a furniture place, well, second-hand furniture at a unit, mainly stuff she retrieves from other people's houses when they can't pay their debts. She also has street soldiers, mainly women who sell drugs in the nightclubs. Scary woman, she is. Doesn't take any shit and looks like a bloke.' Luke smiled weakly.

'So, having this unit filled with furniture is how she could get her hands on stuff quickly in order to make Kev's flat look more homely. That makes sense. So, let's have your story, Luke. Spill the beans. What happened?'

Luke burst into tears as the pressure got too much for him. 'I don't know, Alex. It all went wrong. I've been stupid and now there's nothing I can do.'

Alex could feel his blood boiling but wanted to remain calm. He knew Luke had more to reveal. 'Don't play the hearts and flowers, Luke. You don't get my sympathy vote. Well, not yet anyway. The police have had someone on the door of Kev's hospital room for days and all the time they have let you, his beloved brother in. Although, it's you that put him there, isn't it? Were you planning to go back and finish the job, Luke? Were you that jealous of Kev?' Alex felt he had now dropped the bombshell that might make Luke open up more. But maybe confessing to unrequited love was more embarrassing than admitting he had been constructive in his brother's beating.

Luke looked up at Alex. 'You mean because of Deana, don't you? How did you know?'

'I'm not stupid and I've been around the block.'

Wide eyed, Luke looked directly at Alex. He could see that Alex wasn't going to say much more and that it was time to confess. 'I don't know where to start, Alex, if I'm being honest.' Throwing his hands into the air with exasperation, Luke shrugged. 'Kev was supposed to just get a kicking, nothing like this. You know Kev is gay?' Luke waited for a response, but Alex sat there poker faced. He was getting tired of Luke's cat-and-mouse game. 'Well, anyway, he'd met those two men in a club and given them his address... voluntarily, I might add,' Luke stressed. 'Kev is always giving his address to men he found attractive. Although, God knows why he did it this time; there wasn't anything special about these two men. But Kev can be stupid sometimes, especially when his libido takes over. Two travelling salesmen in a club like that and they had their own agenda and they had been on the lookout for meth. To be honest, that made me suspicious. But Kev was always off his head and didn't see it the same way as me. Most people ask for cannabis or cocaine, yet all those two strangers in suits were interested in was meth? And Dan just happens to be cooking and selling meth? Come on Alex, wouldn't you be suspicious? And then Kev told me that he'd passed out in the club toilets and the sample of Dan's meth he always carried with him had gone missing. Kev thought he might have dropped it, but I think they took it to see if this sample matched what they were looking for. It gets cut so many times by some dealers it isn't worth having, Alex, but we didn't do that, which is why ours just flew off the shelves.' Luke grinned, almost forgetting himself for a moment.

'Fair point... you seem very proud about this meth selling like hot cakes,' Alex snapped, annoyed again that his kids had got themselves caught up in such a mess of their own making.

Nodding his head, Luke carried on. 'Dante's really good, Alex. And having him hanging around here helped. You know I've had to keep my head down after that Liverpudlian business. They were out for my blood, Alex. Which is why...' Luke tailed off sheepishly.

Frowning, Alex was shocked at this revelation. He watched as Luke's face flushed, almost burning. 'What have the gang from Liverpool got to do with any of this, Luke?' Alex recalled the night they had found Luke, badly beaten because of his involvement with a drug gang from Liverpool. But Alex thought he had sorted all that out.

'Well, they found me, Alex. And by then your friend, that new gangland boss, John, had taken over most things. I was told that you had tipped off John about the Liverpudlians...'

Casting his mind back, Alex recalled speaking to John about the Liverpool gang before the court case. John had said he would look into it and nothing else had been said about it. With everything else going on it had slipped Alex's mind. But were they back and involved somehow in all of this? Had they got Deana?

Luke carried on with his confession. 'Well, no matter what I did, Deana was starry eyed over Kev. It was ridiculous the way she hung on his every word. Kev even laughed at me about it; thought it was funny that, once again, I was living in his shadow and called me dull and boring. I might be dull and boring, Alex, but at least I've looked after our mum. Kev never has. He's living the high life and I pick up the leftovers,' Luke spat angrily. 'A bit like you when it comes to your family, eh, Alex?'

Angrily, Alex jumped up and grabbed hold of Luke's shirt and pulled him close. Spit dribbled out of his mouth on to Luke's face as he spoke. He hadn't wanted to lose his cool, but Luke had just touched a very sensitive nerve. 'Don't lecture me on fatherhood, Luke. It's you that nearly got your brother killed. No, I take that back you snivelling bastard, you wanted your brother dead but Dante walked in.'

Stopping himself, Alex swept his hair back and sat down, leaving Luke shaking in his wake. 'Do you have anything stronger than tea?' Alex asked. 'I feel I'm going to need it.'

Breathing heavily and without a word, Luke opened a kitchen cupboard and took out a bottle of brandy. The air was tense and silent as Luke poured some in a mug for Alex and gave it to him, then Luke poured some for himself. Lighting a cigarette, he pushed the packet towards Alex, who took one and lit it.

'Carry on Luke, we haven't got to the good bits yet,' Alex said calmly, after taking a sip of his brandy; it tasted good on his dry throat.

'What else do you want me to say? You seem to know most of it already. I was shit scared that those Liverpudlians had found me. I thought that might have been your doing, mentioning my name to your mate John. Your name came up and they said they knew you and me were working together. So I didn't get a beating, well, not much of one. But how did they find me, Alex? What was I to think?'

Alex rested his elbows on the table and put his head in his hands. 'So, John knows I was dealing with you, is that right? And being hailed as a super grass by the tabloids you naturally assumed I had dropped your name so they could finish what they had started.'

Luke nodded his head. 'Yes, I thought you'd grassed me up, Alex and that's how they'd found me. But I didn't grass you up... I could have done, couldn't I?'

Alex looked up in surprise. Luke's words suddenly sounded

more like a threat than anything else. 'But why would I grass you up, Luke?' Alex asked in a quiet voice.

'Well, it wouldn't be the first time you've turned on your friends, would it?'

Alex smirked and shook his head. 'Don't try that one, Luke. I've heard it all before by bigger and braver men than you. You're the one in the corner here, Luke. So, let's just get to the point, eh?' Taking a sip of his brandy, Alex put the mug down. 'So, you thought I'd grassed you up and you made friends with big boss John and licked his arse like all the rest.'

Luke swallowed hard and rubbed a hand over his face. 'Not exactly, no. I never met John, always spoke to him through a third party. He just wanted to know stuff about you and the pub. Nothing in particular. Let's be honest, there wasn't much to tell. But the heat was on him by what I could gather. I was contacted one day about some new drugs on the market and then two men came to see me. They looked like a pair of undertakers!'

Luke laughed, trying to create a bit of banter, but Alex wasn't interested in Luke's jokes. Alex couldn't believe that Luke had been passing on information about him to all and sundry. Then a fleeting thought passed through his mind. John had turned up at the pub one night unannounced and Alex realised where he had got his address from... Luke. It sickened his stomach to think about this viper stabbing him in the back on a daily basis, while eating with his family and accepting Maggie's help with his mum. Luke had definitely earned his forty pieces of silver. Alex wanted to strangle him there and then.

'Anyway, these blokes,' Luke carried on. 'They wanted to know if I knew anything about these new dealers and did I have anything to do with it. They pushed their way in and roughed me up a bit, so I told them that Kev sold some gear and told them what club to find him in. I told them I didn't know where he got it from or if it was what they were looking for, but they seemed satisfied.' Luke grimaced, but he could see Alex was having none of it.

'And the Scottish woman? Where does she come into all of this?' Alex stared at Luke, realising he had never really known this kid at all. Inwardly, he wished he had left him dying behind that false wall the night he and Deana had found him. How quickly he had turned into an enemy.

'That Scottish woman, Bernie is her name, she's in league with some big bosses. She'd put a tracker on one of those blokes' cars and she found me that way after they'd turned up there. She sent a car for me, well, I say sent, I was dragged into a car and taken to her furniture unit. She's a real scary bitch, Alex! Anyway, she wanted to know what those blokes were after, although she seemed to know half the story already. Her bosses already knew they had been stirring the shit and stealing money for a long time and they wanted rid of them. She held a gun to my head, Alex! And she was prepared to use it!' Luke shouted, trying to defend his actions.

'And I presume you spilled your guts and told her about Dante cooking for you.'

'Yeah but... the thing is, Bernie didn't really give a fuck about the two men. It's your old friend John that they want rid of. That's crazy, isn't it? Why would they want rid of him?'

Alex believed the confused look on Luke's face was genuine and it suddenly all made sense to him now. Bernie, the Scottish woman, must have something to do with that Diamond woman who had contacted him. The Scottish link was too much of a coincidence. They knew that Alex had connections with John and he had just been a pawn in her game. Was that what they wanted in return for helping out Dante that night – help in knocking John off his pedestal? Yeah, that made sense. No one liked a rival in the dealer game and John had lost control of his own patch. Alex had often wondered why he had been released from jail so easily. Well, now he knew. They wanted an assassin. And he was the best.

'Where is Bernie's unit? I feel I should go and speak to this woman myself. Maybe she can tie up any loose ends I still have.'

Standing up, Luke opened a cupboard drawer and took out a notebook and scribbled an address on it. Ripping out the page, he slid it over to Alex. 'You've got to believe me, Alex. Things were out of control here, riots in the streets and pubs getting shot up. I thought I was going to get killed!'

Alex pushed the piece of paper into his pocket and finished his drink. 'I'll not kill you until your mum's dead, Luke. I think that's a fair bargain, don't you?' he said calmly and watched as Luke's face paled.

'But I've told you everything you wanted to know. Why threaten me?' Luke asked as the panic and fear settled over him.

Scowling, Alex shook his head. 'Let me get this straight in my head. A summary if you like, rather than your long-drawn-out babble. You cleared the way for two thugs to kill your gay brother because Deana had a crush on him and not you. To save your own skin you let it be known to John all my private goings on. And Deana; what about her? What do you really know about her kidnapping, Luke? Because I know there is something you still aren't telling me.'

'I never meant to Alex. It was just anger and frustration. As soon as she left, I called the number and told them about the pink car and the registration number. I knew she was heading for London because she'd said so. I shouldn't have done that and I regret it. I didn't know they were going to kidnap her. I thought they were just going to shout at her and threaten her a bit, make her stop dealing. I'd had my misgivings for a while and we were getting in too deep. Even Dante wanted out and argued with Deana about it. But it was like a game for Deana and as long as Kev was on the planet she was going to carry on as that was the only way she could meet up with him. She said she was going to run away with him. That she had enough money to keep them both and didn't give a fuck. I had to stop her. I never meant this to happen. I didn't know she had been kidnapped until you told me.'

Not being able to control himself any longer, Alex threw back his arm and punched Luke in the face, sending him hurling backwards off his chair. 'My daughter has been kidnapped because of your jealousy! You evil bastard. Couldn't you just let her crush run its course, or even better, tell her that Kev is gay? That would have done it, Luke. One fucking sentence. Now, stand up so I can hit you like a man. Get up!'

'You can't kill me, you bastard. I have the gun. I have the fucking gun!'

Alex stood rooted to the spot as Luke's words settled into his brain. 'What gun?'

Luke was curled up into a ball on the kitchen floor, smarting from the punch he had taken. 'The gun with Dante's fingerprints on it. I'll make sure he goes down for murder.'

Alex's mind was in turmoil. 'And if I kill you first, how is anyone ever going to find this gun?'

'I've got insurance. I'm not totally stupid. I knew the moment you put two and two together you'd come looking for me. I picked it up, during the chaos and put it in my pocket. It might be a little smudged, but given the stuff police have these days, they will be able to identify Dan's prints.'

Alex's blood boiled at the sneering, smirking look on Luke's face as he spat out his latest revelation. Still reeling from the punch, Luke managed to stand and sit on the kitchen chair.

'I want that gun, Luke. I'm not having my son doing a life sentence, as well as my daughter missing, presumed dead because of your lies and betrayal. That isn't love or loyalty.'

'Well, you'd know all about that, wouldn't you, Alex? Where was your loyalty to your friends?' Luke spat. 'That gun is the only thing keeping me alive.'

Exhausted by the conversation, Alex gave up. He'd got what he wanted. His gut instinct had told him that Luke was involved, but even he hadn't thought it would be to this extent. Luke was up to his neck in it passing information to John. And the worst part of it was, Dante and Deana had got into John's car and confirmed everything Luke had told him. Establishing Luke as being a good, faithful informer. 'Checkmate it is, Luke. Clearly you are happy to betray Dan, your friend and Deana, a woman you claim to love. No wonder you're all alone in the world. You're a rattle snake.' Alex had heard enough. He couldn't do anything about the gun at the moment, but he could go and speak to this Scottish woman, Bernie. Looking at his watch, he saw that he only had a few hours before he had to meet up with Maggie and John.

'I presume you're going to pass on to your newfound friends that I've been today and that you've told me everything?' Seeing Luke's face drop, Alex smiled. 'No, of course you won't because even you're not that brave, Luke. I think you're going to die a very sad lonely man without any friends or family around you. Please don't contact myself or my family again. Goodbye, Luke.'

Silently, Luke stared at him. 'You're not going to tell Kev, are you?'

'That's for me to know and you to find out, isn't it?'

Crushed, Luke looked down at the floor. His face was starting to swell from the punch he'd received. Sadly, he watched Alex walk down the path and ride off on the motorbike. His heart sank when he thought about Alex's words – that he would die a lonely man. Well, he was lonely and living in these four walls with a dying woman did stupid things to your head at times. Dan and Deana had been the first bit of happiness he had known in a long time, and he hadn't wanted Kev to take that away from him. Even if he had told Deana that Kev was gay, would she have believed him? She had been too blind and in love to hear a word against him. For a short moment in time, Luke had felt what it was like to have a family again. Maggie, Deana and Dante had all cheered up his mum and given him something to look forward to.

Numbly, he walked back into the kitchen. The house seemed eerily silent. His happiness had gone and he had ruined everything. Automatically, he boiled the kettle and set the tray to make his mum a cup of tea. Climbing the stairs with a heavy heart, he tried portraying his usual cheerful self. Putting the cup down beside the bed, he noticed that his mum's lips were blue. Shaking her shoulders, he shouted, 'Mum, Mum, are you okay?' but there was no answer.

Luke sat on the edge of the bed and sobbed. His mother had died. All the time he had been confessing to Alex and not sitting with her, his mother had died alone. It was at that moment he realised the severity of what he had done. Any other time he could have called Dante, Maggie or Deana and one or all of them would have come to his rescue. But Luke realised Alex was right. He was alone now and he had never felt so lonely in all his life. Luke hung his head and began to cry.

## 15

### THE SCOTTISH WOMAN

Riding through the London traffic was no mean feat and Alex's mind was spiralling after his meeting with Luke. He vowed he would make him pay *and* he would get that gun, although he didn't know how yet.

Turning down a street, he checked the piece of paper Luke had given him. Further down the street he saw an open unit with household goods outside on the pavement. It didn't look much, but as he peered closer he saw the furniture and electronic goods were piled high on top of each other, so business must be booming. Alex parked the bike and walked into the unit. He couldn't see anyone around, which he felt was odd – who would leave a unit like this unattended?

'Hello? Anyone in?' he shouted as he craned his neck inside to see if anyone was around.

'Behind you, laddie. I just went to the café to get a coffee and a sandwich.'

Alex spied the woman as she walked towards him. Well, he thought to himself, Luke definitely hadn't been lying about her appearance.

'Aren't you afraid of burglars?' Alex grinned.

'Don't be so fucking stupid, laddie. No one around here is that brave. What do you want?'

'I'm Alex Silva.'

'I know who you are, laddie, and I don't give a fuck. That's not what I asked. What do you want?'

Shocked by her bluntness, Alex pointed to a chair. 'Do you mind if I sit down?'

'I would have thought your arse would be aching from sitting on that bike all the way here, but if you're staying long enough you can sit.'

Alex didn't know whether to laugh or not, but instead he just sat down on the edge of a Chesterfield chair. 'Well, you know who I am, so I presume you're Bernie... who saved my kids. I think I've met your boss. That's if I can call her your boss without sounding rude?'

'Well, you've dragged your feet. I expected you sooner. Aye, Patsy Diamond's my boss, colleague and partner in crime. She's given you enough rope to sort things out or hang yourself. You didn't want it spelt out on a plate, did you? I thought you were an experienced mafia man, but you seem more of a wet lettuce to me,' she scoffed.

Accepting her insults and bluntness with good grace, Alex smiled. 'Well, maybe I am a bit out of practice. It's been a while since I've had to play Agatha Christie.'

'No idea who she is, laddie. I've never worked for her and don't intend to. Got myself a good set-up here and what I do for Mrs Diamond gives me a good commission. So, get on with it, my sandwich is going cold.'

Alex wanted to laugh and correct her about Agatha Christie but could see that apart from not being a book reader, Bernie wasn't a joker either.

'You want to know about the men your son murdered in that druggie's flat? How is he by the way?' Bernie perched herself on the edge of a table and started gnawing at her sausage sandwich.

Grimacing, Alex was reminded of a wildlife programme with the lion eating their prey. 'Kev is on the mend by all accounts. It's going to take time, though. Yeah, the men in the flat, what happened and how come you turned up out of the blue? You can't tell me you were just passing and dropped in for some wacky backy?'

'Well, he's alive and that's what matters. Poor bastard. I wasn't sure he'd make it. And me? I never drop in anywhere unannounced, laddie. I went there to kill those two bastards. Kev was just the bait. They weren't working on anyone's behalf but themselves. They wanted the meth to sell for themselves, all the while everyone was blaming your two sprogs. It's bloody good stuff and could be cut a hundred times and still be good stuff and they knew it. But they weren't prepared to pass on this information to the people that had kept them in work over the years. The Cartel liked your laddie's stuff, but they weren't sure who was making it – they needed the cook, not the bottlewasher, if you know what I mean.'

Alex sat there stunned and Bernie must have seen him pale because she grinned, letting the tomato sauce run down her chin before wiping it away with the back of her hand and licking it. 'Aye, laddie, the Cartel! Big guns, who were prepared to sit back and get to the bottom of it. They didn't want murder, they only wanted the cook,' she emphasised. 'Anyway, your wee laddie turned up just as I got there, so I watched and waited, like you do. That weasel Luke had assured everyone Kev would be alone that night. He'd even stopped buyers using it for the evening, claiming the police were going to raid it.'

Once Alex had got over the shock of the Cartel business, he was pleased that Bernie had brought up Luke. 'You know of Luke. I've just been there and got most of the truth out of him, though I doubt he will ever tell me the whole truth.'

'Nah, he's got more faces than Big Ben. I doubt he knows the whole truth himself. Well, you will get the truth out of me, laddie. Rest assured,' Bernie muttered around a mouthful of sandwich and pushed in a piece of bread that was escaping from her mouth. 'This isn't *Breaking Bad*, Alex. This is real life.'

Alex nodded, although he felt it wasn't too far from it. 'So, these men, if you knew they were skimming, why didn't you just get rid of them?'

'Blimey laddie, you are out of practice. Patience is a virtue, or so they say. My boss doesn't like ripples. She likes peace and quiet with everyone knowing their place. One bad apple in the barrel can cause wars, you know.' She gave him a knowing look. Letting out a large burp, much to Alex's distaste, she carried on. 'One of those blokes came here, showed me the sample to impress me and hoped to get the heat off himself and his mate. What he didn't know was that I already knew most of it, but I let him carry on and then I put a tracker on his car. I knew he would lead me to where I needed to be.'

'Do you have my daughter? Do you know where she is being held?'

'No, I don't kidnap kids. There's nothing more certain to make the headlines than a missing kid or a child killer. But as to where she is... I don't know. And that's your job. Your daughter, you find her. I've done my bit.'

In a strange way, Alex warmed to Bernie. She was blunt and coarse, but she was honest and he liked that. She was also not to be trifled with and didn't suffer fools gladly. And, unlike Luke, he believed everything that came out of her mouth. If she said she didn't know where Deana was, he believed her. But now he could understand her and Patsy Diamond's interest and why they had gone to so much trouble. They wanted Dan's cooking. And John, what about John? Alex thought to himself. Time to bring him into the equation.

'It was my son, Dante, that told John everything. He thought he was a family friend and wanted his help, much to his own detriment. But he's young and stupid.' Alex stopped talking as someone walked into the unit and Bernie walked towards them.

'We're fucking closed. I'm on my lunch break. Piss off!' she shouted.

Alex watched as the nervous man whispered to Bernie, almost pleadingly, and she nodded. Alex was intrigued, and watched intently as Bernie opened a safe near the back of the shop and took out a wad of cash before locking it again, spying Alex as she did. Averting his eyes, he knew she didn't want him seeing the combination and looked around the unit nonchalantly. Taking out a black note pad from the back pocket of her jeans, she scrawled something in it and passed it to the man who presumably signed his name. Then Bernie handed him the cash. 'Friday,' she bellowed, 'and don't be late because Friday has twenty-four hours in it.' Thanking her graciously, the man stuffed the money in his jacket and walked out.

'Never get a minute to myself,' Bernie muttered under her breath. 'People always have a sad story to borrow money, yet he smokes and drinks like a sailor. If he stopped, he might save something. Still, it's all profit and he pays up,' Bernie explained, although Alex felt she didn't need to.

Clearing his throat, Alex broached the subject of John again.

'Gullible, that's what your lad is. Who would trust that

fucking ponce, in his silk suits and with his greasy charm? The tough guy with celebrity friends – he's the one who causes the ripples. He's out there bringing attention to himself, which he loves but it's bad for business. I hear that old bloke, that don in your country, has breathed his last breath, so now John has free rein and there are a lot of names he can point the finger at if need be. He used you like a puppet, promising your safety and the safety of your family, while you never brought him into the picture. Old school loyalty, eh?' Bernie laughed. 'Well, it's a shame he doesn't have any for you.'

Alex's heart sank, and he felt embarrassed as Bernie's words stung a little, because he knew they were true. He had been stupid and had thought of John as a friend. He was just as gullible as Dante. Alex's head spun and he felt sick to the stomach when he thought about how he and his family had been used and how stupid he had been. The sweat on his brow trickled down the side of his face and he rubbed it away with his hands.

Bernie cocked her head to one side with a concerned look on her face. 'You alright, laddie? You look like you're going to pass out,' she asked. 'Here, I've got a bottle of water, take a sip.' Doing as he was told, Alex gulped the water, then put some in his hands and rubbed his face with it.

Finding the words, he looked up at Bernie. 'How fucking stupid have I been?' he whispered. His throat felt dry and he was finding it hard to swallow. Bernie sat in silence watching his inner pain and turmoil.

'Well, I've got work to do, Alex, and so have you. Tell your wee laddie, forty and we're done. No dealer will come looking for him or his sister, and his reputation will be untarnished. As for the gun, there aren't a lot of places it can be hidden. Personally, I would have smashed it up and got rid of it, but Luke would have known he'd be for the high jump when he spilled his guts and would have wanted insurance.' Drumming her fingers on her chin, she looked around the room for inspiration. 'Let me think about it, and you, too. I'm not doing all the work.'

'It's got to be in the house, Bernie. If you had something so precious you wouldn't let it out of your sight, would you? And forty what? Thousand pounds? Is that what you want?'

'Christ, Alex! That time on the run really has addled your brain, hasn't it? Forty kilos. That's what your wee laddie cooks. We'll provide the materials and with what he cooks up, that will last a hell of a long time. Forty kilos and we're done. Apart from what you have to do, of course, but I ain't saying it out loud, but you know what I am saying. Once a criminal, always a criminal. It's in the blood. I honestly can't see you getting a job at Tesco, laddie. You don't have it in you.' She grinned.

Alex listened intently and squirmed at her price. Forty kilos of meth. He didn't like the idea, but he felt Bernie would keep her word. He was going against everything he believed in though, getting Dante to cook drugs. 'Forty kilos? That's a lot of meth, Bernie.'

'What's his life worth, Alex? We're the ones selling it so we take the blame.' Bernie laughed. 'Twenty of that will go to the Cartel. If they are happy, we're happy and so are our customers. No one would link your laddie, apart from Luke, but let's leave him on ice for now.' Wagging a finger in his face, she added, 'but be warned Alex, your laddie does no more cooking after that.'

'If, and only if, I do what you ask, will you keep your word? Will that be the end of it?'

'Don't fuck with me, Alex! I've been straight up to now, haven't I? We'll keep our word, but we don't want your clever kid selling on the market too. He most certainly would end up in a body bag, otherwise. This is a deal and a warning, and you can take it or leave it. Stop wallowing in the past, Alex. What's done is done. Deal?' Bernie wiped her hands on her greasy jeans and held out her hand to shake his. 'And you know what you have to do, Alex.'

Looking directly in her eyes, Alex nodded. 'To be honest, Bernie, you make a lot of sense. You should be a counsellor. Thank you. I accept your terms to clear myself and my family so that we can get on with our lives in peace. Order your materials and I will see that Dante does what you want.' Alex couldn't believe what he was agreeing to, but hopefully the end product would be worth the sacrifice.

'You will never live in peace, Alex. You like the excitement too much. As I say, it's addictive and in your blood, just like it's in mine but I have been instructed to assure you that if you do all that we ask, there could be a special present for you.' She beamed cockily.

'I hope "special present" doesn't mean a bullet between my eyes.'

The smile dropped from Bernie's face, and she took a gun out of the waistband of her jeans, startling Alex and making him step back. 'If that was the case, Alex, I'd have already shot you by now, wouldn't I?'

Alex held up his hands in submission. 'Okay, message received loud and clear. Now, do you mind putting that away.' Grinning, Bernie put her gun back and tucked it under her hoodie.

'But for the record, Bernie I would never go back to my old ways,' Alex replied seriously.

Bernie nodded and stood up, indicating she had what she wanted and had given Alex most of the answers he was looking for. Alex knew she would take the heat off them now. Shaking her hand again, Alex got up and slowly made for the exit without a word.

Bernie stood up and watched him leave. Smiling, she shook her head. 'Not go back to the old ways, eh, Alex?' she muttered to herself. 'You will, Alex, believe me you will. We always do. It's the only thing we know.'

# 16

## THE RECKONING

Once out of sight, Alex called Maggie. He had already arranged for her to meet him in London, and looking at his watch he knew she wouldn't have left yet. 'Alex, where have you been? You've been gone all day. I was just about to leave. What's wrong?'

'Nothing's wrong. In fact, I haven't seen this clearly in years. I need you to do me a favour, Maggie, and don't ask questions. I will tell you everything when you get here. Don't worry, everything is in hand. Just do as I say. Trust me.'

'You know I trust you, Alex. Go on, tell me what you want me to do.'

Alex knew Maggie would be a little shocked at some of his requests, and hearing the anxious tone in her voice made him repeat his instructions again.

'Maggie, I need you to follow this to the letter please. As I say, all will be revealed,' he emphasised.

'Promise. I will sort things out now. See you soon.'

Feeling a bit grimy, Alex looked down at himself. His back was sweaty as he had ridden on the bike most of the day in the sunshine. His hair felt wet under his helmet. He knew this was no way to see John. Going to a local clothing store, he bought a shirt, tie and some trousers, including some deodorant. He would still wear his leather jacket. It looked casual and not like he was trying to impress. This meeting had to appear relaxed and as casual as possible, even though Alex knew it would be far from it. Swallowing hard, he felt pensive. He knew it could be a trap and that Deana's whereabouts was the bait. Whether John was going to tell them anything or not, John knew any information about Deana would definitely get Alex there. John's pretence of being a loyal friend was his cover. Alex knew that now and inwardly cursed himself for believing John in the beginning. Alex had been his fall guy all along.

Going to a takeaway toilet, Alex washed up in the sink and changed into his new clothes. Looking in the mirror, he felt better about his appearance and was much cleaner. Looking at his watch, he realised how quickly time had passed and knew Maggie would be nearly there by now. He got on his motorbike and made his way to their meeting point. He had arranged to meet her three streets away from John's place.

Noting Maggie hadn't arrived or parked up yet, Alex rode around the block of John's house. It was a huge building, with steps leading up to the front door. John had made himself very comfortable at other people's expense, he thought to himself. But Alex wanted to see the back entrance not the front. At last, he spotted it, although there was barbed wire above the brick walls surrounding it. Remembering the last time he had been there, Alex noted that it would be one hell of a walk from front to back, but it would be worth it. Satisfied, he rode around the block again to wait for Maggie.

Seeing her car, he parked behind her. Getting in the car, he kissed her cheek. 'Hi Maggie, you okay? Sorry to mess you around, love. Did you do everything I asked?'

Maggie rolled her eyes. 'Of course I did. But you sounded quite worked up on the phone. Do you want to fill me in?'

Alex hurriedly told her about his conversation with Luke and with Bernie. For the time being he omitted what they had asked Dante to do; he needed to sort things out. Alex took the gun she handed him and seeing the frown on her brow, he smiled. 'Come on Maggie. John may have won the battle, but this is one war he isn't going to win. Thank God I still have a couple of these babies stashed at the pub. Couldn't exactly get one at short notice, could I?'

'Do me a favour, Alex, find out what you can about Deana first before you do anything stupid, okay?'

'I will love.' He grinned. Alex had already dismantled the gun into pieces. The frame of the gun was the bulkiest part. Expecting that John would have his men on standby to frisk them, Alex raised himself off the car seat a little, wincing as he tucked the frame as best as he could between his buttocks. 'Fuck, that's uncomfortable.'

'I hope you don't wince like that when you sit down at John's.' Maggie half laughed. She couldn't stop herself from smiling. 'I see that's why you've worn wider legged trousers. Not your usual style, but it gives you leg room, or should I say bum room.' She giggled.

'Very funny.' He smiled, glad that it had taken the pensive look off Maggie's face. 'To make matters worse, I have a smaller size of old man's Y fronts underneath to keep things tighter and in place. Christ, my balls feel like they are being strangled.' He grinned.

'Alex Silva wearing Bridget Jones' knickers.' Maggie smiled as she watched him spread around the other smaller components of the gun around his underarms and inside jacket pocket. 'If they find the barrel, Alex, won't they know what it is?'

'I don't think so. I hope not. Let's be honest, Maggie. This is all last minute without preparation. I know what I have to do, but in the past I've been more strategic and less impulsive. Time is not on our side and I can't cancel John's invitation, can I? Now that would look suspicious.'

Maggie listened and watched intently as Alex prepared himself. She felt nervous and her stomach was in knots. She knew part of Alex's plan, but the latter part made her cringe inside. 'Did you get the train tickets?' Seeing Maggie nod and hold them up, he took them and put them in his breast pocket. Alex strategically went through what Maggie had to do to make this work.

'Do you think it will work, Alex?' Maggie asked worriedly. 'What if something goes wrong?'

Although his mind was focused on the job in hand, he turned towards her and kissed her on the cheek. 'Fingers crossed it will work, Maggie, or that was our last kiss.'

Alex saw Maggie pale as they both got out of the car and made their way to John's.

They rang the doorbell and a man in a black suit and tie answered the door. It was standard practice for gangland, or any kind of mafia group.

'We are expected, I'm sure you know that.' Alex smiled. The man opened the door wider to let them in. Alex flashed a glance at Maggie. This was to be her acting debut and he prayed she could pull it off. He could see that she was nervous, and to be honest he felt the same way. God only knew how many people were in the house waiting for them or what the outcome would be. If there was a crowd of people inside, his plan was doomed.

Another man stood in the marble hallway with its antique, luxurious surroundings, and came towards Alex. 'You still don't mind if we check you over, do you?'

'Not at all boys. You carry on. I've been in prison so I'm used to being manhandled by men.' Alex laughed, trying to make light of the situation to ease the tension. Squeezing his buttocks together, Alex put his hand in his breast pocket. Brazening it out, he smiled. 'There's nothing in here but two train tickets from Kent, but you can look if you want to.' Alex took out the train tickets to prove it, feeling the barrel of the gun in his bulky leather pocket, which seemed to hide it. Maybe it was his guilty conscience, but he felt it stuck out like a sore thumb. Thankfully, and much to Alex's surprise, the man just rubbed his hands up and down his waist and legs with distaste and nodded to the other one. 'Seems clear.' Swallowing hard, he winked at Maggie. 'Your turn love.' He laughed.

'Mrs Silva,' said the other one.

Stubbornly, Maggie stuck out her chin. 'We've been invited by John himself, who I personally have known for years, and you want to frisk me? Where is he? Does he know you're treating me like this?' she snapped. 'Don't you dare touch my tits!'

'Come on, Maggie, leave the man alone, he's only doing his job,' Alex butted in and the man looked at Alex, almost thanking him for intervening.

'Well, do you mind if I look in your bags? It seems you've come with a lot of shopping. Aren't there any supermarkets in Kent?' the man retorted as he looked down at Maggie's shopping bag for life and her overly large handbag, raising his eyebrows.

'It's just a spot of shopping. Anyway, I needed some new underwear. I don't get to come to London that often, but if you want to check my handbag and sniff my Tampax, you're welcome. As for the shopping, I have the receipts so keep your hands off the bread.'

'Proper little spitfire, Mrs Silva! I'm just doing my job.'

'I will leave my shopping bag in the hallway here, if you want.

Makes no difference to me. Where is John? I thought he would be here to greet us. I'm sure he doesn't want to know that you want to touch me up. I really don't have time for this. Here, keep my handbag and you can search it at your leisure. I haven't brought any mysterious presents that are ticking,' she scoffed.

One man peeked inside and moved his hand around a bit. 'Looks alright.' Alex wished he had put the frame of the gun in Maggie's handbag, considering how little they had searched her. If anything, the two men looked bored and pissed off with Maggie. Alex stood there listening and watching Maggie wind the men up and her outburst had taken the intensity out of their search. They wanted it over with as quickly as possible. The shopping bag, overflowing with groceries, had been looked at, and again one man moved a few things off the top, but considering Maggie wasn't taking it in with her, he slowly slid it under a table in the hallway. Picking up an intercom phone, they buzzed through to John. 'Mr Silva here boss... and his wife,' they added while casting a sarcastic glance at her.

Alex looked at the shopping bag, and mentally hoped their curiosity wouldn't get the better of them. The double doors opened widely and John came out to greet them in the hallway. 'Alex, Maggie. How lovely to see you. I hope these two gorillas haven't harassed you too much. Sorry, I was on the phone.' Wrapping his arms around Maggie, he kissed her on the cheek, then turned and hugged Alex. The two men seemed to relax more seeing the casual friendliness.

John ushered them both into his study, which contained a desk and two Chesterfield sofas. Looking around, Alex noted there weren't any windows in the office. Antique paintings hung on the wall and looking at one more closely, Alex thought he recognised it from somewhere. Suddenly, it came to him in a flash. That very same painting had been above Pereira's bed in

Portugal. He remembered looking at it when he had put the pillow over the old man's face. Fuck, Alex thought to himself, John had been very hasty in robbing a dead man.

John was his usual charming self, offering them both drinks from a well-stocked drinks cabinet. One bottle stood out and a wry grin crossed Alex's face. 'Is that Sambuca, John?'

Surprised, John looked at the front of the bottle. 'That's very sharp eyed of you, Alex. Do you want one?'

'Well, I'm not driving. Might as well. It's been a long time, and it's not something you have in a local pub.'

'What about you, Maggie? Or would you like a gin and tonic? That used to be your tipple, didn't it?' The smile never left his face as he oozed politeness. Not waiting for her reply, John handed her a drink. Alex noted that although John had made a show of putting ice and a slice of lemon in the glass, he hadn't opened a bottle or picked up a decanter to pour Maggie's drink. Alex felt his hackles rise and flashed a glance at Maggie, giving her a knowing look. Alex looked at Maggie's drink and slowly shook his head, indicating for her not to drink it. Maggie held it to her lips, supposedly to take a sip, but never let a drop pass her lips. The drink had already been prepared before they'd walked in so was either poisoned or drugged, Alex was sure of it.

'And you don't mind if Alex drinks the Sambuca, Maggie?' John asked nonchalantly. 'Or would you prefer he drank something else? We all bow to the boss lady when she speaks,' laughed John.

'No, that's fine.' Maggie grinned. 'Alex doesn't often get a chance to drink the good stuff. Just the one, though, Alex, eh?'

Alex realised that his suspicions had been confirmed when he saw the mask slip from John's face as he realised he had made a fatal mistake. He had given Maggie her drink first out of politeness and expected Alex to have either the same, or a whisky, which was his usual tipple. Alex felt his gut instinct had paid off again, and noted that John had picked up his own drink from his desk. 'Sorry, I'll finish this. I've started without you.' He smiled at them both.

Once John had got up and topped up his own drink, which Alex noticed was from a totally different decanter to the one he had offered Maggie, he sat opposite them. 'This is nice, Alex. It's always good to meet up with old friends. We have history, unlike my new celebrity friends. Oh, they all want selfies and the like. Makes my head spin sometimes.'

'Less of the old you. Just because you have friends in high places,' Maggie cooed. They all laughed at Maggie's joke, taking any tension out of the meeting. Alex was glad he had suggested Maggie come. He knew John's men in the hallway would be listening at the door and all they would hear was laughter and light-hearted banter. As he had done himself in the past, hearing that everything was okay, he would have gone and made himself a well-earned coffee and he presumed that was what those two gorillas would do too.

Alex looked at his watch and cast a glance towards Maggie. The chit chat was over and John had relished boasting about his newfound status and friends. He was on the cover of magazines with the showbiz elite, who, Alex knew too well, would drop him like a hot potato if need be. None of that impressed Alex. It was as though John's need to be popular ruled his every move. Alex felt he was a joke and letting himself be used for the sake of fame.

'So, John, old friend, you said you might know something about Deana and where she is? We've given up hope to be honest as there is no trace of her anywhere. I presume it has something to do with my past.' Alex added, 'I thought that would come back and bite me on the arse sometime, but not as quickly as this.' Mentally, Maggie laughed at the inuendo of something biting

Alex on the arse, because she could see Alex's smile was more of a grimace.

'Possibly.' John's face was serious now and the smile disappeared. 'I have this.' John walked over to his desk and opened a drawer. Alex instantly tensed, not knowing what John was going to pull out, but John held up a notebook and walked towards Alex. 'I've done some digging, Alex and this address has come up. I think she may be there. I haven't checked it out, but this is all I've come up with from informers on the street. I wanted to speak to you first.'

Alex looked at the address, which was totally different from the one he already had and looked at John carefully. 'How did you get this?'

'I said I would always try and help you if I could. I don't know if it's kosher, but it's worth a try. Do you want me to send some men there with you to take a look?'

'You could come with me,' Alex answered, knowing he was throwing down the gauntlet. He knew John wouldn't dirty his hands looking for Deana. Those days had long gone, Alex could see that now.

'Sorry Alex, but I've got things to do. I know it isn't much, but it might be worth checking out. And, like I say, I could send a couple of the boys with you.' Inwardly, Alex cringed. His mind was picturing the scene of how four people would walk into this address and only two of them would walk out.

'No, I'll go John. It could be a wild goose chase, and you all have better things to do. Do you know this area?'

Pursing his lips, John shook his head. 'I can't say it rings any bells.'

Maggie's blood boiled with every fake smile and joke John made. Her drink remained on the table before her. Alex was right, she thought to herself. This was a trap. John was planning to wipe her family out in true mafia style. The rage inside her was building up and she couldn't help herself. 'I'm surprised you don't know the place, John, because you probably put Deana there yourself, you bastard!' she blurted out, not only shocking John, but Alex as well.

Alex cast Maggie a warning look. 'Ignore her John, you shouldn't give her gin. She's upset about Deana, that's why she's snapping at everyone. Sorry mate,' Alex apologised, then cast another glance at Maggie.

John looked from Alex to Maggie and back again. 'Women not knowing their place in my home doesn't impress me. Keep a civil tongue, Maggie.'

Although blazing with anger, Maggie looked at Alex, who was almost pleading with her to behave. It wasn't time yet. 'Sorry John,' she answered. The words almost choked her, but she had to go along with Alex's plan.

John smiled. 'Let's put it behind us. I understand you're not thinking straight.' His smarmy answer made Maggie want to scream, but she held it in for Alex's sake.

'Can I use your bathroom, John? Where is it?' Alex stood up and looked around.

'There is one in the hallway; you can use that if you wish.'

Inwardly, Alex smiled. He knew there was no way John would let him walk aimlessly around his house. He wanted him under guard and the hallway with the two men out there was a sure way of doing it. Walking into the hallway, Alex looked around. True to form, the two men were missing and the coast was clear. But no sooner was he walking down the hallway than a door opened and one of the men cocked his head through.

'Where's the loo?' Alex asked, and without answering, the man pointed to a door. Once inside the bathroom, Alex pulled down his trousers and the overly tight Y fronts and pulled out the frame of the gun buried between his cheeks. Feeling almost faint with relief, he quickly put the frame, barrel, spring and slide back into place. He had done this many times in the past and it took less than a minute. Now he could put his plan into place.

\* \* \*

As Alex left, John took a sip of his drink and smiled at Maggie. 'Still the spitfire, eh, Maggie?' Nodding towards her handbag, John raised his eyebrows. 'What's in the bag? A surprise for me?'

Keeping her cool, Maggie feigned ignorance. 'Well, I haven't bought you anything, John. Is that what you expected? I'm sure you don't need anything from me.' She half smiled, although this time John wasn't smiling. He looked deadly serious.

'Empty the bag. Has Alex gone that mad that he would dare to put a weapon in your handbag and then let you make a fuss about my men searching it?'

'How do you know I made a fuss if you were busy on the phone, unless you have the place bugged and were listening?' Maggie picked up her bag and passed it to him. 'You open it, John. I have nothing to hide.'

Spying her, John looked down at the bag. Maggie had given it so freely, it knocked him off his guard. He had expected her to object, but she hadn't. Slowly he bent over and tipped the contents onto the floor. Seeing there was nothing incriminating in there, he almost blushed, and handed the bag back to Maggie. 'Apologies, but you can't be too careful, especially after that outburst.'

'I'm angry and upset. My daughter is missing and everyone I know is under suspicion, John. My nerves are fraught,' she lied, while leaning down and putting the contents on the floor back into her handbag. John said nothing and took a sip of his drink.

\* \* \*

'How's it going guys?' Casually, Alex walked up to the two men in the hallway. Surprised, they turned to face him. Alex had his loaded gun in his pocket. Moving closer to one man, he shot him in the head. Swiftly he turned and shot the other man before he could take his gun out of his holster. Looking down at the two dead bodies on the floor, Alex glanced at the hole in his jacket pocket and sighed. The thickness of his jacket had dulled the noise somewhat, but it had made a bloody mess of his beloved jacket. Opening the door to John's office, Alex felt the tension and cast a glance at Maggie. It was time to leave.

'Well, John it's been nice, but we should be making a move. You're a busy man and we have a train to catch.' Remembering his manners, he waved the paper in the air. 'And thanks for this, I'll let you know the outcome.'

Suddenly John's face changed into a snarl. 'Do you really think I'm going to let you walk out of here, Alex? Maggie's outburst is the only truthful thing that has been said in here today, isn't it?'

Calmly, Alex opened the good half of his jacket wide. 'You know I am unarmed, John. Your two men out there frisked us before we came in, which I found quite strange considering they knew we were coming and as old friends you had invited us. That's not how you treat your friends, is it, John?'

'We're not friends, Alex. I told you once, that bounty on your head will never be paid by me. You're a menace, Alex, a rock around my neck. Even in prison you couldn't keep your nose out of things and those fucking kids of yours have been the icing on the cake. You know what I have to do.' John quickly took out his gun from the inside of his jacket and pointed it at Alex.

Standing there calmly, Alex looked down the barrel of the

gun. His heart was pounding, and his throat felt dry, but he had expected this. Saying nothing, he let John finish speaking. 'I know you lied about killing Pereira. There was no way you could leave the country without a passport. As for Pereira, he was an old dying man. Finished. His time was over and he didn't die fast enough, but you didn't kill him.' John was breathing heavily as he pointed the gun at Alex shakily.

'If you're going to shoot John, shoot. But, yes, I was in Portugal. I put the pillow over Pereira's head at his request. He was sick of you all and he tipped me off about you. I really didn't mean to kill one of his men on the balcony though, but it was just collateral damage – you know how these things are.' Alex grinned, especially when he saw John's face turn ashen.

Cocking the barrel of his gun, John cast a glance at Maggie. 'Don't worry, I'll make it nice and quick for you. Finish your drink, it will make it easier. I'm sure we can find a big enough hole to bury you both in.' John grinned, then suddenly staggered backwards on to the sofa, holding his stomach. Blood seeped through his shirt as the shot fired out. Alex, still tightly holding his gun in his pocket, had fired first.

'Everyone listens to a dying man's confession, John. You know that.' In quick succession, Alex fired twice again into John's torso. Maggie looked up at Alex and then at the doors. 'Don't worry, his goons are dead. No one's coming, unless there's someone here who we don't know about, but I doubt it. Leave now Maggie. Go!' Alex commanded.

Stunned, Maggie looked at John's lifeless body, his blood pouring out of the bullet holes in his white shirt, leaving a pool beside him. 'Is there anything I can do, Alex?' she asked meekly.

'Yes, get the fucking hell out of here. You don't need to see the next part. Go home, I will see you there,' he almost shouted.

Although she was hesitant about leaving him, she also felt

relieved. The ghoulish part of Alex's plan was something she wasn't looking forward to and she was glad of the escape. Doing as she was told, she picked up her bag and skirted past John's body, taking one last glance at Alex before she left. Walking into the hallway, she was shocked to see the two dead bodies of the men that had opened the door to her initially. Taking in the scene, she paused for a moment, her heart pounding in her chest. Seeing that one of the men's eyes were open wide, almost staring at her, made her feel sick and she wondered for a moment if he was still alive. The white marbled floor had pools of blood pouring down it, making the whiteness stand out even more. Swallowing hard, she crept past them tentatively, half expecting one of them to grab at her ankles or leg. Breathing a sigh of relief when neither moved, she opened the door and left.

Once outside, she filled her lungs with air. She felt everyone in the street was looking at her and knew what had happened, but they were just going on about their daily business. None of them knew about the blood bath she was leaving behind her. Finding her feet, she walked quickly on trembling legs before bursting into a run back to her car.

She hated leaving Alex to clean up the mess alone. Breathless, she approached her car, fumbling for her keys. She kicked off her shoes knowing the soles would have blood on them and didn't want any trace of it in the car. Putting them in her bag, she almost fell into the car and her hands trembled as she reached for the cigarette packet and lit one. Breathing in the nicotine, she opened the window and rested her head back on the seat to catch her breath and calm her nerves. Getting her second wind, and feeling much calmer, she started up the engine and headed for home.

\* \* \*

Hearing the door close behind Maggie, Alex walked into the hallway, ignoring the bodies that lay there. Kneeling down, he reached for the shopping bag Maggie had brought in full of groceries. He pushed past the food and took out a large plastic blue bag advertising frozen chips. Inside the bag was a small axe, safely disguised amongst the chips and buried underneath all of the other shopping.

Searching through the rest of the shopping, he found the roll of thick garden rubble bags and pulled three off the roll. Making a hole in the sealed end of one of the bags, Alex put it over his head and pulled it down, almost like an overall to avoid any blood stains. Then going back into John's study, Alex manoeuvred John's body and raised the axe. With two hefty blows, one after the other, he decapitated John. Lifting his head up by the hair, Alex put it into another bag and tied it. The third bag was for his rubbish. He put the axe inside it and his bloodied makeshift overall. Then Alex went through John's jacket pockets and found his mobile. Working solely on adrenalin, he ran into the hallway and searched the dead men for their mobiles too and stuffed them into his pockets. Back in John's study, he reached for the bottle of Sambuca. He was glad that he had spotted it earlier and Alex took his time, pouring it over John's body and around the room. Then Alex took out his lighter and lit a piece of paper, holding it like a torch away from himself before dropping it on the alcohol-covered floor. Immediately flames erupted and Alex took a moment to look at John's burning, decapitated body.

'Flambe John,' he said to himself, as a wry grin crossed his face. The fire took hold quickly, catching the varnished desk, books and oil paintings. Alex opened the study doors wider and ran down the hallway, opening all the doors he could. His eyes began to water, and he started to cough. Already he could feel the sweat trickling down his back from the heat. Picking up the bag containing John's head and the rubbish bag now containing the axe, overalls and the empty bottle of Sambuca with his fingerprints on, Alex ran down the hallway towards the back exit. It seemed like a long, lengthy process searching for the right door, but at last he found it. Coughing and almost choking, he kicked it open into the fresh air, leaving the door ajar to let more oxygen in to feed the raging fire.

Looking up at the barbed wire above the walls, Alex cringed. Then he noticed the back gates were bolted from the inside, with no padlocks. Was John so arrogant that he presumed no one would dare attempt to break in? It was sloppy. Looking up, Alex spied the CCTV cameras, but hopefully, the fire would burn any evidence. Hurriedly, he walked away, not wanting to cause any alarm by running. Suddenly, he heard a loud shattering of glass behind him and knew it was the windows of John's house. He could hear people shouting now and began to pick up his pace. Almost running around the corner, he looked up and saw black smoke in the air. Taking out the helmet from the back of his motorbike and wiping his red, sore eyes, he put it on, and placed the two plastic rubble bags in the helmet box. He was pleased to see that Maggie's car wasn't there and that she had followed his instructions and left. Trying hard to focus, Alex rode out of the ensuing mayhem. He would have liked a cigarette to calm his nerves, but he knew there was no time to lose. Revving up his bike even more, he could hear the sirens of the fire engines in the background. Trying hard to focus on the road, he headed for Bernie's.

## 17

### THE FALLOUT

The journey to Bernie's place seemed twice as long as before, the London traffic busier than usual. Alex wondered if he was making a mistake. What if Bernie had closed up and left early? Riding through London traffic with a head in your motorbike box wasn't an ideal situation if you were pulled over by the police!

Arriving there, he saw that the furniture had been moved from off the pavement, but the shutter was only halfway down, which meant she was still inside. Breathing a sigh of relief, he parked outside the unit. Approaching it, he bent down and put his head under the shutter. 'Bernie,' he called, 'are you there?'

Seeing a pair of denim-clad legs walk towards the shutter and pull it up, he stood back. 'Just checking.' Alex took his helmet off. 'Are you alone?'

'Yes laddie, I'm alone. You'd better come in.'

Alex walked back to his bike and opened the box on the back and took out the plastic rubble bag containing John's head. It felt heavier than before and peering closer, he could see there was blood in the bottom of the bag. Scrunching the bag closed more tightly, he walked into the unit. Immediately, Bernie spotted the bag and pulled down the metal shutter, letting it bang to the floor.

Folding her arms, she cocked her head onto one side. 'Well, it's not bin day, so what's in the bag?'

Alex smiled. He liked Bernie's attitude and her no-nonsense approach to business – she seemed fearless.

Alex put the bag on the floor and opened it. 'I figured you might want proof that the job is done, and I haven't let him escape to another country and live out his life in comfort.'

Squinting her eyes, Bernie knelt down and looked in the bag, then back up at Alex. Chewing on the side of her mouth, she met Alex's eyes. 'I don't think I've got anything in my drugs cabinet to fix that headache. Either that or it's one hell of a bad haircut.' She smiled. 'On the radio, I've heard his place is on fire. They wouldn't normally tell us about a house fire, but he was quite the celebrity,' she added sarcastically. 'As you say, that could have just been bullshit and a cover story to let him disappear for old times' sake. People try lying to me all the time. Even my wife,' Bernie added. 'She lies about her age, weight and waist size. I don't even think she knows the truth.'

Alex nodded. 'It sounds like we're married to the same woman, because I've got one at home just like that.' Alex grinned. 'But there's not a chance I would have let John go. He was prepared to kill me and my wife, and I know he's behind Deana's disappearance.'

Standing up, Bernie looked Alex up and down and took stock of him. 'I hear they used to call you the Silva Bullet. Well, I'm going to call you Swifty Silva, because I didn't think you'd get back to me this quickly.'

Alex smiled, watching as she took out her mobile phone and started taking photos of John's head from every angle.

'Now the question is Swifty,' she said. 'I've got my proof that cheating scumbag is dead, but what are we going to do with a head in a bag?' Letting out a huge roar of laughter, Bernie slapped Alex on the back, making him stagger.

'I hope I'm not in any of those photos Bernie. I don't like evidence.'

'What? You don't want a selfie with Mr Popular? Don't be so cynical, Swifty. Take a look.' Bernie handed her mobile phone over for Alex to look for himself. 'Personally Swifty, I'm tempted to put a cigar in his mouth. That is not a good passport photo, is it?'

Satisfied, Alex handed the mobile back. 'Not really, but at least he's not smiling.' Instantly, they both burst out laughing. 'So, I suppose I'd better dispose of it.' Scrunching the bag together, Alex was about to pick it up when Bernie stopped him. 'No you don't, laddie. Look.'

While they had been laughing, Bernie's phone had buzzed, indicating a message. After reading it, Alex's jaw dropped. 'You're going to what?' he asked disbelievingly.

'We're going to freeze it and see that it gets to Portugal to the Portuguese bosses who think they can take over from him' – Bernie pointed to the bag – 'as a warning to not mess with us. Can't send it FedEx, though.' She grinned. 'But that's one part of our pact done and dusted, Swifty. Well done.'

'I know. The next one is Dante and that mountain of meth you want. To be honest, Bernie, I have no idea how long that stuff takes to cook or whatever. It really isn't my field of knowledge. And I doubt Dan has ever done a batch that size. So, is there a time scale?'

'First of all, let me get the ingredients together. I'd say about a week. Your wee laddie will know, but I appreciate your honesty. I'll be in touch. After all, I know where you live.' Bernie drummed her fingers on her chin. 'Just a thought, but do you know of a local hood called Nick?'

Alex looked blankly at her and shook his head. Bernie carried on. 'Well, I might have something for you considering how hard you've worked. I've done my own fishing for you and a very nervous, angry man came to see me and was surprised to hear that your Deana wasn't home yet.'

Stunned, Alex stood rooted to the spot, not knowing what to say. Moistening his lips with his tongue, he looked at her confused. 'Who? I don't know what you mean. No one has been in touch. Why does he think Deana should be home by now?'

'Mmm, not sure of all the details yet, as I say, but he was agitated and twitchy. Looking over his shoulder like a cat on hot bricks. But he did say that John had shot his friend in cold blood and how easily it could have been him. He said, he knew he would be next because of your daughter... well, he said "Deana" so I presume they've spoken. He's slipped her a mobile phone apparently but didn't have chance to get the new number. He said he knew he was a dead man walking if John ever found out, which is why he came to me to help him get him out of the country without anyone knowing. He said him and his mate hadn't taken her to where they were supposed to, but to a flat of one his mates who was away at the moment. Does that ring any bells?'

'How do you know that he's telling the truth?' Alex asked as he thought of the empty flat he and Maggie had visited.

'Because he was scared shitless. And he knows he's fucked up. Sucker for a pretty face is Nick, but he was angry, too.'

Frowning, Alex squared up to Bernie. 'When were you going to tell me about this, Bernie?'

'When I got more information, Alex. I wasn't holding back. I just didn't expect to see you so soon. Cut the accusations, eh? Don't spoil a good thing with your suspicious mind, laddie.'

'I have an address but then John had an address for me when I went to see him but they didn't match,' Alex said, although his mind was spinning. If Deana had a phone, why hadn't she called home?

'Well, maybe you should go to both flats and look again?'

Alex rolled his eyes. 'You know, that's the second time today someone has advised me to go to an anonymous address. I wonder what's waiting for me inside, eh?'

Angrily, Bernie slapped his face. 'Don't compare me to that boil in the bag down there... do you fucking hear me, laddie? I've done my best to help you!' she spat. 'If I was going to shoot you, I would have done it already. You could already be joining him in that bag. Don't fuck with me, Alex. I'm not in the mood.'

Realising that he had said the wrong thing, Alex apologised. He hadn't meant to upset her. But it had been a long day, and his nerves were raw.

'My guess is laddie, she's been moved from one place to another by the sounds of it and I think Nick has tried tipping you off.'

'Where is he now? Can I talk to him?' Alex urged.

'No, not yet. He doesn't know John is dead. I offered him protection from John for a price. I don't break my word, Alex. The same as I wouldn't to you. Let me speak to him again, but I wanted to speak to you first to see if your daughter had been in touch.'

Alex sat down and rubbed his hands through his hair. 'I haven't taken a breath yet since I got out of prison. I presume this is the surprise you said might be in store for me?' Alex asked hopefully.

'Nope! And it isn't a bullet either. Patience laddie, all will be revealed. My boss lady doesn't rush into anything. You have to prove yourself, first. Too many people have thought they could take the piss just because they are dealing with a female. Present company accepted.' She smiled. 'Go home, laddie. Take the weight off your brain, have something to eat, fuck the wife, watch the football. That's what I usually do when I need to unwind. Leave him with me. After all, Alex, two heads are better than one.' Bernie gave out a guffaw, which led to an enormous fart, making Alex wince and laugh at the same time.

'Nice meeting you, Bernie.' Alex held out his hand to shake hers. He didn't know her story but he felt she was a person to be trusted. You got what you saw, including farts!

* * *

Later that evening, Alex walked into the back door of the pub exhausted. Home had never looked so nice and a warm feeling washed over him. *Home.* He had never thought he would feel secure anywhere again, but that's what this was. The Silva home, somewhere they could all rest their weary bones. Although, he thought to himself, it would be a whole lot better when all of his family were back together again and this whole business was behind them.

Surprised and full of relief, Maggie greeted him. 'Alex, how are you?' she whispered. 'Where have you been? I've been so worried.' Not saying a word, Alex pointed upstairs to where their living quarters were. Maggie shouted through to the bar that she was taking a break and almost ran upstairs before giving them a chance to answer.

Shutting the door behind her, she sat on the sofa beside him. 'Where have you been? It's been hours and I've been going out of my mind, especially when I saw on the news that John's house was on fire.'

'I heard that. And I am sorry I didn't call and for worrying you, but as you can see, I am home safe and sound. Pour me a drink, would you? My throat feels like sandpaper.'

Eager to please, Maggie jumped up and poured him a large whisky, including one for herself. She was desperate to know what had happened after she had left and what had taken him so long. 'Your eyes look red and sore, you should bathe them.' Maggie stroked his face. 'Let me run you a hot bath, you look done in.'

Almost too tired to talk, Alex gulped back his drink in one. 'That sounds good. Before I go into any detail, just let me say, I believe Deana is alive and in a safe house somewhere. I think she has been given a mobile phone. What I don't know for sure is why she hasn't called us. If she had one, she would call the pub, wouldn't she? Have you had any missed calls? Has Dan?'

'If Dan had had any calls from Deana he would have told us, wouldn't he? That's not something he would keep secret from us. I haven't had any either... but how do you know this, Alex?' Curious and desperate to know the truth, Maggie urged him to speak. 'For God's sake, tell me!'

'Because,' Alex whispered, 'the person I took John's head to, told me.' Maggie linked her arm through his and squeezed her eyes tight. 'You went through with it? When I heard about the fire, I thought you'd changed your mind. He was already dead,' Maggie whispered.

'I got rid of the evidence, but I needed proof that he was dead. You know that, Maggie. I told you that. Once done, I took it to the person that needed to see it. It's done now and I just want to put it all behind me.'

'Is this source reliable? About Deana, I mean,' Maggie stammered. 'They could be fobbing you off with some story.' Tears brimmed on her lashes. 'I should have stayed with you, Alex.'

'No!' Alex barked. 'You needed to get back here and keep everything normal. Do not bring any suspicion here. People know that I knew John. Let's hope no one points the finger this way, that's the best I can hope for. Where is Dante?'

'He went to see Kev at the hospital, and now he's in his room, why?'

'I need to speak to him. How is Kev, by the way?'

'On the mend apparently, but it's going to be a while yet. What's going on, Alex? Please don't keep me in the dark.'

'Dan has to clear his and Deana's debt and regain his freedom by cooking a whole batch of stuff for them.' Maggie was about to butt in, but Alex stopped her. 'It's a one off and then it will be over. But we still have a problem with Luke. He has Dan's gun. God knows where he is keeping it but that is my next objective. Then we can all move on, Maggie.'

Glumly, Maggie gave a weak smile and squeezed him tighter. 'You've had a shit day, love, and so have I. My nerves are fraught. Talking of Luke, Kev told Dan their mother had passed away. I suppose I should go and see if there is anything I can do.'

'No, don't. Leave Luke to it. He's no friend of ours, Maggie. I know you liked his mum but he's got the evidence to put your son away for life. That's not a friend. Leave him be and let him rot.'

'I know, I know. I will steer clear, Alex. I have a thousand questions but they are going to have to wait and so can Dan. I'm going to run you a bath. You've had nothing to eat, I bet.' Seeing Alex shrug, she knew the answer. Standing up, she went to the bathroom and when she came back she saw he had dozed off. Picking up a blanket from the sofa, she threw it over Alex to keep him warm. 'Night my love. Get some sleep.' Kissing him on the forehead, she walked into the bathroom. It would be a shame to let a nice bath go to waste...

**18**

THE END OF THE ROAD

Famished, Alex sat at the breakfast table and ate the full fry-up plus extras that Maggie put before him. 'God, this is good Maggie. You know, I only married you for your fry-ups.' He grinned between mouthfuls.

Pensively, Dante ate his toast. He could see his parents laughing like their usual selves but couldn't understand why his dad had spent the night sleeping on the sofa. Surely, married couples only did that when they argued, didn't they?

'You two okay? How's your back, Dad? That sofa isn't that comfy, is it?' Darting a look from one to the other, he sensed nothing strange apart from their confused looks.

'Ah, I see. You want to know if we've been arguing and why your dad spent the night on the sofa?' Maggie smiled, pouring more tea for everyone.

Wiping his mouth, Alex shrugged. 'Why not just ask? I had a busy day yesterday with one thing and another and when I came home, I fell asleep on the sofa. No big deal, okay? Anyway Dante, I need to have a chat with you after I've finished this, but food first. My stomach feels like my throat's been cut.'

Dan's heart sank and he rolled his eyes to the ceiling. Suddenly he had lost his appetite. 'I take it I'm in trouble again?'

Alex shook his head but carried on eating in silence.

Putting marmalade on her toast, Maggie smiled. 'Leave him to eat his breakfast, Dan. He'll be more approachable with a full stomach. You're not in trouble, so don't panic. It's just a favour. Okay?'

Dan knew his father was never too busy eating to lecture him, so whatever it was he would find out when his dad was ready. 'Dad, did you hear Luke's mum's died?'

Alex stopped eating and put his knife and fork down. Once he'd finished chewing what was in his mouth, he picked up his mug of tea and took a sip. 'You're not going around there, Dan. I'm sorry about his mum, but it hasn't come as a surprise, has it? She's been in God's corridor for a long time.'

'Alex!' Maggie stopped him. 'That's an awful thing to say. She was a nice woman.'

'She was, but it's a bloody shame none of her niceness rubbed off on her sons, isn't it?' Turning to Dan again, Alex picked up his mug. 'Well, you're obviously wanting a conversation, so let's have it. No, me and your mum are not at loggerheads. No, you're not going to visit Luke; he grassed you up and he's got the gun you used and won't get rid of it. He calls it insurance; I call it blackmail. He's willing to let you swing, Dan, so no, I don't give a fuck about Luke. Let him stew in his own juices.'

Dante's jaw dropped; he hadn't expected this. 'He's had the gun all this time? When did he take it?'

Showing his annoyance at such a stupid question, Alex couldn't help snapping, 'Well, the night you used it, of course. When else would he pick it up, the two-faced lying bastard. He's no friend of yours, Dante, believe me. And yes, he's had it all this time.' Alex felt now was time to spill the beans to Dan and let him know the truth. 'It was Luke who set Kev up to be beaten up. He didn't expect things to get so out of hand, until you unexpectedly turned up all guns blazing. But if he would do that to his own brother, why would he give a fuck about you?'

Dante took a moment to let what Alex was saying sink in. He had trusted Luke and thought him a friend, or a kind of brother. 'Does Kev know what he did?' he muttered, not knowing what else to say.

'Not yet, but he will. And whatever Kev decides is his business. If he forgives him and lets it go, that's up to him, but I'm not letting Luke get away with any more lies. Granted, he's already threatened to grass you up if I beat the fuck out of him, which I am very close to doing, and I presume he would want his own back if I told Kev. But who is to say he won't grass you up anyway?'

Stunned, Dan looked at Maggie. He suddenly felt sick. 'You're prepared to let me be arrested just to tell Kev the truth? Is that what you're saying, Dad?'

'Stop it, Dante,' Alex threatened. 'Kev will know in my own sweet time. I will not do anything until after their mother is buried. That is my respect to her and she deserves to have her family at her funeral. It seems their mum was the only anchor that kept the boys together... and the drugs of course. I would like to think that you and Deana have a closer relationship.'

'We do, Dad,' Dan stressed. 'Talking of Deana, have you found anything more out about where she is?' Dan knew it was a touchy subject, but he had been out of his mind with worry. All he knew of was the hushed conversations his parents had together. He felt useless, but more to the point, he felt guilty. If anything had happened to her, he would never forgive himself. He didn't want to contemplate the worst; what if she was dead and buried somewhere? Night after night, it had given him nightmares. They would never know where she was. Feeling the bile rise in his throat, he swallowed it back and took a drink of his own tea to wash it down.

'I've got a fair idea of where she is and I am going to get her today, hopefully. It's been a long bloody week, but I swear she will be home before I have to go back to prison.'

Wide eyed, both Maggie and Dan stared at him. Maggie wasn't aware of this, but then again, Alex hadn't had the energy to fill her in on the details. Tears brimmed on Maggie's lashes. 'You know where Deana is? Really Alex, you know where my baby is?' Reaching out her hand, she put it on top of Alex's and squeezed it.

'I believe so, and I believe she's still alive, although I don't know what condition she's in. But, with a little love and care, she might be okay again after her ordeal.' Alex sighed. 'That's the part I'm afraid I really don't know.'

Maggie and Dan urged him for more, and Alex told them most of the conversation he'd had with Bernie, informing them that Luke also knew Bernie and that was how Alex had found her. When he saw Dan's face pale again, Alex's dark eyes flashed at him. 'Yes Dan, Luke is up to his neck in it,' Alex sneered. The very thought of Luke angered him.

'Did you burn down John's house, Dad?' Dante asked tentatively, knowing he was on thin ice.

'Did you go boasting to him that you were a drug dealing gangster making loads of money? Don't ask me questions like that, Dante,' Alex barked angrily.

Embarrassed, Dan blushed. His father had already given him the answer; he didn't need to ask further.

A puzzled frown crossed Alex's face. 'What I can't understand though, is that this man who deposited Deana where she is says he gave her a mobile phone, but surely she would have called us?

I don't know whether he's lying or not, but Bernie isn't someone you lie to easily.'

'Maybe she's ill, Alex, or afraid to come home,' Maggie said slowly. 'What if she's afraid to contact us?'

Alex patted her hand reassuringly, although he didn't feel too sure himself about what he would find when he found Deana. He had two addresses, but his money was on the flat he and Maggie had visited. It made sense and Bernie had said that Nick had dropped Deana off at an apartment while the owner was away. And that night he and Maggie had gone to the flat, the woman they had spoken to had told them there was no point knocking on the door because the man who lived there was away. She'd had no reason to lie to them, so that part must be true.

Alex thought about what Maggie had said. What if Deana was afraid to come home? She knew what she had done and the trouble she had caused. Maybe Deana thought that if her family thought she was dead she could start again somewhere else. Alex cringed; it was an awful thought, but it was a possibility. Dismissing it, he felt his mind was playing tricks and coming up with the worst scenarios. Deana *would* come home. Even knowing the consequences she would be facing, she wouldn't leave her family forever wondering without some form of contact. All of these wild thoughts spiralled around his mind. No wonder he felt weary.

Breaking the silence, Alex dropped the biggest bombshell of all. 'Dan, the opportunity to make things right with no repercussions, means you cooking more meth. And I mean a bloody lot of it, so I hope you can do your sums. Somehow, the ingredients are going to be dropped off and then you need to get to work. Payback time.'

'What? But you said I wasn't to do it again. And how much is a lot?'

Exasperated, Alex hit the table with his fist. 'I am not the one asking, son. You're being told, not asked. Christ, you and Deana have had one hell of a ride on other people's patches. If you do this, you're in the clear and no one will come looking for you. It will be over. The only loose end is Luke and that bloody gun. He's told me he's got it in a safe place and there's a letter explaining everything so even if I kill him it can still be revealed. It could all be bollocks, but after finding out what a sly bastard he is, I kind of believe him.'

'When you put it like that, Dad, so do I,' Dan admitted. 'But regarding the meth, where am I supposed to cook it? I used to do it at Luke's house, and I've never done a really big load before...'

Feeling drained with all of the questions, Alex let out a huge sigh and threw his hands up in the air. 'I've got no idea, Dan, but you won't be doing it at Luke's, that's for sure. So, I presume here. As for the size, well, here's the sticky bit.' When Alex slowly mouthed the amount both Maggie and Dan fell into silence. They didn't know what to say. 'Dad,' Dan answered after a moment. 'I've never done anything like that. It could take a week, maybe two. I really don't know. And what if I get it wrong? There was no pressure before, but now it has to be right, doesn't it?'

'Well, you seem to have got it right up to now, or else they wouldn't be asking for more. Let's see what happens when they drop the ingredients. I can't answer your questions, Dan, because I don't have the answers.' Alex shrugged and sat back in his chair.

Looking down at the table, Dante looked at his father under his lashes. 'Me and Deana have caused you a whole heap of shit, haven't we? You've rarely had five minutes alone with Mum, and that's our fault. Sorry doesn't seem enough, neither does thank you for getting us out of this hole that we dug for ourselves. I can't turn back time, but I can learn from it. You humble me, Dad.'

'Stop talking shit, Dante. You wouldn't be sorry if you hadn't got caught. Just do your part. If they are willing to accept it, then so can I. Believe me, I'm no angel and in no position to judge anyone.' Alex said the words softly as he held a hand to Dan's shoulder.

'Good morning peeps!' Mark and Olivia stood in the doorway smiling. 'Chef let us in. Mark's going to drop me off at work, but we wondered if Dan wanted a lift to school?' Olivia was smiling strangely, while Mark was discreetly nodding his head towards Olivia, giving them all a strange look.

Suddenly, the penny dropped for Alex. 'My, my, you look smart in your new uniform, Olivia.' He grinned and encouraged Maggie and Dan to join in. Mark stood behind Olivia and gave Alex the thumbs up.

'Oh this.' Olivia beamed. 'It's my first day today. I'm cleaning the leisure centre this morning and then I go back later and clean when the school is finished.' She grinned.

'You're cleaning the leisure centre and the school?' Maggie asked.

'I clean for the council and any premises they need cleaning. So, it could be anywhere.' Obviously very pleased with herself, Olivia did a little twirl like a young girl showing off her party dress. Mark encouraged them all to give her a little round of applause. 'I will wait for you in the car, Dan. I just want to make sure George has his bag and stuff.' With that she trotted off downstairs as pleased as punch.

The smile dropped from Alex's face, and he looked up at Mark. 'Did she really come here this morning to show us a tabard with a council logo on it?'

Mark pulled out a chair and sat down. 'Two sugars in mine, Maggie. To you, Alex, it's a tabard. To Olivia it's the world. It's making her smile for fuck's sake and that's all I want. If this tabard makes her feel like a princess earning her own money and giving her an ego boost why should you care. Just go with it you lot, eh?'

Alex couldn't help but laugh and nodded. 'If it works for her, mate, who are we to question it. Anyway, Mark I need a favour.'

'One good turn deserves another, Alex.' Turning to Maggie, Mark looked at the unused bacon in the pan. 'Is that going spare?' Seeing Maggie nod, he smiled. 'Nice one. Put two slices of bread around it will you?'

'In your tools and stuff, do you have a battering ram. You know like the kind of thing the police use to batter doors down.'

'Yeah, I know what a battering ram is, Alex. Why?' Taking the sandwich from Maggie, Mark bit into it.

'I need to borrow one and I wondered if you had one, or something similar.'

Puzzled, Mark paused from taking another bite. 'What's going on, Alex? Why would you need a battering ram?'

Knowing that asking such a question would raise eyebrows, Alex shook his head. 'You don't need to know Mark and I don't want you involved. But if you have one, could I borrow it?'

'Dan, fuck off and meet George in the car, I need to talk to your dad.' The seriousness in Mark's tone and face astounded Alex. Dan raised his eyebrows, kissed Maggie on the cheek and left. 'Right, are you ramming a door or gates? Why, where and when? Involving me, shit. Come on Alex, what is it? And don't fob me off; I know something is going down. You want my tools; you tell me why.'

Maggie stood up. 'I'm going to leave you two to it. I have work to do.'

Watching her leave, Alex stood up and rested his arms on the sink while looking out of the window thinking. 'It doesn't matter, Mark. I'll sort something else out.'

Concerned, Mark stood up beside him. 'You look stressed and

tired, mate, and if your answer is to ram doors in to relieve the tension, then tell me.' Mark grinned.

Weighing up the odds, Alex continued looking out the window and took a deep breath before speaking. 'Well, the truth is Mark, Deana's been kidnapped. I have two addresses where she could be and the only way I'm getting in there is to ram the door down. I don't intend calling the police for reasons I don't want to go into, but you know who I was and the people I've mixed with. I want to get my girl back and the only way is to ram the door down. Is that enough facts for you Mark? And I don't want to hear anything I've just said coming out in the pub during one of your drinking binges with your pals. I've already lost what I thought were friends, I can't afford to lose any more.'

Mark let out a low whistle and looked almost hurt. 'Thanks for the vote of confidence, Alex. Well, I think I can keep my mouth shut, when it calls for it. I'm offering to help you, Alex, because apart from my drinking buddies, I don't have any real friends either. But I must say, you don't do things by halves. But don't you mobster guys have skeleton keys and things for when you can't get into locked doors?'

Alex held out his hands and smiled. 'You watch too many movies, Mark.'

'Well, maybe I do, but people lock themselves out of their cars all the time. My mate's a locksmith and he turns up at houses when people have locked themselves out. Why don't we just do it the easy way, Alex? That's what mates do. You can fill me in on the rest when I've dropped tabard woman off at the leisure centre.' Laughing, Mark went downstairs and left.

'Why the hell didn't I think of that?' Alex thought to himself and grinned. Oddly enough he felt like a weight had been taken off his shoulders confiding in Mark.

Seeing Mark leave, Maggie went back upstairs. Leaning on

the door jamb, she folded her arms. 'We all have to trust somebody sometime. He's more genuine than some of the friends you've had.'

'Come here.' Alex held out his arms for Maggie to walk into. 'I just don't want to get him involved, Maggie. This is deep shit we're in.'

'He's a grown man, Alex, and it's his choice. I knew he would offer if you opened up a little. We all need a little help sometimes. Anyway, postman's been and this looks important.' Pursing her lips, Maggie handed Alex a large A4 envelope. 'Look at the address, it's from the courts.'

Frowning, Alex tore it open. Reading it, he looked up at Maggie. 'My appeal hearing is tomorrow?' Confused, he showed her the letter. 'I haven't made an appeal, Maggie.'

Maggie sat down and read the document line by line. 'Well, someone has, and it's tomorrow. Does this mean you might not be going back to jail if they agree your appeal? Don't these things usually take months and months?'

'Not if you know the right people, I suppose. And obviously, whoever's done this appeal and put it to the top of the pile, knows the right people. I can't believe it Maggie, and to be honest, I don't want to think about it. My mind is focused on getting Deana home. I dare not even think about freedom in case it falls flat on its arse. This is just raising my hopes to be with my family. Don't set your heart on it, Maggie, please,' Alex stressed, seeing how much Maggie's face had lit up.

Holding him tighter, Maggie kissed him. 'You know, I once saw an old black and white movie with a famous line. "Don't reach for the moon when we have the stars already." Or something like that.' She smiled and hugged him even tighter. Maggie desperately wanted her family back together; she felt they had all suffered enough.

# 19

## FREEDOM

As Alex heard the hustle and bustle from downstairs, he thought about the day ahead. Before he went back to the apartment where he thought Deana would be at, he wanted to check out the address John had given him first. Whatever this place was, John had intended it to be his and Maggie's last resting place if he hadn't killed them at his house first. Thinking about John's house, Alex recalled some of the news reports he'd heard. The fire brigade had found three burnt bodies and they assumed one to be John but hadn't confirmed it yet. Well, they would, but they hadn't reported that his head was also missing. Then his mind wandered to Bernie and what she was planning to do with John's head.

Suddenly another thought came to him and hope rose inside of him and his stomach churned. Bernie! She had said that there was a surprise for him – could she have meant the appeal? Perhaps his freedom was his payment for killing John, and Dante's cooking was payment for the kids' stupidity. Luke still nagged at him, but he would deal with him later. He had to admit that Bernie's boss was a very powerful person with a lot of influential people in their pockets. Bernie had mentioned the Cartel. Well, that said it all really, didn't it, he thought to himself.

Dressing in his scruffiest jeans, T-shirt and an old fleece, considering his once beloved leather jacket was ruined, Alex's first job was to empty the motorbike box of its contents. He should have done it last night, but he had forgotten about it.

The gun in the plastic bag was going to be easily dissembled again and broken up and scattered somewhere. The bottle of Sambuca could easily be smashed and put in the pub's bottle skip, but it would need a good cleaning first. He doubted if anyone would find it, but better to be on the safe side.

Alex had decided to keep the motorbike but to have it transferred over into his own name. He liked it, and it had come in very useful. Maybe that was his present to himself, he thought. Deana's stupid car flashed through his mind. That was still at Luke's garage, tucked away safely. Maybe Mark could use the parts or even sell it on. Either way he wanted rid of it.

A wave of emotion overcame him as he thought about his appeal. What if nothing happened and it was all a bad joke? The only way to find out, Alex thought to himself, was to contact the police. The paperwork looked real enough with its official stamps, but doubt had crept in, and lastly guilt. If he hadn't been so magnanimous in wanting to start afresh and volunteering to go to prison in the first place, none of this would have happened. Cursing himself, Alex thought how stupid and selfish he had been. There had been no need for him to do it. Okay, he would have had a suspended sentence hanging over him, but he would have had his freedom. Wracked with guilt, he sat down, glad to be alone for a few minutes with his thoughts. Hindsight was a wonderful thing and if only he'd had a crystal ball, none of this would have happened.

The kids had run wild in his absence and lied and betrayed

everyone, thinking they could stand on their own feet. It had been their first taste of freedom in years and they had run amok. Maybe, he thought to himself, he would have done the same at their age. God knows, he had done a lot worse! But now it was time to get his family back on the straight and narrow again. And the appeal was his chance to do that.

Mustering up his courage, he called the police station and explained about the appeal letter. It was a long, drawn-out conversation, but it seemed they knew about it and strangely enough wished him luck with it. Once he had put the phone down, Alex smiled, so it was real and pending. His stomach was full of butterflies and he could feel his breakfast rising. But no, he was to go to an appeal tomorrow and try to convince an appeal board that he was turning over a new leaf. It was a lifeline. It had been a long time since he had been afraid, but tomorrow's hearing overwhelmed him with fear. He wasn't sure Maggie could take another emotional blow, and he needed to be there for Dante and Deana. Because he was determined to bring his daughter home today but God only knew what state she would be in.

* * *

Alex parked the motorbike in their own car park. It was mud splashed and dirty from the roads and needed a good wash. It felt like therapy getting out the pressure jet wash, and cleaning the bike took his mind off things for a moment. Looking up, he saw Maggie pop her head around the back door, obviously wondering what the noise was. Seeing him, she left him to his own devices and went back inside.

'Nice bike,' he heard above the sound of the jet spray. Turning around, Alex saw Mark and nodded. 'Just giving it a clean.'

'This year's number plates, I see.' Mark couldn't help but notice, but he also looked over the bike lovingly. Engines and motors were his true love. 'Yours, I presume?'

'Not quite, but it will be.' Alex carried on rinsing off the soap suds as Mark stood watching Alex.

'Well, I can see you're building yourself up for a big day, so let's get it over with. I've got what we need. Come on, Alex, we can go in my van. Wherever we need to be, no one takes notice of a mobile mechanic van,' Mark muttered under his breath.

Giving Mark a weak smile, Alex was surprised. Mark, the fun-loving laughing man they all knew, had suddenly turned into a serious grown-up. There were no jokes or banter, just serious conversation. 'Are you sure you want to do this?' Alex asked. 'You could just give me the gear and I'll see you later.'

'Put that away and get into the van, Alex. I'm not stupid. You're putting off the inevitable. You want to go but are afraid of what you'll find,' Mark whispered, without mentioning Deana's name. Nodding, Alex put the pressure wash away and then climbed into Mark's van. 'I want to stop off at this place first. There is something I need to see.' Without a word, Mark read the address and frowned. Putting the address in his Google Maps, he drove on in silence. Mark could see Alex was deep in thought, and didn't disturb him with questions or mundane details. Casting a furtive glance sideways, Mark could tell Alex was a troubled man.

Eventually, they drove into a back-street industrial unit that looked like it hadn't been used in ages. There was scaffolding, possibly holding the units up, Alex thought to himself. Wincing inside, he dreaded the idea that Deana had been brought here. He was glad Mark was with him and would have hated to let Maggie see this place. Alex looked around; a couple of units were just square boxes with metal shutters. As they both walked further into the courtyard, Alex saw one that appeared to have a living quarter above it. Noting the unit number on the piece of paper, he knew this was the right one. Walking ahead of Mark, he saw the shutter hadn't been quite pulled down, but there was also a side entrance. 'I'll go in first and make sure the coast is clear. I don't know what to expect in here, Mark, so watch your back.'

Mark shook his head, determined to go with Alex. Looking up at the rusty metal unit surrounded by scaffolding, Mark's stomach somersaulted. How would he feel, if he thought his son had been brought here against his will and left? The very thought sickened him and he was determined to see it through with Alex, no matter what.

Entering the cobwebbed, derelict building, Alex and Mark looked at each other pensively, then they saw a side staircase. Without a word Alex pointed to it and slowly started to climb it. Seeing a door wide open, Mark was going to step forward, but Alex stopped him and indicated the other closed doors. Quietly they placed their hands on the handles and flung the doors open widely, just in case anyone was inside, but they could both see that the place was deserted. Mark took a sigh of relief and biting his bottom lip nervously, he looked at Alex. 'Now what? There's no one here.'

Alex walked towards the open door, the only room they hadn't yet checked. 'Someone has left in a hurry. Do you see the bolt on the outside?' Mark nodded. Nervously, he walked behind Alex, all the while looking behind him and listening out for anyone that might come behind them. Entering the room, they had to adjust their eyes to the darkness of the boarded-up room. Alex glanced at Mark. 'She's been here, or someone has.' Alex looked at the pitiful duvet in the corner of the cold, deserted room, stripped bare of anything. There was discarded food and wrappers.

'What the fuck is that smell?' asked Mark, almost retching.

'That's her toilet, Mark.' Walking over to the boarded-up window, Alex pushed at the planks of wood and noticed one was loose. 'Look, there's blood on here. She tried escaping.' Alex pictured Deana being held here and it sickened him.

Using the torch on his phone, Mark held it up to see more clearly and pulled at the board. 'You're right, the glass is broken this side of the window. There's no way she could have got out of here with all that scaffolding outside though – she'd have broken her neck. Come on Alex, you're torturing yourself here.' Mark pulled Alex by the arm, even though he was locked in thought. 'Deana's not here so let's see what the other place looks like. Come on Alex!'

Mark couldn't wait to get out of the cold, dingy smelling room. It felt eerie and gave him the creeps. Ushering Alex out of the room, Mark almost marched to his van, gulping in fresh air.

Alex looked at the road ahead. 'Let's see if the next place is an improvement.'

Nervously, Mark started the engine but left the window open. The smell of sweat and faeces made him want to retch, and when he had watched Alex pick up the duvet and smell it, he knew he'd smelled Deana's scent on it, by the look on his face. It was beyond Mark's thinking that anyone could do that to a young girl, no matter what they had done.

Taking out his cigarettes, Mark lit one and handed the packet to Alex. He hoped the nicotine and smoke would clear his nostrils.

The block of flats they arrived at some time later looked more promising. The tower blocks were painted and clean and some balconies had hanging baskets on.

'Let's knock first and see if anyone answers,' Alex instructed. He knew this flat belonged to someone on holiday, but he could be home now. And if so, where was Deana? Alex wondered.

When no one answered the door, Alex felt on safer ground. There was no one in the corridor, so he nodded to Mark to use whatever he had brought with him to open the door.

Fumbling with what Alex thought looked like Allen keys, Alex could see Mark was nervous but determined. Alex's face fell after Mark's second attempt, and he cursed him inwardly. Sweat appeared on Mark's brow and after another try, they heard the door unlock and open. 'Double lock, they're always the worst,' Mark whispered. 'But I did bring the ram just in case you were wondering. It's in the van. It wasn't going to be a lost cause,' Mark snapped. He hadn't meant to but, seeing Alex's exasperated glare, he couldn't help it.

Ignoring Mark, Alex flung the door wide open and ran inside, kicking every door in the hallway wide open. At last, he heard a shout and scream and saw a door with a bolt on the outside. Mark had closed the front door behind them so as not to alert anyone. With all of his might, Alex kicked and kicked again at the door. 'Deana,' he shouted. 'Deana, is that you?' Mark helped to give it one last kick and the door flung open.

With blind panic and hysterics, a screaming, frightened Deana hurled a lamp and any object she could find at them. Mark held up his arms to shield himself, but Alex ran towards her and grabbed her shoulders.

'It's me, Deana! It's Dad! It's me!' Alex shouted. Pulling her closer, he wrapped his arms around her and hugged her tightly. 'It's Dad, Deana. You're not dreaming. It really is me,' he stressed, trying to get through to her puzzled, confused brain.

Disbelievingly, Deana looked at Alex and opened her eyes as much as she could. They were swollen from crying. 'Dad, I prayed you'd come. I called for you and you didn't come, Dad,' she said, over and over again, while sobbing onto his chest. Alex felt heartbroken as he looked at her pale, frightened face. He couldn't help his own tears from falling. Looking around the room, he felt it was a far cry from what he had seen earlier. This place looked like a comfortable kid's room, full of posters and there were a couple of bags of food. Tinned beans she could take the top off and eat, bread and apples. Alex realised that whoever had brought her here, shouldn't have. This was not the designated place John had in mind for Deana to rot in. John hadn't dared kill Deana, but he had been prepared for her to rot and starve to death without blood on his hands. But someone had tried keeping her safe.

Deana was holding him tightly, almost squeezing the life out of him, and Alex held her away from him for just a moment. 'Deana,' he half whispered, trying to get through to her. 'I was informed you were given a mobile phone. Who brought you here? Did you know the men? Come, sit down on the bed beside me. Look, there's Mark, you are safe with us now.' Soothing her almost like a baby, he pointed to Mark, who brushed his own tears away and smiled.

'Some fucking holiday resort you picked, Deana.' Mark grinned in his usual style, trying to take the tension out of the situation.

'There were two of them,' she stammered with a croaky voice. Still trembling, she held Alex's hand firmly. 'One of them... Nick, brought the food, the other one was horrible!' With that she started crying again and clung to Alex. 'I couldn't get out, it's too high. I couldn't get out, Dad.' She cried onto his shoulder. 'I didn't dare eat all the food in the bags. No one came back, Dad. They left me here. No one came.' Spit dribbled down her mouth and looking down, Alex could see she had wet herself with fear. Mustering all his strength, Alex tried to remain calm. He felt like screaming himself. He had been helpless, and if it hadn't been for the tip off, he may never have found her. The very thought of it made him want to vomit, but he held it back.

He recalled that Bernie had used the name Nick, too. He was the man who had tried to help Deana. Alex pointed to the two shopping bags. 'Empty what's left in those bags, Mark.'

'Not that one!' Deana pointed to one of them. 'I used that as a toilet.' Looking down, she felt ashamed. 'There was nowhere else, Dad,' she whispered.

Mark emptied what was left in the other bag on the floor. There were a few bags of crisps, some bottled water and a white loaf of bread, but nothing else. 'Open the wrappers, Mark.'

Mark looked at him oddly but opened the crisps. The packets were still sealed. Confused, Alex held Deana and watched Mark. There was no mobile phone. 'You should have eaten the bread, Deana,' said Mark. 'This will have gone mouldy.' Opening it, Mark paled. 'Oh, fuck Alex, look at this.' The sliced bread had what looked like a fist hole in the middle of it, even though the wrapper had been put back together making it look unopened. Mark looked in closer and buried in it was indeed a mobile phone.

Wide eyed, Deana dried her eyes with the back of her sleeve and her jaw dropped. 'I never opened it,' she said slowly. Rooted to the spot, she watched as Mark tried turning the phone on.

'It's new Alex. And the battery is half charged.'

Alex felt crushed; her salvation had been within arm's distance. The man had tried, possibly thinking that was the first thing she would open. Whatever he had done, even buying the mobile phone, he had done hastily. But he couldn't have done any more.

'Nick went and did the shopping while the other one put the

bolt on the door,' Deana whispered, her voice almost non-existent.

'Let's get out of here, Alex. We've no time to waste. Can you stand Deana? Are you okay?' Mark interrupted. Seeing her nod, Alex helped her to her feet.

'I need to trash this place, Mark. Make it look like a burglary and get rid of those bags. You take her down to the van, I'll only be a minute.' Mark nodded and picked Deana up in his arms as he carried her to the lift. Methodically Alex ran around the flat, tipping things over and smashing them. Looking around him, he felt satisfied. He picked up the bags from Deana's room, and getting a knife from the kitchen, he took the bolt from the outside of the door and stuffed it in his pocket. He knew there would be fingerprints, and he tried to clean what he could, but he didn't want to start a fire. And, if anyone called the police about a burglary, it would look real enough.

## 20

### HOMEWARD BOUND

Mark drove as close to the back door of the pub as possible. 'Let's smuggle her in. No one can see her looking like that,' Mark said as he cast a glance in the back of the van towards Deana. She was emaciated and filthy; her blonde hair was straggly and greasy around her shoulders and her hands were scratched and torn. It made him shudder.

'Mark. Thank you for coming with me today and helping me. I don't know what else to say.'

'Good, then don't say anything. Because I don't want to discuss it or think of this again. Let's just get her inside to Maggie.'

Alex carried Deana inside. She looked weak and a shadow of her former self. God knows what she would have looked like if they hadn't found her. Mentally, he didn't want to go there, but he couldn't help considering the alternative. She was home, and that was all that mattered for now.

Mark went into the bar and looked for Maggie who was busy serving customers. 'Alex has a present for you.' He beckoned.

Pausing, she looked Mark directly in the eye, knowing what

he meant. Handing a tray to another waitress, she almost ran behind Mark up the stairs to find Alex and Deana. Collapsing onto her knees, she burst into tears. She had never thought this moment would come. She had longed for it but couldn't believe Deana was actually back home. Reaching forward, she put her arms around Deana and hugged her so tight, she couldn't breathe.

'Cigarette break, I think.' Mark nodded to Alex. Taking the hint, Alex stood up and left the two women in his life sobbing and holding each other. He had seen enough heartache and tears for the moment. There were no words, and he knew they wouldn't just be able to pick up where things had been left and carry on. So much had changed in a short space of time. Deana's life would never be the same again.

Pouring himself and Mark two large whiskies and two pints of beer, Alex took a tray and walked out into the empty beer garden.

Gulping his down in one, Mark put the glass on the garden bench and looked at Alex. 'I needed that. So, what happens now?' Emotionally drained, Alex did the same. 'I really don't know. Physically Deana will heal, but mentally, I'm not so sure. I want to gun the bastards down, Mark, but what's the point?' Alex knew he had already killed the one man responsible for all of this.

'That other bloke sounds like he tried to help. How the fuck did he know she wouldn't eat the bread?' The air was tense and sombre; the memories of that first room still sickened him.

'You're right, of course. He tried. And I really do need to shake that bloke's hand. He did what he could, the same as I would or yourself. But we'll probably never know who he is. I have an appeal tomorrow, which will hopefully mean I won't have to go back to jail,' Alex said, trying to change the subject. Seeing Mark's eyebrows raise in surprise, Alex told him about the letter that had arrived. 'Shit or bust, Mark, that's the point, isn't it. I fucked up with my male pride and look where it's got me.'

'Don't blame yourself, Alex. True, I think you should have taken the easy option and left court with Maggie that day, but it's done now. What's the point in beating yourself up about it? I'm sure you did that many nights in your prison cell. Now you can hopefully put it all behind you and become a boring bastard like me and just live a boring life. Although, since you moved into the area, it's been far from boring!' Mark looked at Alex and together they smiled.

Alex raised his glass against Mark's and chinked it. 'Here's to boring. Cheers.' They laughed and Alex hoped that this was the start of a new and better life for all of the Silvas.

* * *

Gently, Maggie had bathed Deana. Sat in a hot bath full of bubbles, Maggie had soothingly sponged her back with warm water and washed her hair. She had wanted Deana to tell her what had happened, but she remined silent, taking everything in and afraid of her own shadow. Each time she heard footsteps up the stairs she froze. 'I'll leave you to have a soak, Deana. No rush, take your time. I'm going to put the kettle on and make you a hot drink.'

As Maggie was about to leave, Deana called her, 'Mum, don't shut the door, please.' Maggie saw the pleading look in her eyes and swung the door even wider. 'Let me know if it's draughty, and we can half close it, okay?' It broke Maggie's heart seeing her like this.

Alex came upstairs and walked into the kitchen to find Maggie busying herself making tea. Giving her a knowing look, he queried where Deana was.

'In the bath,' Maggie mouthed, 'she wanted me to leave the door open.'

Alex cast his eyes to the floor and nodded. 'Give her time, love. She can have the windows and doors open if it makes her feel secure. I've been incarcerated, Maggie, and being behind locked doors is no fun. It fucks up your brain if you let it. I found it hard to sleep when I came home because, in prison the nights are noisy. Suddenly, I came home and it's silent. With Deana, all she has heard is silence and so the noise will deafen her. We're humans and we need human contact. Give her space.'

A worried look crossed Maggie's face. 'Do you think they raped her, Alex? Should we have her checked over or something? What about pregnancy?' Maggie panicked.

Pondering for a moment, Alex shook his head. 'I don't know for sure, but I don't think so. And we may never find out – we have to let Deana tell us in her own time. Don't push it, Maggie and don't torture yourself. And where would we take her to get checked over – the doctor, the hospital? And what would we say?' Seeing the dawning realisation on Maggie's face, he kissed her on the cheek. 'Put some cream on her wounds and be there for her, but no pressure. We'll face the next hurdle when we get to it. Just be pleased to have her home.' He knew she would be a mother hen and want to know everything at once, but he knew his way was the best way. Let Deana get used to the idea of being home first, then they could ask the tough questions.

As Maggie left the kitchen, Alex felt drained. Everyone wanted answers from him, and he felt he had nothing more to give, but he needed to mentally prepare himself for tomorrow. Closing his eyes, he thanked God that Deana was home and prayed that all would go well tomorrow. He needed a shower. He felt grubby after the morning. He stood under the warm water, and as it rained down on his body and washed away the stench of the day, he felt close to collapsing. In the privacy of the downstairs bathroom, he let his own tears flow and once he started, he couldn't stop. Deep sobs wracked his body that he had kept inside him all day. Deana was alive and home and that was all that mattered.

* * *

Taking in a mug of tea, Maggie put it down on the bath rack next to Deana. 'Get that down you love, while I look in this cabinet for some creams and bandages to sort out your cuts and bruises.'

'How's Dante, Mum?' Deana muttered. Surprised, Maggie turned to look at her.

'Much the same as always. He's been worried about you, though.'

'He's told you what we did, hasn't he? Do you and Dad hate us?'

'Do we look and sound as though we hate you, Deana? Would your father have run all around London looking for you if he hated you? He's due in court tomorrow for an appeal to keep him out of prison, but all he could think about was you. There was no way he could go back to prison without you being home. We're family, Deana, and we are your parents; we love you no matter what... even if you were a pair of prats!' Maggie smiled, feeling that was an understatement.

'Dad's got an appeal? Does that mean he could stay home?' Maggie nodded. 'Oh God, that would be great, wouldn't it?' Deana half smiled and picked up her mug and sipped her tea.

Maggie smiled. They had a long way to go but there was hope on the horizon.

* * *

'Deana's home?' Disbelievingly, Dante ran into the lounge and grinned. Lying full length on the sofa staring blindly at the television, was his big sister. 'Deana!' Falling to his knees, he wrapped his arms around her. Maggie left them to it and continued putting out dinner. She had informed Phyllis that Deana was unwell and that she wasn't coming down for the rest of the day. She also filled her in on Alex's appeal and told her they were going to have a quiet family evening off together.

Phyllis had brushed her off in her own matter-of-fact way and told Maggie to leave her to it. Maggie's broken family needed healing and with friends like Phyllis and Mark, Maggie felt stronger already. Popping her head around the lounge door, Maggie halted. Before her was one of those images she would never forget. Dan had climbed onto the sofa with his back against Deana, and she had put one half of her dressing gown around him, holding him tight. Together, they were laid like spoons in a drawer in silence. Glad to be reunited.

Nothing much was said during the course of the evening. Everyone was locked in their own thoughts. As he went to bed, Alex left all of the landing doors open and winked at Maggie. As Deana walked into her own room, she looked around it, as though seeing it for the first time ever.

Alex spent the night dozing off and on. He noticed that Deana was sleeping with the lamp on, like she had done as a child. At some point during the night he woke up to find a figure standing beside him. Blinking, he saw that it was Deana. 'Are you okay, Deana?' he whispered in the darkness. Behind him Maggie roused and switched on the lamp.

'I just wanted to know that you were here and that it wasn't a dream. I've dreamt so long about being home. It is real, isn't it, Dad?'

Alex pulled back the duvet, and opened his arms to welcome

her in. 'It is real, Deana. You're home and safe. Nothing can hurt you now.' Hearing Dan come into the room, Maggie smiled. 'Couldn't sleep, love?'

'Just wondered if Deana was okay.' He yawned and scratched his head.

Alex chuckled. 'Well, it's just as well this is a bloody king-size bed. Come on, get in. Christ, this is just like the old days.' Almost hanging on to the end of the mattress, Alex smiled, happy that his family were all together again. Things would get better, he thought to himself. This was what they needed: each other's strength to keep them going.

The next morning felt almost surreal. Each in turn, they all turned up at the breakfast table while Maggie made tea and toast. Bleary eyed, Alex came through and sat down. 'I'd forgotten just how much room your kids took up in your bed,' Alex laughed. Even though tired, he felt happy.

Deana sat down and picked up a cup gingerly with her bandaged hands. 'What have you told everyone about my absence? I need to know what you've said.'

'We told people you'd gone away for a few days with friends. That's all they need to know. Dante here has done some of your homework so college doesn't need to know any more,' Alex announced. 'As for anyone else, it's none of their business.'

'You've done my homework, Dan?'

Half expecting her to go bonkers, Dan nodded. 'Done my best, sis.'

'Thank you.' Leaning forward, she unexpectedly kissed him on the cheek.

'Remember that, Dante,' laughed Alex, 'because you will never get another one.'

Deana looked around at her family. 'Mum, Dad, I'm sorry. Sorry for everything. Absolutely everything. And I am sorry to you, too, Dan. You warned me it would blow up in my face and it did. Look at me, I'm a mess. If this is the price of fame, then I don't want it.'

'Who the hell said you were famous?' Dante laughed. 'Forget it, Deana. Just get well. I want my crabby sister back. It doesn't feel right you being so nice all the time.' He grinned.

'Morning, morning, morning!'

Maggie's eyes rolled to the ceiling, and she grinned as Mark made his way into the kitchen. 'Christ, he's better than an alarm clock. Move up, Dante. Make space for Mark.'

'How's the walking wounded?' Mark grinned at Deana and impulsively, she stood up and hugged him.

'Thank you,' she whispered, making him blush.

'Sit down, Deana, tabard woman is here.' Giving him a strange look, Deana sat down again.

Dan winked at her mischievously, making her even more curious. Just then, Olivia came upstairs, as predicted, in her council polo shirt today and her tabard.

'I just came to wish you luck today, Alex. Mark said you had an appeal.' She grinned. Thanking her graciously, Alex grinned back. 'New polo shirt?' He felt he had to say something as she stood there flashing the logo at them all.

'Yeah,' Mark laughed. 'It looks like you get one piece of uniform a day. Tomorrow she might even get the trousers,' he laughed, then winced in pain as Olivia dug him in the ribs with her elbow.

'You look pale, Deana, and what have you done to your hands? Mark said you've been doing some outdoor glamping with your friends. I'm sure I've got some special hand creams from my Avon selling. I'll bring some around later.'

Alex breathed a sigh of relief. Mark had come up with some

kind of cover story and Olivia, who lived in her own world most of the time, had accepted it.

'Good luck, mate.' Mark held out his hand to shake Alex's. 'Text me, if you can, later. I'm dropping Olivia off at work, so I presume you'll be gone when I get back.'

Alex stood up. Words weren't needed as he opened his arms and hugged Mark. 'Thanks man, I'll be in touch.'

Wide eyed, Deana looked around the table. 'Olivia's got a job?' she asked, amazed.

'Now known as Tabard woman,' Dan laughed. 'She never takes it off. She has six hours in between shifts and keeps it on all the time. Bloody hell, I hope they give her two of everything; she will smell worse than the toilets she's cleaning otherwise!' For the first time since she had come home, the usual, uncontrolled laughter escaped Deana. It was hearty and genuine and Alex looked at Maggie and grinned too.

'Oh my God, Dan. Do you think her hand cream is the council's as well? Unless she just wants to flog her Avon to me.' Deana's face creased up with laughter, melting Alex's heart. Finishing his tea, he licked his lips and put his cup down. 'Well, I'm going to leave you two to it and get a shower. I need to look my best for today.'

'I've got your suit out, Alex. It's on the back of the door,' Maggie shouted after him. Today was judgement day, but Alex knew no matter what, his family were going to be okay.

## 21

JUDGEMENT DAY

Maggie went with Alex to the appeal court. She needed to give him the same moral support he had given her over the past few days. With Deana missing, her life had been a nightmare and she couldn't have faced it without him. More to the point, she knew she wouldn't have been as successful as Alex. She would have trusted all the wrong people and probably ended up dead herself. The very thought of it made her shudder. Swallowing hard, she waited while Alex gave his name to a woman on reception and was scanned and led through a barrier. Maggie waited on the opposite side and waved goodbye. Wringing her hands together, she went outside and sat on the stone steps outside the court. The sun was shining, and people were walking past her chatting and laughing with each other. She wondered what their plans were for the day. Nervously, she looked behind her at the court doors and wondered if Alex had been called in yet. Soon they would know his fate.

Alex's hands were hot and clammy as he stood before the appeals board and the judge. After flicking through their paperwork and nodding to each other, at last, they addressed him. 'Mr

Silva, it seems you have decided to appeal against your voluntary decision to serve your two-year sentence. Can you tell us why?'

Swallowing hard, Alex had to think on his feet. He didn't know what circumstances he had supposedly appealed on, because he'd never appealed for this hearing.

'I feel sir, that I acted hastily and that my family need me. I've appealed for them, not for my own selfish reasons. They suffered during my very public court case and afterwards. I know I have done wrong, but I've tried to help the police and the FBI in all their investigations, which is why my sentence was reduced dramatically, and I am very grateful for that. I want to rebuild our lives and not prolong their suffering any more. I would prefer to have the suspended sentence that I was originally offered.' Alex felt he had said enough. They knew what and who he was. He was pleading for his life, but by the looks on their faces they already knew what the outcome would be, as they whispered in each other's ears.

'We have a letter from the governor of the prison you resided at. He says that you were a model prisoner and helped him discover a drug ring in the prison. He personally feels you deserve a second chance.'

Alex stood rooted to the spot. His legs felt weak and his mind wandered to Maggie waiting outside. They talked about his employment at the pub and that his family were doing well. Mentally, Alex squirmed at that, but on the face of it, Deana was at college and Dante was going to stay on at school. To the outside world, Alex presumed it did look like they were rebuilding their lives or trying to anyway. They mentioned his recent measles and asked how he was feeling now. They praised him for how he had reported himself to the police on a daily basis and got a sick note from the doctor. Nodding, Alex told them he felt much better and thanked them. His mouth felt dry and he licked his lips, moistening them.

One of the judges made it clear they didn't want him freed. They felt he was a menace to society and that he should be locked away. Men like Alex Silva, he said, should be made an example of. Alex was then asked to step outside, assuring him that it wouldn't be for long. He felt sick. Those men in there were deciding his fate and already he could see one was totally against him. Pacing up and down the corridor, he looked at his watch. It seemed like an eternity before he was called in again. Taking a breath, he walked forward and stood before them again.

After a long-winded speech, the judge picked up a large stamp. 'Approved,' he said, stamping the appeals form which, supposedly, Alex had filled in with his lawyers. Alex stood there in shock for a moment and looked at them, hardly believing his ears. 'Thank you,' he muttered, and relief washed over him. They told him he was free to go, but the remainder of his sentence would be suspended. Alex listened as the judge told him this was his last chance and to make good use of it and how he never wanted to see Alex before him again.

'You're free to leave, Mr Silva.' The words echoed in his ears, and his legs felt like lead unable to move for a moment, although he wanted to run outside to Maggie and scream he was free to the world outside. Instead, he thanked them again and walked out. It felt like he was in a trance and he half expected them to call him back. Hastily, he picked up his speed, scanning the corridors for Maggie, surprised that she wasn't there. Opening the court doors, he looked down at the steps and saw Maggie sat there forlornly.

'Maggie!' he called. 'Maggie. It's over. I'm a free man!'

Standing up, she ran towards his open arms. 'What happened? I was so afraid a policeman would come out and tell me you were being taken back to prison in handcuffs and they wouldn't give me a moment with you alone.'

'I've still got a suspended sentence hanging over me, but tonight I'm in my own bed. Oh God, Maggie, let's make this work,' he gushed and held her. He couldn't believe his luck, and he felt that he owed whoever had instigated all of this his very existence. He knew that Bernie's boss, the elusive Patsy Diamond, obviously had the judge in her pocket. It seemed this woman had everyone in her pocket. But, at this moment, he didn't care. Whatever the future held, he would face it. He didn't know what the price of all this was, but, felt sure he would find out soon enough.

'Let's go home, Alex; I've had enough of courts and police. Let's go home, before they change their minds!' Linking her arm through his, Maggie almost dragged him behind her as she ran to the car.

\* \* \*

As Maggie drove them back to the pub, she decided to get something off her chest. 'I've been thinking, Alex. It's time this family talked more and that's what we'll do from now on. Honesty, Alex. We will have a full family meeting and each story can come pouring out. This is the first day of the rest of our lives, so let's do it openly with each other for once. I'm sick of secrets and whispers. Mark knows more than I do and I am your wife. I know we have a couple more hurdles to jump, but I've had an idea about Luke.'

The very mention of his name angered Alex, but Maggie stopped him as she continued. 'Let me finish, please. My thinking is Dante's gun is in that house of his and we need to get him out and us in to find it.'

'And just how do we do that?' Alex looked out of the window as he listened to Maggie.

'The funeral, Alex. That's the only day we know Luke will be out most of the day. But firstly, we have to go and see him and offer our condolences. By that, I mean me, the female touch. We need to find out what day the funeral is and offer our help. He has no one else. He might be suspicious, but I think I can convince him.'

As much as Alex hated the idea, he felt himself warming to it. If they knew when he would be out, that would give him a chance to search the house. Alex also thought about Mark's skeleton keys and how easy it had been to get into the other flat with them. Maybe he could borrow them for one last time.

'Alright, let's do it your way. But the funeral won't be for a week or more. The woman is hardly cold.'

'Right, I'll call him and ask him how he's doing and what I can do to help. Maybe we could do the catering.' She grinned.

'Oh my God, not another wake in the back room,' Alex laughed.

'Actually, Alex,' Maggie mused, 'that's not a bad idea. At least we'd know where he is at all times.'

'And it would give us a couple of hours. To be fair, it's not a bad idea, Maggie. But it's not the last hurdle. Dan has still got to cook a shitload of stuff. Christ, will this never end?'

'It will. We're nearly there. We just need to hang on in there, and we can if we stick together.' Maggie smiled and put her foot down, heading for home.

Alex's phone buzzed. Reading it, he saw it was a message from Mark that simply read, 'YAAAY!' Alex smiled and quickly showed it to Maggie. 'A man of few words.' He laughed.

Once home, Maggie felt lighter and happier. Going through to the bar, she checked everything was okay, even though she knew it would be. Phyllis and Pauline could run that place with their eyes closed. The chef knew his job and the kitchen assistants and waitresses busied themselves serving the customers. Maggie felt a hushed silence as she walked through the bar. Seeing Mark and Olivia she knew he had tipped off the other regulars. 'Drinks on the house!' she shouted towards them. 'Go on everyone, order a drink and celebrate my Alex's freedom.'

While everyone was congratulating Alex, Dan and Deana came downstairs, hearing the noise. Each in turn, they hugged Alex. Maggie slipped away into the hallway and picked up the telephone to set her plan in action. 'Hello Luke, it's Maggie. Don't put the phone down, please. I've been busy lately, but I wanted to ask if there was anything I could help you with. I was wondering about your mum's wake. Would you like to hold it here? It might help and I can sort the food for you... if you like.'

'Why would you do that, Maggie? Why do you care? Alex has made it very clear he hates me and that you all want nothing to do with me any more,' Luke said sadly.

'I liked your mum, Luke. She was a decent woman who deserves a decent send-off, that's all. I know Alex can be hasty and angry and to be honest he has a right to be. But I'm asking, not Alex. Look, think about it. I'm sorry I called.' Maggie waited, while she heard Luke pausing on the line.

'The wake at yours would take a load off, but would Alex mind? I'd pay of course.'

'This is my pub, Luke not Alex's. I've never stuck my nose in yours and Alex's business and I'm not going to start now. And as for paying, I've offered. All those nurses who helped your mum deserve a decent drink after all the help they gave. Maybe you could get each of them a gift or something? That would be nice.'

'I never thought of that. Yeah, that would be a good idea.'

'And what about,' Maggie carried on, worming her way in,

'people not buying loads of flowers but giving to the charity of your mum's cancer. Of course, there would be your flowers, but you know what I mean.' Again, she heard Luke pause, deep in thought.

'You know, Maggie, that's a really nice idea. Yeah, if you want to come over, we can go through a few things if you like. Maybe... maybe you could help me get some presents for the nurses and the like.'

Maggie felt like punching the air. She was playing Luke at his own game and she would save her own son in the process. Nothing and no one would threaten her family again.

## 22

### THE SNARE

'I don't like you licking arse, Maggie, but you're the boss and if you think it will help, I'll wait until the funeral – that's all.'

Surprised, Maggie raised her eyebrows. 'The boss? Since when was I the boss?' she laughed.

Giving her a knowing look, Alex grinned. 'Since I put this gold band on my finger, or are you just deluded?'

Maggie picked up her tea towel and flicked Alex with it. Then she grinned and kissed him. 'You need to be patient, Alex. Luke is suspicious, but he's already fallen into my trap. And he's got no one else,' Maggie stressed. 'He needs help. Funerals need a lot of organising. There's an awful lot of paperwork to fill in, not to mention the emotional support. Believe me, Alex, people who have lost a loved one don't really get to grieve until way after the funeral, because there's no time.'

'Fair point.' Alex shrugged. 'I've never really thought of it that way. Good luck with your manipulation.'

'I like to call it my feminine charm, you cheeky bugger.' Looking up, Maggie saw Dante and Deana enter the lounge. 'The very two people I was just thinking about.'

Oddly they both looked at her and waited, without saying anything. 'Dan,' Maggie began, 'I think you should go and see Kev. I'm sure he could do with some emotional support. Put his mind at rest and tell him that I'm helping with the funeral arrangements and holding the wake here, at the pub.'

'Really? You're having the wake here? What about Luke? That would mean he's coming too.'

Raising her eyebrows, Maggie smiled. 'Why didn't I think of that?'

'Could I go and see Kev?' Deana asked. 'I'd like to see him.'

Alex stopped smiling and looked at her seriously for a moment. 'Are you up to going out?'

'I could go with Dante,' she said hopefully. 'I have to go forward, Dad. I'm not overly confident, but I don't want to become a victim. I'm alive, Dad. I've been given a second chance and so from now on, this is the first day of the rest of my life.'

Alex looked down at the floor silently. He hadn't expected this so soon, and to be honest, the paternal side of him didn't want Deana out of his sight at the moment. Thinking about Kev, he looked up at her. 'Deana, I think there's something you need to know about Kev. He's not the man you think he is...' Alex looked at Maggie for support, hoping she would somehow help him ease the way. Alex felt he had to tell her that Kev was gay and had no interest in her, apart from friendship.

Sitting on the sofa beside him, Deana gave a weak smile. 'I know, Dan filled me in on that. I've been so stupid. Christ, poor Kev must have cringed inside at times.'

Alex reached up and took her face in both hands. 'Any man would be flattered to have your attention, Deana. You're beautiful, but that man is just not Kev.'

'I know. That's why I'd like to go and see him. Not only to see how he is, but to set things straight between us. I don't want him having to dodge a bullet every time he sees me. We could still be friends.'

Alex nodded. 'I'll drive you both to the hospital and wait outside. Just take things easy, Deana.' Taking her hand, Alex kissed the back of it.

Pausing, Deana looked around the room before speaking. 'You know, Dad, being locked up, the way I have been, gives you time to reflect and think about all the things you would change about yourself and do again. I'm sure you know what I mean. I guess it's like prison...' She tailed off and seeing Alex nod, she gave a wan smile. 'I need to apologise to Kev. I forced him to come to my birthday party, just to make me look good. It was pathetic. He's fun to be around, and I should have just left it at that, but you know me – all or nothing. I've been a silly schoolgirl with a crush and it's time I grew up.'

Alex put his arms around Deana and held her close. 'We've all had crushes and unrequited love. Look at your mother and Brad Pitt, but she's getting over it.' They all laughed, easing the tension.

\* \* \*

Later that day, during the lull of the afternoon when the pub was quiet and the lunch time rush was over, Maggie felt it was a good time to go and see Luke.

'Hi Luke, I'm here as promised. What do you need me to do?' She grinned. Mentally, she felt her smile was as false as his. As she stood at the door, Luke looked around her up the street.

'Are you looking for someone, Luke?' she asked puzzled.

'Erm, no Maggie, I just didn't expect you to be on your own. I thought Alex might come.'

Maggie shrugged. 'Do you want me to ask him to come?'

'No, it's fine. I just thought Alex might not let you come on your own, given the circumstances,' he muttered.

'The circumstances are' – Maggie pushed past him into the hallway – 'that your mum has passed away and you need help. Isn't that what friends do? I bear you no ill will Luke. Life is too short.' Through gritted teeth, Maggie smiled sweetly like Mary Poppins, all the while plotting his demise.

As Maggie looked at Luke, she could see how dishevelled he looked. It looked like he had worn the same T-shirt for a couple of days and the house was untidy. 'First of all, young man, why don't you go and get a shower while I put the kettle on and then you can tell me how far you've got up to now.'

Smiling, Luke raised his arms and sniffed his armpits. 'Phew, I see what you mean. Maybe I should. I haven't registered the death yet, although I have an appointment. Mum's at the funeral directors I've chosen, or rather she did. She sorted a lot out before she died, because she knew what was coming and wanted to make it easier.'

'Go on then, stinky, and we'll talk when I can sit in the same room as you without having to hold my breath.' Seeing Luke's smile as he walked up the stairs, Maggie felt she had just earned his trust. A small part of her felt sorry for him, but then she remembered what he'd threatened to do to Dante and she hardened her heart against him.

\* \* \*

As Alex sat outside the hospital, his mind wandered to Maggie. She had been gone hours, and he wondered what could be taking her so long. He hated the idea of a very unscrupulous Luke taking advantage of Maggie's good nature. He knew she was doing it for the family, but he also knew what a big heart she had and knew she would go that extra mile. She rarely saw the bad in anyone. That was one of the things he liked about her, no, loved about her. Picking up his mobile, he was tempted to call or text but thought better of it, and didn't think Maggie would thank him for interrupting her.

Just then Deana and Dante came walking towards the car. To Alex's mind's eye, Deana still looked pale and seemed a little nervous at times. 'How's Kev doing?' Alex asked out of politeness.

'He's on the mend, Dad, although I'm not sure there isn't a bone that hasn't been broken. Most of him is in plaster cast! But he's not on so many pain killers now and can talk more. I told him I was sorry for being a silly little girl and how uncomfortable I must have made him, but he was okay about it. He said he was the silly one and should have come out of the closet years ago but that he was afraid to. Poor bugger, Dad. Imagine being afraid of who you are. It's not fair.' She sighed and put her seat belt on while he started up the engine.

Alex shrugged. 'Sometimes life's not fair, Deana. But you should always be proud of who you are. Kev will feel better once he admits who he is and people have different attitudes these days. Once he does that, there will be no more misunderstandings in the future.'

'I'll tell you what's not fair, that you get to sit in the front of the car all the time and I'm squashed up in the back,' Dan laughed.

Deana was full of chatter and banter with Dan, and even though Alex had been reluctant about her seeing Kev in case it opened up old wounds, even he could see that it had done her a world of good.

* * *

Seeing Maggie's car, Alex was curious about her meeting with Luke. Considering how long she had been with him, he obviously hadn't slammed the door in her face, Alex thought to himself. Walking into the pub, Deana opted to go upstairs and not in the pub with everyone looking at her. She still felt self-conscious, especially with her hands bandaged. Sticking his head around the bar, Alex saw Maggie in her usual stance behind the pumps, pulling pints and laughing with the customers. 'You got one of those frothy coffees for your husband?' Alex grinned.

'Can you believe that, boys?' Maggie laughed to a group of builders who were working nearby and had become regular customers. 'A beautiful woman who owns a pub with as many pints and bacon sandwiches as you can eat, and my husband wants a coffee!'

'Is she flirting while taking your money, boys?' Alex joked with the men, and they all laughed and cheered.

'Here's your coffee, you cheeky monkey.' Maggie smiled.

'You're a lucky man, Alex.' One of the builders shouted and raised his glass to him. Suddenly a dark cloud fell over Alex. Looking at Maggie again, he saw her slim body, pert breasts and blonde hair. She was funny and cracked jokes around the bar all the time. It was a side of her he hadn't seen much of lately. But she was the hostess with the mostest, and everyone loved her. Suddenly, he felt he had neglected his lovely wife. He hadn't taken her out for a very long time just them two. And here were a handful of men, although only joking, admiring his wife and he had been too wrapped up with everything else to pay her proper attention. She deserved spoiling, he thought to himself.

He had a sudden urge to take his wife out on a date. To show her how much he loved her. Just because they owned a pub with a restaurant didn't mean they had to spend their life there, did it? Surely other publicans must eat and drink elsewhere.

Sitting at the back of the bar near the hatch, Alex watched Maggie organising everyone, sorting out orders, keeping customers happy. He sipped his coffee and admired how efficient she was with the staff and the respect she got back from them. He'd never really noticed before, but then he hadn't been there much of late and when he had he'd been distracted. Now, he was determined to change all of that.

Just then, two workmen walked into the bar with a clipboard and asked for himself and Maggie. Alex stood up and walked to the front of the bar. 'Can we help you?'

'It's just that couple of extra barrels you ordered. Can you sign for them and we'll leave them round the back?' Confused, Alex looked at Maggie. 'Have you ordered extra?'

The workmen handed Alex the clipboard. 'Check the invoice, Mr Silva. You will see that it's all in order.'

Alex scanned through the first page of the clipboard and turned to the next page while he could feel Maggie's hot breath on his neck as she peered over his shoulder. 'What does it say, Alex?'

'Oh God, yeah, sorry guys,' Alex apologised. 'It's been one of those days. Yeah Maggie, I rang it through for you. Isn't it for that wake you're catering for?' Alex spied the bottom of the second page and read the words written there again. 'Two weeks, Swifty Silva and son.'

'I'll come out the back with you and sort it now.' Alex grinned, winking at Maggie before she could answer.

Out the back, Alex spied the two barrels and looked at the men. 'Bernie said you were expecting this delivery. Do you need a hand getting them down the cellar?'

Nodding, Alex apologised again. 'The trap door is here that goes down into the cellar, if you don't mind.' As Alex went to roll one, he felt it was heavier than it looked. They appeared to look like the usual metal barrels that the beer was delivered in, but these were plastic. Alex met the eye of one of workmen, who gave him a knowing look and a lopsided grin. 'Everything is there, Mr Silva. Any problems, you know who to contact.' With the barrels safely tucked away in the cellar, Alex decided to call Dan.

Both Deana and Dan walked down the cellar steps. 'I believe these are yours. Do you want to check everything is in there that you need?' Alex asked.

With a bit of muscle, Alex and Dan got the lids off the barrels and looked inside. The different bags of ingredients meant nothing to Alex, but Dan clearly knew what he needed. 'Check it over Dante. This is your baby, not mine. You have two weeks maximum. Can you do that?'

'Dunno Dad, but I'll give it my best shot.'

Deana looked on, puzzled. 'Are you cooking meth again?'

'Yeah, he is. And the price is your freedom from what you've both done. I'm surprised they haven't asked for their money back. By the way, where is the money?'

'It's stored in some old wardrobes in a storage facility. It's safe but what do we do with it?' Dan cast a furtive glance at Deana, hoping she was going to butt in and suggest something.

Deana eventually spoke up, much to Dante's relief. 'We didn't expect to make that much money, Dad. If they don't want it back, I would still like to use it to pay for my university fees and so would Dan. That was why we did it. We don't have a penny to scratch our arses with, do we?'

'That's not a good enough reason to deal drugs, Deana. Other people have student loans and pay them back,' Alex snapped, then bit his tongue. He had asked for honesty and he had got it. 'Well, the bottom line is, you can't just put the cash you have stored into a bank. They would definitely know you were dealers. Those are the only people I know that have great sums of cash, apart from lottery winners.' Musing to himself, an idea came to Alex. But he needed to talk it over with Maggie first. 'At some point your mum wants a family meeting. She wants no more skeletons in the closet, which I think is fair.'

Both Dan and Deana nodded. 'When can I start this, Dad, because I'll need use of the freezer. At least one, anyway.' As Dan peered in closer, he smiled. 'Everything is in there, even the jars and trays. They've thought of everything. We used to use Luke's mum's baking trays, but these are great.'

Alex shook his head as he repeated Dante's sentence to himself. 'Luke's mum's baking trays? Christ, all of this was madness. You are going to have to sort a freezer out with your mum. The biggest one will be the restaurant kitchen when everyone has left. That means working through the nights and making damn sure it's clean before the staff arrive. All I can say is, if you need any help I'm here. I've no idea what to do, but we can all fetch and carry, eh, Deana?'

'Absolutely Dad. But once Mary Berry gets going it's going to look like an episode of *Master Chef*. This is my price for freedom...' Deana tailed off. 'Thank you, Dan. Whatever you need, okay?' she said as she hugged him.

Alex clapped his hands together. 'Never mind that now. Like I said, you can all air your thoughts and stuff when we have a moment to spare. You just check everything, Dan. It's not Tesco. We can't just pop and get a missing ingredient.' Alex sighed and walked back up the cellar stairs and into the pub. Things were about to get very interesting.

\* \* \*

Alex sat at the kitchen table and meticulously started filling out the passport forms he had picked up from the Post Office. It was time they all had a holiday and now he was a free man he could travel freely without pretending to be anyone else. There was a form for each of them, but as he filled in the boxes he began to wonder who might vouch for them and countersign the form. He doubted the police would do it, but he didn't know any other civil servants. Putting the form down, he felt crushed.

He heard Maggie's footsteps as she walked into the kitchen. 'Oh,' she laughed. 'Have I caught you writing love letters to other women?'

Alex held up the passport forms with a sad look on his face. 'I thought we could all do with a holiday soon, but who would sign the forms? No one I know...' Putting them down, he rubbed his hands through his hair. 'Best laid plans, eh?'

'Jen, the nurse, will do it for us. So don't despair. It's a lovely idea, and if that's all we have to worry about, that's fine with me. I take it that delivery is for Dan's handy work?' she scoffed.

'Yeah, we've hit a sticky wicket on that one. We need a freezer and somewhere to cook it. Presumably that's something we have to sort out.'

'Fair enough, we can sort that. We've taped off the freezers before.' She winked and Alex remembered the dead body they had once stored there. 'I can sort that out, but he can't work in the day.'

Alex agreed and made a note to talk to Dan about how it might work.

'So, tell me about Luke. How did it go with him? Did he suspect anything?'

'He has no idea what he's doing. But I've made him a list to contact his mum's bank. Direct debits are still going out of her account even though she's dead. And he has no death certificate yet!' Maggie shook her head in disbelief. 'One thing I do know, Luke and Kev are going to be very, very rich men. From what I can see their mum had insurances going back years. There's a lot of money coming their way and the funeral has already been paid for.'

'Lucky boys. Well, she's done her best by them and Luke did look after her, even I can't deny that,' Alex muttered under his breath.

'Well, I've done what I can until everything is registered. Now while I'm here, I'll fill in one of those forms and then we can all go and have our photos taken.'

'The last time I had my photo taken was when I had a number in front of me in the police station! Then again, most passport photos look like that! Come on, use this pen.' Alex laughed, but he couldn't stop thinking about Luke...

## 23

### THE DEMISE OF LUKE

Over the next few days Maggie was constantly in touch with Luke, much to Alex's distaste. He hated the way she talked to him on the phone full of enthusiasm and ideas for the funeral, but he kept quiet.

Wagging a finger at Alex and giving him a meaningful look, Maggie scoffed, 'Don't look like that. The day he's here for the wake you'll have plenty of time to search his house and that's what you want isn't it? First, we have to regain his trust. Do you think I'm enjoying it? We're both as fake as each other. He's suspicious of me and I'm damn sure he thinks I'm going to ask him for the gun so it will surprise him when I don't.'

Alex just nodded. Maggie being charming and joking with Luke made his skin crawl. Taking a breath, he wanted to talk about something else and mention his idea about what to do about the money the kids had stashed away. Granted, it wasn't a great idea, but it was the only one he could come up with and he wanted to see what Maggie thought about it. He liked these early moments in the morning, when they had just woken up and Maggie went and made a cup of tea and brought it back to bed for both of them. Snuggling up while they sipped their tea was golden hour. It was a rare bit of time that they really had together before the staff turned up, the kids wanted breakfast and Mark popped in for his usual fry-up. It had become their routine, and a good time to talk.

'Have you ever thought about the money the kids have got stashed away?' Tentatively, he broached the subject.

Maggie sipped her tea and shrugged. 'To be honest, Alex, no I haven't. It sounds silly, but it never occurred to me, what with one thing and another. Is it a lot?'

'I haven't seen it yet, but I get the feeling it's a bloody lot.' Alex plumped his pillow up more behind his head. 'It can't be put in a bank all at once. People know the only income we have is from this place. It would have to be drip fed...' Alex tailed off, hoping Maggie would come up with the same idea, but seeing her blank expression, he knew he had to suggest the unmentionable. 'We, or rather you, could launder it through the pub. It would take time and we don't overdo it, but it's an option.'

Maggie's jaw dropped. 'You want us to launder money in the pub?'

'Have you got any better suggestions? It's just sitting there at the moment and sooner or later the mice will eat it, unit or no unit. So, what do you think?' Alex pushed.

'The tax man will have a field day thinking we're making so much money,' Maggie laughed. 'We're a country restaurant-cum-pub, not the Hilton. We could give it to charity and wash our hands of it.'

Now it was time for Alex to laugh. 'Bollocks, Maggie. Even they would wonder where we've got it from and we'd be found out eventually. No.' Alex was adamant that the money was there to be used. And if it could, as the kids suggested, give them a leg up and pay their university fees, then why waste it? He just had to find out a way to make it legal and plausible. 'Money laundering is the only option, Maggie. It would take months, but it could be done. Our holiday could be paid in cash and the rest, well, I don't know until I see how much there is. Just think about it, Maggie. Don't give me an answer now. It's your pub, but done properly there would be no risk. We do it at the right time of the seasons. Summer holidays when we are busier, Christmas when all restaurants and pubs double their money. You started up the delivery service, and the private functions. Your accountant can already see that you've made a real gold mine of this place,' he stressed, knowing it could be done, but that she had to agree. He could see her mind turning over his proposal but decided not to push it any further. Finishing his tea, he threw back the duvet. 'I'm going to take a shower before the morning rush.' He kissed her and left the room, leaving her to think.

\* \* \*

'Last day today of college and I can't say I'm sorry.' Deana yawned as she entered the kitchen in her pink pyjamas and fluffy pink slippers. Her bandages were off her hands now and healing normally. 'The college is having a party but I'm not going.'

'Why not?' Maggie asked. 'It might do you good. How do you think your exams went?'

Deana rubbed her face with her hands. 'Thankfully they were over before I was kidnapped. The results will be out in the summer. I won't be sorry to see the back of that place and start again. My university placement depends on the grades I get.' Mournfully, she looked at Maggie. 'Even though me and Dan were up to no good Mum, I never let my school work slip and neither did Dan. We have our goals in life and want to achieve them. So hopefully, things should go well.' She smiled weakly.

Maggie patted her hand. 'Well, whatever happens Deana, I'm proud of you and I know you'll get whatever university you want. When you have your mind set on something, you can achieve anything.' Maggie looked at Deana and although she appeared to be getting better, she could still see the dark circles under her eyes. Maggie didn't really want her to go away to university while she was still recovering from her ordeal.

'Poor Dante, he's still sitting his exams and cooking by night. He's got a few weeks left yet, but he's working hard, Mum. I was up with him last night, I couldn't sleep,' she muttered under her breath. 'I thought he could do with moral support.'

'I know love, and I'm sure he appreciates it. We're standing around like lemons and Dan is lost in a world of his own. He prefers to work alone, a bit like his dad.' Maggie smiled. 'He's trying to make things right, Deana and to be honest the poor bugger must be on his knees, but he won't give up.'

Just then Alex walked into the kitchen, still rubbing his hair from the shower, leaving it damp and tousled near his shoulders. 'Is Pablo Escobar still in bed?' He smiled and sat down.

'If you mean Dante, yes, he is. He's not due in until this afternoon for an exam, so he's making the most of it. I'm going to take him some tea and a sandwich. He needs a lie-in.'

Now in a routine, Alex finished cooking breakfast and laid an extra plate on the table with a sandwich on it.

'Who's that for, Dad? Dan's having his breakfast in his room.'

'Give it five minutes, Deana.' Alex smiled, pouring another mug of tea. Deana looked puzzled then suddenly they heard the front door open and a voice bellowed up the stairs. 'Morning everyone, are you decent?' Mark's heavy footsteps bounded up the stairs to the kitchen. Alex looked at Deana and winked. 'Told you to wait.' Alex looked at his watch. 'Bang on time.'

Pulling a dining chair out, Mark sat down. 'Is that for me?'

he asked innocently and picked up the sandwich without anyone answering. 'Good bit of bacon this.' He munched. 'I've just taken Olivia to work. Christ, she never takes that tabard off. I think it's tattooed to her body. She's even got a badge now for security with her photo on, so I presume she'll pop around later to show you all.' He grinned and slurped his mug of tea.

Walking back into the kitchen, Maggie feigned surprise. 'Ooh Mark, fancy seeing you here.' Seeing him eating his sandwich and drinking his tea, she smiled. 'Make yourself at home.'

'Thanks, Maggie. Must say, I love this mug you've bought me with my initial on it. Makes me feel right at home.'

'That's because no one wants to drink out of a mug your beard has rubbed against,' Deana laughed.

'Olivia loves my beard.' He grinned, stroking it lovingly. 'She rubs conditioner and stuff in it.'

Deana made a face. 'Yuk, too much information!' She stood up. 'I'm going to take a shower.'

'How is she?' Mark whispered seriously under his breath.

'She's getting there.' Alex nodded. 'Normality is the key, and you turning up for your breakfast annoying her is normal.' Alex laughed and pulled at Mark's beard. 'You know how to wind her up. How is Olivia doing with her job? You don't seem very happy about it.'

Mark shook his head. 'I'm not. But if it keeps her happy and gives her something else to think about, that's okay. I don't want to sound snobbish, but I earn enough. I don't want my wife cleaning toilets. Is that unreasonable?'

Maggie grinned. 'What would we do without the cleaners in this world, Mark? They are the rock of any workplace. You're just worried people think you're not earning enough any more. But she's making her own way, Mark. Be grateful, some women have affairs to kill the boredom.' She laughed, seeing Mark's face drop with horror.

'Only joking, love.' Maggie grinned. 'Anyway, changing the subject for a moment, I haven't had the chance to thank you for helping Alex get Deana home. Bacon sandwiches and free pints are here whenever you need them. And as for Olivia, leave her be. I've offered her a few shifts behind the bar or waitressing when we're busy.'

Mark's eyes widened with horror. 'Oh God, no, don't do that Maggie. That means she'll know how much time I spend in the pub when I say I'm working. As for the business with Deana, Maggie, I didn't do anything. Just mates offering support. Forget it.'

Alex erupted with laughter. 'You bloody hypocrite. Firstly, you tell her you're on a diet but come here for a fry-up. Now you're telling her you're on a call out and you're leaning on the bar. Come on Mark, you can't have it both ways. Be a kept man. Personally, I recommend it,' Alex boasted jokingly and got a clip around the ear from Maggie for his cheek.

'Yeah, but you get a fry-up and a free pint Alex. I come home to a tuna salad and a bottle of water because it's good for me,' Mark retorted and stuffed the rest of his sandwich in his mouth, making his cheeks bulge.

Maggie's phone started ringing and when she answered it, Alex knew it was Luke. Pausing for a moment, he looked at her expectantly. 'Luke says he's registered the death. The funeral directors can now organise the funeral, which means we'll get a date soon. Patience is a virtue, Alex.'

Curiously, Mark looked at them both. 'Have I walked in on something?'

'No Mark. It's a long story so I will cut it short. Actually, I need to borrow something off you.' Alex went on to explain that Luke was blackmailing Dante over the gun with his fingerprints on it. 'The wake is being held here for his mum's funeral and I need to get into his house and look for it. It's the only opportunity I have. Could I borrow those keys from you that helped us get into the flat?'

'Nope. Cos, I will come with you. I might as well be hung for a sheep as well as a lamb. I've come this far with you, Alex.' Pausing for a moment, Mark looked at Alex and licked his lips. 'I take it Dante had this gun as his fingerprints are all over it. Did he use it?'

Not wanting to lie, Alex nodded. 'Right on both counts, Mark. When we have a moment and a drink in our hand, I will fill you in on the whole sordid story, but in the meantime, I need to stop Luke and his power over us. All I want to borrow is the keys. I think I've dragged you into enough of my troubles.'

Both Maggie and Alex could see Mark weighing up the odds.

'Well, I think two people searching a house would be easier and faster. You can have the keys, by all means, and if you don't want me to come with you, that's fine. But I've come this far with you, Alex.'

'Okay, Mark. Let's see if you're free that day.' Alex smiled, touched by the friendship Mark offered him.

'I'll be free whatever the day, mate. That's what mates do.'

Alex let out a huge sigh. He felt he had involved Mark too much already and didn't want to involve him any further. 'Actually, you might be able to help me with something a little closer to home. I need a car crushing. Deana bought a stupid car. You've seen it; it's that bright pink one that was parked outside.' Seeing Mark frown, Alex carried on while Maggie excused herself. 'I have to get rid. It's been bought with dishonest money, but that's all I'm saying for now.'

'I remember that car. Can't you respray it? Olivia loved it, especially the colour. I'll buy it for her... at a discount of course.'

'You can have it, but I don't think Deana would want to see it around.'

'Mmm, I see what you mean. I tell you what. Why not sell it for parts? I make a good profit doing that. It's an idea.'

'Mark, if you want to do that then the car is yours but keep it out of sight. Weirdly enough, it's parked at that Luke's house in his garage. I've nowhere else to hide it.'

'I'll definitely come with you when you go to his house then. And I'll drive the car to my mate's old garage. We'll rip it apart and sell the parts. Three-way split.'

Alex shook his head. 'Absolutely not, Mark. Take the fucking car and if you can make anything on it, then be my guest. I don't want to hear another word.' Alex felt this was something he could give Mark after all his help and something he would enjoy doing. Alex held out his hand to shake Mark's. As far as he was concerned, it was a done deal and Deana would just have to swallow it.

## 24

### THE WAKE

Standing in the church with Dan and Deana was a sorry affair, Maggie thought to herself. It was a real shame that someone who had lived so many years only had a handful of people at her funeral. A few carers had turned up out of respect and some neighbours, but none of these so-called neighbours had showed their faces while this poor woman had been alive. But suddenly at the mention of free food and drinks they had offered their condolences to Luke and come to the funeral.

Deana and Dan had gone with her to visit Luke and offer any help as part of Maggie's plan. And Luke looked more than pleased to see Deana and asked the usual questions about how she was but Deana had just told him she didn't want to talk about it and that ended that conversation. Luke hadn't even mentioned Alex coming to the funeral and she was glad about not having to make excuses. It was a subject neither of them wanted to broach.

Kev had turned up in a taxi designed for wheelchairs, and as the funeral got underway her mind wandered to Alex and Mark. She wondered what they were doing and prayed to God that they would find what they were looking for.

\* \* \*

Alex winced as Mark's huge bulk got on the back of the motorbike, almost feeling the tyres go down beneath him. Alex had his own biker gloves but had got another pair for Mark. He wanted to leave no trace of fingerprints in Luke's house, and he had pre-warned Mark that everything had to be left just as they found it. The basement was Alex's main target. He didn't want to imagine what Mark would think of the cannabis forest down there but he couldn't worry about that now. It was time to get on with the job in hand. They both had to travel together, because Mark was going to drive the car off. Alex wasn't sure that was the right thing to do, but hopefully they would have found what they were looking for by then and Luke wouldn't be able to do anything about it.

Alex was pleased that some of the neighbours had gone to the funeral, because them turning up wouldn't raise concerns.

'Nice house.' Mark let out a low whistle and looked it up and down. 'Christ, that kid has come into this? It must cost a fortune. Garage, basement, fuck's sake, Alex. Places like this aren't cheap.'

'No and it has no mortgage apparently. She must have bought this very cheap when her and her husband were first married or something.'

'Hey Alex, he's got one of those doorbell cameras that alert your phone. It's the same as ours, that's why I recognise it.' Looking at the door, Alex didn't remember seeing that before. Maybe Luke was becoming paranoid. 'If we walk up the front, Alex, his phone will go off and alert him.'

Damn, Alex cursed inwardly. 'Then we're going to have to get around the back. Actually,' Alex said and looked at the house next door, 'I have an idea.' Going to the neighbour's house, Alex knocked on the door. No answer. Then for good measure, he knocked on the bay window loudly. Still no answer. Beckoning Mark over, Alex whispered, 'I bet they're at the funeral, Mark. If we can get into this house, we can climb over the fence to Luke's. Are you game?'

'Fuck Alex, you don't do things by halves do you? Yeah, I'm game.' Mark took out his keys and fiddled with the lock, which opened much more easily than the flat lock had. Shutting and locking it behind them, Alex went through the house to the back and walked out of the back door, which wasn't even locked, much to his surprise. 'Great security,' Mark muttered.

Alex waited while Mark's huge bulk climbed the fence. He was very impressed that a man as big and as wide as Mark could climb it so easily. Once inside Luke's house, Mark looked at Alex expectantly. 'What now? Where do we start?'

Alex handed him the gloves and led him down the basement. 'Fuck, this is creepy. It's bigger than your cellar, Alex.' Remembering where the lights were, Alex flicked them on. Strangely enough, there wasn't a cannabis plant in sight, which took him by surprise. Had they used up the cannabis plants that Luke had nurtured? Then Alex remembered the allotments Luke had sometimes used to store things. The plants were probably there, which meant the gun probably was, too. That meant that this was a wild goose chase, and Luke was one step ahead of him.

Mark looked around innocently. 'Nothing down here, Alex. It looks like it's been cleaned to within an inch of its life.' As Alex looked around properly, he could see that Mark was right. There wasn't a thing out of place and it was spotless. Nodding, they both made their way upstairs. Careful not to disturb anything, Alex searched Luke's bedroom but found nothing. Then he had an idea and searched Luke's mum's bedroom, even going through her coat pockets in her wardrobe. Still nothing.

They both wandered around the house looking through

cupboards and drawers, but there was nothing to be found. After three hours, Alex shook his head, disheartened. 'It's not here, is it?'

'Doesn't look like it. Let's check the garage. What if he's put it in Deana's car?'

Alex cocked his head, indicating for Mark to follow him to the kitchen door that led into the garage. His eyes lit up at the thought of the idea. It would be the perfect place to hide it, he thought to himself. He cursed himself for not thinking of it sooner.

Mark opened the car door, noting the blood stains and looked up at Alex. 'I see what you mean about Deana not wanting to see this car around. She's been through the mill if that's how they carjacked her.'

Nodding, Alex swallowed hard. 'She has Mark. That's why I want it gone.'

Checking the car over, Mark even looked up the exhaust, but they both shrugged when they came up empty handed. 'I don't think you should take the car today, Mark. Luke will know we've been. I thought we might have found the gun, and it wouldn't matter. But we can't give the game away.'

'I agree. Especially after climbing over that bloody fence. I swear I've got a splinter in my arse.' Mark grinned.

Taking out his mobile, Alex messaged Maggie. 'No,' was all he wrote, knowing she would know their search had been fruitless. With a heavy heart, Alex checked everything was as they had found it and then left Luke's house.

\* \* \*

Standing by the coffin as it was lowered into the ground, Maggie felt herself shudder and linked her arm through a tearful Luke's.

She noticed that Luke hadn't offered to push Kev in the wheelchair and could sense an animosity between the brothers, but she wasn't sure why.

Deana had pushed Kev as far as she could up the grass, but the wheelchair kept getting stuck and so he watched the coffin being lowered into the ground from afar. 'Will you throw this on top of the coffin for me, Deana?' he asked, teary eyed as he handed her a rose he had been holding. Deana did as she was asked but could feel the daggered look from Luke as she threw the rose on the coffin. As she glanced up at him he seemed almost triumphant, she thought to herself as he stood there with Maggie, knowing Kev couldn't get any closer. A few of the others had offered to lift his wheelchair closer but Kev had declined.

Once the ceremony was over, everyone got into their cars and headed for the pub where Maggie had laid on quite a spread of sandwiches and cakes for more than enough people.

On entering the pub, Maggie suggested that Kev use the back entrance, which had a ramp for wheelchairs. Once the small gathering went into the back room, Maggie and Deana made a point of filling everyone's glasses and unwrapping the cling film off the food. Some people were looking at Kev oddly. He was wearing black baggy shorts, because he couldn't wear trousers with his leg in plaster and he had a black vest with his arms stuck out in plaster. Deana had wrapped a black jacket around him and put a tie on him.

He must have been freezing in that cemetery, Maggie thought to herself. Surprisingly enough, once Deana knew there was no future for them, they had become good friends.

Conversely, Luke wore a respectable black suit and tie and played the gracious host, thanking everyone for coming. Seeing everyone standing around making small talk, Maggie felt she had to do something to liven things up or the wake would be over sooner than she or Alex had hoped.

'Luke love, it's a little quiet in here, why don't I let some of my close friends in. I know they didn't know your mum but it might create a little bit more atmosphere. After all, a wake is supposed to be a celebration of someone's life. This lot look like we've just buried them.' She smiled.

Luke looked around the room glumly. 'I see what you mean. Not exactly the life and soul of the party, are they?'

Maggie went out to the bar and cherry picking her friends who she thought would be suitable, she beckoned them in. 'Jen, come and have a drink with this lot. It's the most boring wake I've ever known. I need someone sensible and who can string a sentence together.'

'Dad's in the pub with me, though. Is that okay?'

'That's fine.' Maggie laughed. 'The regulars will look after him. Are Olivia and Emma around?'

'Yes, I've just seen them. Olivia's having a well-earned sandwich and a catch up with Emma and Mark's working.'

'Go and fetch them please. This party is going tits up,' Maggie stressed. Turning, Jen went and gathered the troops, including another couple she thought she could rely on as well. Suddenly, the room was full of chatter and as the drink flowed, Maggie felt more relaxed. Looking at her watch, she breathed a sigh of relief. She needed to give Alex time, or all of this would have been for nothing.

'Mum, why is Olivia wearing her tabard when she isn't working?' Deana whispered. 'And she smells of cleaning fluid.' Making a face, Deana indicated with her head to where Olivia was stood.

'Mark's right, she has it glued to her. Ignore it.' Maggie looked over at Olivia, who was informing everyone about cleaning products. But people seemed pleased of the light relief, and she was making them laugh, Maggie noticed. Maggie heard her mobile buzz, indicating she had a message. Seeing it was a message from Alex, she crossed her fingers and read it. 'No,' it read. Suddenly, her heart sank. Looking around the room at everyone, she felt like leaving the party or asking them all to leave. It had all been pointless, she thought to herself. What a bloody waste of time! She felt like screaming inside after all the effort she had put in.

Jen had left the door to the function room ajar, in case Larry needed her, and as Maggie looked up, she could see him wheeling himself in the room. Maggie laughed and caught the eye of one of the guests as they looked on with amusement as Larry stuffed sandwiches up his jumper. Giving Maggie a sorrowful look, Jen walked forward to take charge of the wheelchair and get him out of the pub.

'Hey! That's my bloody jacket!' Luke shouted as he turned to see what everyone was giggling and talking about. 'Give it back you old bastard.' Stunned, the room went quiet as everyone stared at Luke. His face was flushed with anger.

'It's my jacket,' Larry answered. 'I've had it for years. Leave me alone.'

'I'm sorry Luke,' Jen apologised. 'Let me get him out of here and I'll bring your jacket back, I promise.'

'Just get it off him now,' Luke snarled. 'I'm not waiting; my keys and everything are in the pockets.' Luke marched over to Larry and started pulling at the jacket, trying to strip him of it. 'Give me my coat,' he shouted again. Larry fought back, pushing Luke away. Maggie stepped in. 'Luke, your guests.' She indicated, looking around the room and trying to calm his anger. He was blazing and she couldn't understand why.

'Leave this with me. I'll sort it; he doesn't know what he's doing,' Maggie pleaded. 'Don't spoil your mother's wake over a coat.'

'Luke, leave it. Let the women sort it out. Come and have a drink,' Kev shouted, looking the worse for wear after mixing alcohol with the medication he was taking. Deana had warned him not to drink on his painkillers, but obviously he'd helped himself to the bottles of alcohol on the table.

Other people in the room tried pulling Luke away as he ignored Maggie and carried on yanking on the cuff of his jacket. The sleeve was almost hanging off Larry now.

'I'll prove it's mine!' Larry shouted. Putting his hand in the pocket and fiddling about, he pulled out what looked like a sandwich bag. But when Larry shook it open and put his hand inside, everyone stood rooted to the spot, staring as Larry held up a gun.

Dante immediately recognised it and widening his eyes, he gave Maggie a knowing look.

'It's a bloody gun!' one of the carers shouted. 'Call the police, everyone hide!' Larry sat there, waving the gun around aimlessly, thinking it was a game as everyone started to make their way outside.

Dumbstruck, Luke looked around at the mob gathering outside the door. 'It's not mine.' He shrugged. 'Don't look at me. That thieving old man must have stolen it from somewhere else. My wallet and keys are in my jacket pocket. I just wanted them back, what's wrong with that? How did I know he had a gun in his pocket?' Again, he repeated himself. 'It's not mine,' he half shouted, almost in panic as he realised what was happening. Everyone had seen the fuss he had made over his jacket, and Luke could see everyone staring at him accusingly. Inwardly cursing himself, he wished he had never brought it with him. He had been half tempted, when he'd had a moment alone with his mother this morning, to bury the gun with her in her coffin, but had thought better of it. Now he wished he had.

'Well, it's not mine either and it was in your pocket. The old man was struggling to get it out,' a woman shouted. Luke recognised her as one of the carers who visited his mum.

'Come on Mary, you can see he's mad.' Luke grinned, trying to turn on the charm although Luke could see she was angry and didn't believe him.

Disgusted, the carer glared at him. 'How dare you. The man is ill. Can't you see that? Don't blame him for your shortcomings.'

Everyone seemed frozen in time as they looked on. Maggie was shocked and tried ushering everyone out of the room. Larry was laughing and joking. 'You see, I told you it was my jacket.' He grinned. Suddenly, he fired the gun. Everyone screamed and ducked for cover and there were gasps of horror as Larry waved it around. 'I had one of these in the army.' He smiled and shot aimlessly at the ceiling, laughing as bits of plaster fell off onto the sandwiches.

Snapping out of their mesmerised, hypnotic state, everyone fled the room, almost tripping over each other in their haste to leave. Deana pushed Kev out of the room without a backward glance. Suddenly sirens and blue lights could be seen and police mobbed the pavement as they got out of their cars. Someone must have called them when Larry had first pulled out the gun.

One officer entered the pub and held up his hand. 'What's going on? Who's in charge?' they asked calmly.

Maggie stepped forward. 'I am. This is my pub, and this is a private wake,' she explained, much to the officer's amusement as he looked at his colleague. 'There's an old man in there, Larry,' she stuttered. 'He has dementia and doesn't know what he's doing half the time. Anyone will tell you, we're used to it.' Maggie tried explaining, although her nerves were taut and her voice trembled. 'He took one of the guests' coats and an argument broke out. Larry pulled a plastic bag out of the pocket and there was a gun inside it.' Tears from shock started to roll down her cheeks as she tried to compose herself. 'He doesn't know what he's doing, and he's in his nineties.'

Jen stepped forward. 'I'm Larry's granddaughter, he lives with me. I don't know why there was a gun in that young man's pocket. I'm afraid for Grandad. What's going to happen to him?' She panicked. 'He could shoot himself.' Her face turned ashen and she turned to Maggie for comfort.

Hearing another blast of gunfire, the police looked at each other and started talking on their radios, asking for back-up. Bravely, one officer opened the pub doors, while the other one did his best to create some crowd control and ushered everyone out of the pub to the other side of the street for safety. People in the neighbourhood came out to see what was happening.

Inside the pub, the policeman was confused. The place was deserted, but he could hear a male voice singing. 'Hello?' he called out. 'This is the police.' Confused, the policeman saw a wheelchair coming through a side room and quickly tried gathering his thoughts.

Wheeling himself out of the room, smiling, Larry looked up. 'Ooh, I like your hat.' He grinned, while still holding the gun.

Shocked, the policeman noticed the gun, and Larry's nonchalant attitude. 'Are you alone, sir? Are you okay?'

'No, you're here,' said Larry, waving his arms around the room. More or less holding his breath, the officer waited for someone else to shout or come out of the side room but nothing happened. Realising the man was not quite in his right mind, the policeman smiled. 'I'll swap you if you like, Larry. You can have my hat, if you give me that,' he said nervously, pointing at the gun.

'Oh, go on then. This is rubbish anyway, and it's bloody heavy,' Larry complained and held out the gun to the policeman. Swallowing hard, the policeman stepped forward, taking his hat off and slowly, not wanting to make any sudden movements that would scare Larry, placed his cap on Larry's head and held out his hand for the gun. His heart was pounding in his chest as he looked down the barrel of the gun and wasn't sure how the old man would react.

'Fair swap.' Larry grinned and handed it over without issue. 'Where is everyone?' he asked, looking around the room. More sirens filled the air, and more police officers ran into the pub. Seeing the officer turn, holding the gun, they stopped anyone else from entering. 'This is Larry,' the officer said lightly. The police stood there, open mouthed.

Taking the lead, a female officer stepped forward. 'My, you look nice, Larry. Why don't you come with me and show everyone outside your posh hat.' She smiled.

Larry adjusted his police hat to a jaunty angle and laughed. 'It's better than yours.' He pointed to another officer's hat and grinned. Larry had no idea of the seriousness of the situation; it had all been a game to him and he had already forgotten most of it. Taking hold of the handles of the wheelchair, the policewoman started to wheel Larry outside, all the while telling him how lovely he looked in his hat. When everyone on the opposite pavement saw Larry coming out, they screamed and ran for cover. The police officers that were holding them back did their best to quiet the screaming crowd. 'Shush everyone, let's not make a bad situation worse. Don't frighten him.' Seeing everyone, Larry shouted to them and waved innocently at them. 'Coo – wee, everyone!'

Back inside, the police looked around the function room and noticed a man lying on the floor.

'Male. Caucasian. He's not moving. Send an ambulance,' one officer said into his radio.

Kneeling down, two officers shook the man on the floor and tried shouting to him to stir him. Then they turned him over onto his back. Looking at each other, they knew it was pointless and shook their heads. The floor was covered in blood. Noticing two bullet holes in his chest, they stepped back and looked at the other officers in the room. Two detectives came running into the pub, spying the body on the floor. 'He's dead, sir. Two bullets to the chest.' They pointed. Asking what had happened, the detectives tried piecing everything together. 'How did the gun get here? Isn't this place Alex Silva's pub? Is he here?' one of them scoffed, knowing it belonged to the infamous Silva family.

'Silva isn't here, sir. It's the old man outside in the wheelchair who fired the shots.'

'Yes, but where did he get the gun from?' They hastily walked outside to the waiting crowd.

'This is Maggie Silva, sir. She owns the pub.' Maggie was annoyed at the way the detective looked her up and down. She knew she was already guilty in his eyes; her surname went before her. With Jen at her side, Maggie explained the situation. Everyone nodded and agreed with her story. 'So, are you telling me someone brought this gun in with them?'

'They must have. It was in Luke's pocket.' For a moment Maggie looked around, her eyes scanning the street for Luke. 'Where is Luke? Has anyone seen Luke?' she shouted to the crowd. Everyone looked around in silence, trying to do a head count.

Raising one eyebrow, the detective looked at his colleague and then back at Maggie. 'So there is one male missing?' the detective asked. 'The same male that you say brought the gun into the pub?'

'He's done a runner,' Phyllis piped up. 'You need to catch him before he buggers off.' The policemen looked at the jeering crowd and tried silencing them.

Kev spoke up. 'Luke's my brother. This is our mum's wake.

We've just come from her funeral. Where is he? You know where he is, don't you?' Seeing Luke's absence, an overwhelming feeling of foreboding came over him. Instantly, Kev seemed to know that Luke was dead, that he had been shot and no one had even noticed or heard him cry out above their own screams and blind panic to escape.

'I think you had better come with us.' Kev looked down at the wheelchair as the detective indicated for an officer to push him into the pub. An eerie silence fell upon the crowd.

As Kev was wheeled into the function room, he saw Luke lying on the floor, covered in blood and obviously dead. 'Is that your brother Luke?' Stunned, Kev nodded. He couldn't believe his eyes. Luke was dead. 'Yes, that's my brother Luke.' He nodded, his mouth felt dry, and he swallowed hard and tried moistening his lips with what spit he had left.

'Why would he have a gun, Kev?' the detective asked, noticing Kev's injuries.

'I dunno... he was heavily into drug dealing, or so he said.' Kev shrugged. 'Maybe that's why? I've no idea. He lived with our mum, but she was blind and went to bed early. I have my own place, but Luke often boasted about his dealings and his money. I know I was wrong not to inform anyone, but he's my brother and I thought he was bullshitting most of the time.'

Looking him up and down, the detective queried Kev's injuries. 'Got mugged or something, did you?'

Kev shrugged. 'My flat isn't in the good part of town. It happens all the time; I'm sure you know the estate. Anyway, I don't really remember. Woke up in the hospital like this. I only came out today for Mum's funeral.' Kev half smiled, knowing they would check out his story.

The ambulance men started preparations to take Luke's body away. There was no real need for forensics, but red tape called for it and the police would follow procedures. Even though they knew what had happened.

'What about prints?' the other detective asked.

Raising one eyebrow, he looked at his colleague and grinned. 'What about them? Whose fingerprints are we likely to get off it? That old man out there has held it, our officer quite rightly held it as he bravely took it off him, and that poor bastard has held it,' he answered, looking at Luke's body bag being wheeled out on a stretcher. Remembering himself, he looked at Kev. 'You'll need to come down the station with us. We'll arrange transport.'

Outside, word was spreading and people from streets away turned up to find out the gossip. Looking up, Maggie saw a motorbike approaching. 'Alex! Alex!' She waved for him to stop and pushed her way forward. Slowing down, Alex saw the police cars and the ambulance outside the pub. He couldn't even imagine what had happened, although his first thought was Maggie. He couldn't park any closer and was stopped by the police who were diverting the traffic away from the scene of the crime. Alex could see the police already coning off the area and a body bag being taken into the back of the ambulance. Shocked and surprised, he took his helmet off and turned to look at Mark, behind him, who was doing the same.

'What the fuck is going on here, Alex?' The policeman was about to divert him when Alex explained he lived at the pub. The policeman nodded and asked him to park further up the street so as not to obstruct the ambulance.

In a blind panic, Mark shouted out Olivia's name. 'I'm here, Mark.' She waved. A police officer was about to stop her running across the road, but she barged her way past him, explaining it was her husband, and ran into his arms sobbing. 'That man was going to kill us all, Mark. I could have been killed,' she wailed and buried her head into his shoulder. Casting a furtive glance towards Mark, Alex slowly walked towards Maggie.

'Who's in the bag?' he asked calmly. His first thoughts now he knew Maggie was safe, were for Deana and Dan. A cold shudder ran down his spine as he looked into Maggie's pale face waiting for an answer. The crowd had quietened down somewhat now and were more interested in watching the proceedings, while the police officer was taking their names and statements.

'Luke. Luke is dead. He had a gun with him, in his pocket,' Maggie stressed carefully, so as not to cause suspicion. 'Larry stole Luke's jacket and took the gun out. No wonder Luke went bonkers,' she whispered, all the while giving him a knowing look. 'Now we know why.'

Horrified, Alex looked around at everyone, trying to take it in. 'Larry shot Luke?' Seeing Maggie nod her head, Alex winced, as though in pain. 'Oh my God, Maggie. Don't you know what this means?' Innocently Maggie shook her head.

Alex didn't want to say any more, but his mind was in turmoil. Luke had said there was a letter in the event of anything happening to him. Where was it? Who had it? Musing to himself amongst the chaos, he realised he'd been looking in the wrong place. It had probably crossed Luke's mind that Maggie befriending him and helping him was just an excuse to gain entry into his house to snoop around. If he had something as precious as a gun to prove someone's guilt, he would keep it close by. And that was what Luke had done. It had never left his side. All the time he'd been searching Luke's house, it had been in Luke's pocket. Wrapping his arms around a shaken, trembling Maggie, he whispered in her ear, 'Will this nightmare never bloody end?'

## 25

### THE ALIBI

One by one people started to leave. They all had a story to tell, not only to the police but to their own loved ones over the telephone.

'Are we allowed to go into the pub, officer?' Alex asked politely. 'Or do you want us to go to a bed and breakfast somewhere?'

The officer went over and spoke to the detectives, who eventually came over. 'You can go inside Mr Silva, just don't go into that room. We will be taping it off. We will want to speak to your wife and kids at some point.' Then, as an afterthought, the detective looked at Alex. 'Where were you while all of this was going on?'

'I was out with my friend and neighbour. We turned up after the event had happened. I really didn't want to hang around while there was a wake going on. Your officers saw us turn up when everyone was on the pavement.' Spying him closely, the detective nodded and told Alex he would be interviewing him as well.

'Well, there is nothing I can tell you, but sure, why not?' Alex shrugged.

Seeing Alex was busy talking to the police, Mark slowly walked towards them. 'Come to our house and have a cuppa to calm your nerves. You can't go back in there yet. Just see the pub is secured before you come, eh?'

For the first time, Alex looked at the detective, then back at Mark and grinned. 'Mark, there are a load of police swarming the place. I doubt anyone is going to break in.' Casting a glance at the detective, Alex could see that even he was amused by Mark's comments.

'Just give us a few more hours, Mr Silva. Forensics need to go in there. We know where to find you when we want to talk.'

'You go in, Alex. Olivia wants me to drop her off at her mum's, which I think might be for the best. Then she can tell her story and calm down. I'll be about an hour. Make yourselves at home.'

'Are you okay, Mark?' Alex whispered.

'Dunno, Alex, I haven't had time to let it sink in yet, but I can't believe it though.' Mark made the pretence of lighting a cigarette and turned his back to the police, still hanging around. 'Where do we say we were, Alex?'

Puzzled, Alex looked at him. 'Well, we can't say we were burgling the dead bloke's house, can we?' Alex stressed.

Nervously, Mark looked around. 'Mmm, well, I don't want them sniffing around and looking too closely at some of them dodgy number plates outside my house.'

'We'll say we were looking around scrapyards for parts. You're a mechanic, so there's nothing unusual there and no one saw us.'

Satisfied, Mark nodded. 'Sounds good to me.'

Alex beckoned Maggie over 'We're going to Mark's. Come over when you're finished,' he told her.

Dante and Deana joined their dad. 'I'm just going to hang around with Kev for a minute. The police are sending a special van for his wheelchair. They want him to go with them now.' Alex nodded. Remembering his manners, he walked over to Kev. 'How are you Kev? Not exactly the wake for your mum you planned mate.' Alex wasn't quite sure what to say in the circumstances.

Seeing Kev's serious face as he looked up from his wheelchair, Alex noted there wasn't a tear to be seen. 'I'm okay, Alex. Hasn't really sunk in yet. What the fuck was he thinking of?'

Giving him a weak smile, Alex shook his head. 'Who knows, Kev. He must have had his reasons.'

Kev met Alex square in the face. 'Yeah, I'm sure he did,' he replied.

Looking up at Deana, Alex told her not to be too long as the police would want to talk to her and then he walked away. He wondered what was going through Kev's mind. The serious look Kev had given him had chilled him a little.

Walking alone to Mark's house, he saw that it was empty but that Mark had left a bottle of brandy in the middle of the coffee table. Finding a glass, Alex poured himself a large drink. He felt agitated. What mess were the police going to discover about his family's attachment to Luke? Gulping the drink back, Maggie was soon behind him with Dante. 'We'll both have one of those. Deana won't be long. They're just pulling out the ramp for Kev's wheelchair.'

Alex sat down on the sofa. 'We need to get our stories straight.'

Feeling more composed, Maggie sat down with him. 'We know what happened, Alex. We were there. You weren't,' she scoffed. 'Christ, we were terrified.'

'I'm not talking about today,' Alex began. 'Those coppers out there are going to want to know how you knew Luke. When you met him. After all, he didn't just pick out your pub from a hat to hold a wake in, did he? They know you know him; they will have done their homework before they interview you. They will know by that copper on Kev's hospital door that Dante visited him. So, there is a family connection. Do you understand?'

Stunned, Maggie and Dan looked at him. 'I never thought about that, Alex,' she said, 'but you're right, everyone knows we knew him. We were at his mum's funeral. The carers have seen the kids around his house. There's no lying our way out of that.' She picked up her own brandy, taking a huge gulp. 'As for anything else, Alex,' Maggie snapped, 'it was you that brought him into our lives.'

Alex held his hand up to stop her ranting. 'Let's not play the blame game, Maggie. My association with Luke finished when I went to prison.'

Dan looked at the floor. 'It was me and Deana that sought him out Mum,' he muttered.

Deana burst in, interrupting them. 'Is everything okay?' Seeing Dan's sheepish face and feeling the animosity in the room, she sat down. 'Kev's gone with the police. What's wrong Dad?'

'I am trying to get our stories straight about how we knew Luke. Your mother feels it's my fault, but I haven't been around for the last few months, have I?' Alex snapped accusingly. 'The police will want to know what our connection with him is and they aren't stupid. They will know about Luke's background. For fuck's sake, am I the only one who's thinking straight here?'

Tears brimmed on Maggie's eyelashes and one escaped down her cheek. 'We're not thinking, Alex, because we're still in shock. That gunshot could have been aimed at any one of us. Larry was waving the gun around like a bloody flag! Have you considered that? You could have come home to one of us being put in the back of an ambulance in a body bag!' she cried. Reaching over, she put her arms around Dante and cried.

Letting out a sigh, Alex softened his voice. 'Maggie, love. We don't have much time. We don't know when the police will come knocking for us, so can you hold on to your emotions for a moment and think?'

Nodding, she dried her tears and released her grip on Dan. 'What about: he came into the pub one day and we got chatting about his mum. People tell bar staff all their problems for the price of a pint.' She sniffed.

Musing, Alex weighed up her story. 'Have any of the others ever seen Luke in the pub apart from today?' he asked, as he watched them shake their heads slowly.

'Well, that's not a solid story then. We need something else.'

After a few minutes, Deana spoke up. 'I have a story, that isn't a lie, it's just not that long winded...'

Alex shrugged. 'Go on. Don't keep us in suspense. The coppers could be walking up the path any minute.'

'Kev worked at the pub as an agency chef for a while. He introduced us to Luke and told us about his poorly mum. Our mum, being Mother Teresa, offered to help Luke and support him and Kev. We all became friends, or something like that...' Deana stammered.

Alex's eyes widened, and a grin spread across his face. 'Now that is a good honest story. The bar staff met Kev and knew he was an agency chef. Actually, that's quite good Deana, but there is a but,' he added. Seeing their blank expressions, Alex carried on. 'Would Kev admit to introducing Luke to us all? He has to confirm all of this and they already have him at the police station.' Alex's heart sank. It was a good plausible story, but what had Kev already told the police?

Pursing her lips, Deana stuck her chin out stubbornly. 'He won't tell them anything, Dad. He already whispered to me that we need to talk. Let's be honest, Dad, Kev's up to his eyes in this as well. He's already called Luke a dealer. He's laid the bait for the police. He has his reasons.' Deana tailed off and shook her head when Alex asked her what she meant. 'I've said enough for now. But let's go with this story: you didn't know Luke very well, because you were in prison. Mum went and babysat, or mother sat, Luke's mum to give him some free time. Kev was a good chef and we all got on, no biggie. We all became friends. Any one of those carers will confirm that!'

Alex felt there was an underlying story Deana wasn't telling him. How could she be so sure about what Kev would do? Although even he had to admit it was plausible. Opening his hands wide and shrugging, he looked at the three of them. 'Well, if that's the best we've got, so be it. Any other suggestions?' Alex was about to speak when there was a knock at the door. Cocking his head between the blinds, he could see two uniformed officers. 'They're here. We've got our story. Let's use it.'

Being sat in front of the police again, Alex felt nervous. This was becoming a habit. Initially, they wanted to talk through the events, which Alex couldn't help with, so he offered to make everyone tea. Anything, he thought to himself, just to get out of the lounge and away from their beady eyes. Eventually, after asking the same questions, they turned to Alex. 'Where were you today, Mr Silva?' they asked politely. Clearing his throat, Alex repeated the alibi he had agreed with Mark. Satisfied, the police asked if Maggie and the kids would go down to the station and make statements. Alex felt useless and at a loose end as he watched them drive off in the police car. Looking towards the pub, he could see the mayhem and police cars had disappeared. It all seemed surreal. His head was aching and he looked around Mark's house knowing Olivia would have paracetamol somewhere. It had been a long day and now this. Slouching on the sofa, he put his arm around the back of his head and shut his eyes for a moment, his mind turning over recent events. He kept coming back to Luke's letter, fearing the next knock on the door from the police wouldn't be so pleasant.

\* \* \*

Maggie had closed the pub for the next week. On the day of the shooting, she had already told everyone they would still be on full pay for however long they needed off, before stepping back into the scene of the crime. But they would need time to get over the shock. Strangely enough, although people were shocked at the shooting, it wasn't as though some gunman had burst through the doors, threatening them and scaring them half to death. It had been Larry and a tragic accident. It seemed to make people feel better in an odd way, that it had been an accident and the only one to blame was Luke.

Maggie had found it eerie going back into the pub after a couple of days. Nervously, she looked at the function room still with the police tape over the door, even though the police had given them the all clear. They had finished with their investigations in the function room. It was a clear-cut case.

'Come on Maggie love,' Alex whispered in her ear and handed her a cup of tea. 'Let's see what the damage is.' Swinging the door open wide, he stepped in first. 'Christ, I'd forgotten about the food,' he cursed, holding his breath. 'Couldn't the police have binned it?'

Maggie surveyed the room, mentally re-enacting the wake. The tables were still full of half empty glasses and bottles. Foil trays laden with sandwiches and light bites were stale and had flies buzzing around them. Maggie cast her eyes downwards. There was an outline of where Luke's dead body had been, and she shuddered, wrapping her arms around herself. Maggie's eyeline followed all the dust and plaster on the sandwich trays and looked up at the bullet hole in the ceiling. 'What's that dark patch on the carpet, Alex?'

'It's blood, Maggie. Stained right through the carpet and dried. I'll take it up and we will get it replaced.'

'Don't you think this has taken the shine off our home, having someone die in it? When someone is killed in your home, it leaves a kind of shadow over it, like that blood stain,' she muttered.

'They didn't die in our home, Maggie. This is downstairs in the pub, not our living quarters. I'll get this sorted today, and everything will be back to normal in here.' Alex smiled. 'Maybe we could use some of the kids' money to change this room completely. It could still be used as a staff room, but we could brighten it up more. God knows, we know the money is there.' He smiled, giving her a squeeze, while trying to cheer her up.

'Have you heard from Deana and Dan? How is Kev doing?'

'Not yet. Deana was right though. Kev has come up trumps. There is something behind all of this they are not telling us, Maggie. I just know it. We did say no more secrets, but I feel there is one, don't you?'

'Well, whatever it is, I'm pleased Kev has let them stay with him at the house. Dan had to finish doing that cooking stuff and we had nowhere to do it, what with the police hanging around. Kev had discharged himself from hospital anyway and wanted to go back to the house. When Deana suggested she and Dan stay there with him, he was pleased, even when Deana told him what Dan had to do, he agreed to it. You know Kev, he doesn't care.'

'Well, I'm grateful for that, at least,' sighed Alex, 'although I don't like Kev knowing our business. And I still have Luke's letter on my mind. Even to the point where I am actually wondering if there is a letter? What if Luke was bluffing?'

'It's only been a few days, Alex. Who knows what will turn up? Let's just bide our time and play it by ear. We will cross that bridge when we have to. In the meantime, let's get some bin bags and start clearing this room. I want it stripping to the core.' Maggie smiled. 'It's a definite clean-up day, Alex. I am going to have a ring around and see if any staff want to help. I'll call Phyllis first.'

Alex went over to see Mark and wondered if he fancied helping him with the carpet and told him Maggie's plan. 'I know a good cleaner who permanently wears a tabard,' Mark laughed and winked at Alex. 'Olivia!' he bellowed through the house. 'Maggie needs a cleaner!'

While they cleared the function room, Alex heard banging and chattering. Standing up, he looked out of the door to the pub. 'Bloody hell, Mark, the cavalry has arrived. I know Maggie said she would make a few calls, but this is an army. Christ, look at them all.' Mark and Alex stood in the doorway, arms folded, as the chef and the kitchen assistants strolled past them rolling up their sleeves to scrub the kitchen. Phyllis and Pauline were busily filling the dishwashers with all the glasses from the bar, while Olivia was in her element showing the young waitresses how to hoover properly and clean the toilets, much to their disgust.

'I don't know about you, Alex,' Mark laughed, 'but I'm hiding in the function room. It's safer than being trampled on by this lot.'

Within a few hours, the pub was shining like a new pin. The function room had been stripped bare, with no traces of blood, as Olivia mopped the floor to within an inch of its life. Alex glanced at Maggie and saw her smiling and laughing again. Only a few hours ago, she had looked around an empty dead room, disheartened. But now, it had burst into life again full of hustle and bustle, with staff doing their jobs and joking with each other.

Observing Maggie in her element, Alex couldn't help smiling. It gave him a warm feeling inside, watching her. She needs this place, he mused. It had become part of her. Her aura was one of warmth and love for the place. And he'd do everything he could to keep it that way.

## 26

### HAPPY ENDINGS?

Opening the door, Kev recognised one of his mother's old carers. 'Kev,' she breathed, obviously in a hurry. 'I've got something for you. I meant to give it back to Luke on the day of the funeral, but, well...' She tailed off, not wanting to mention Luke's death. Reaching in her pocket, she took out an envelope and handed it to Kev. 'What is it?' Kev asked.

'Oh, Luke was having a mournful day I think and wanted to set things in order for your mum should anything happen to him. Anyway, he'd written instructions in this letter, presumably for you about your mum's care.'

Kev spied the envelope curiously. 'Have you read it?' he asked. 'What does it say?' He remembered Deana mentioning something about a letter that Luke had said he'd written incriminating Dante.

'No, of course not. It was given to me for safety. Look, it's still sealed,' she stressed and pointed at the envelope. 'Anyway, got to go. Bye, love.' Hurriedly, she ran down the path and into her car, waving as she drove off.

Staring at the envelope, Kev held it up to the light. Remembering what he had been told, he didn't think it would be anything else. Picking up his mobile, he called Alex. 'Alex, it's Kev. Can you come around here asap, please?' With that, Kev didn't wait for an answer but ended the call. He wanted Alex to open the sealed envelope himself.

Alex looked at his mobile oddly.

'What's up, love? Cold call?' Maggie asked, seeing Alex's confused face.

'No, it was Kev. He's just asked me to go round and then put the phone down.'

A wave of concern came over Maggie. 'Maybe I should come with you. I hope he's okay.'

'No, I'll go.' Alex had a strange feeling. Why would Kev call him? He normally called Maggie or Deana, so why him? Although Dante and Deana were living back at home now, at least once of them popped in every day to see Kev, so what was the urgency?

Picking up his motorbike helmet, Alex rode to Kev's, all the while wondering what he could possibly want. Maggie had offered for Kev to stay with them while he was still in plaster, but he'd declined because they lived upstairs above the pub and it would be impossible.

Alex opened the front door and walked in. That had become the norm lately, as Kev was still in his wheelchair and struggled to wheel it to the door. 'Kev? Kev!' he shouted.

'I'm here, Alex. Give us a minute. Bloody hell, I'm going to have muscles in my spit by the time I've wheeled this thing around. I've got something of yours.'

Puzzled, Alex, took the hint and pushed him into the kitchen and then sat down. 'Okay, what is it that's so important?'

Without saying a word, Kev pushed the envelope towards him. 'This.'

For a moment, their eyes met and Alex looked down at the letter, afraid to touch it in case it burnt his fingers. 'Deana said that Luke had written a letter about Dan and that it's never been found. But that it's got a lot of incriminating evidence in it.'

Nodding, Alex looked at the letter again. 'Where did you find it?' Kev went on to tell Alex the story of the carer and watched Alex's jaw drop. 'Have you read it?'

'No. It's not for me. Look at the front of it.' Reading it, Alex could see that all it said was, 'To whom it may concern, only to be opened in the event of my death,' in capital letters.

'What else did Deana tell you, Kev?' Alex asked cautiously.

Kev's voice was serious and monotone. 'She told me everything. She's become a good friend and felt I should know the truth about my brother. She knew you couldn't tell me because Luke had this over you, so she did.' Kev picked up the letter and waved it in the air before Alex. 'She was upset Alex, so don't blame her. But she told me there was a letter and that Luke was blackmailing you about the gun. The very gun that saved my fucking life, Alex.'

Alex sighed as he realised that Kev wasn't going to use the letter against him – the total opposite, in fact. 'That's right. Apparently, Luke took the gun the night you were beaten up.'

'You mean, the night he set me up, Alex. I thought you were a straight-talking man. I've thought about Luke, Mr Goody Two Shoes brother, and things that have happened in the past. This isn't the first beating I've taken, but none have been as bad as this. And there have been police raids on the flat before, you know? But lying there in that hospital bed, you've got nothing else to do but think, Alex. It all added up to Luke grassing me up. I don't know why I never realised it before. I never suspected my brother. Is that stupid?'

'Not really. Look at Cain and Abel.' Alex didn't know why he had quoted the bible, but it just seemed there had been sibling rivalry for centuries.

Kev let out a huge sigh. 'I know you think I'm a waster, Alex, and I don't blame you. But, for all of my dealings, it wasn't me who double crossed the Liverpudlians, was it? It was Luke they wanted to murder, not me. I'm an honest drug dealer, if there is such a thing.' Kev smiled. 'Even when I was pulled into the station to make a statement about Luke, the coppers knew who I was. That's why they believed Luke was a dealer. Apparently, I was already in hospital when he sold a bulk load of cannabis plants to some moonlighting druggies in a pub. Oh, they've recovered them, Alex, after the idiots were boasting about how many plants they'd got. They were cleaned out the same night by a gang of hoods who overheard them. Then apparently, the police have found the farm. I dunno how, they never said.'

Shocked, Alex stared at him. Then he recalled the day he had gone with Mark to the basement and found it was empty. He had presumed Luke had moved the plants to the allotment.

'That basement has been scrubbed to within an inch of its life, Alex. Then I get a letter through the door informing me that Luke was planning on selling this house without telling me. And then I discover Mum had money I never knew about. Luke always said she only had her pension, but that was a lie too. I couldn't look after my mum, Alex. I'm ashamed to say it, but I don't have it in me. I hated seeing her like that and if it had been up to me, I would have put her into a really posh residential home. I mean a good one,' Kev stressed. 'Not some shithole. But Luke insisted he would look after her and that she wanted to be in her own home, so I paid the bills...' Seeing Alex's surprised look, Kev laughed. 'He didn't tell you that, did he? Yeah, I paid for everything, Alex.'

'I did think you were a waster, Kev. Come on, every time I saw you, you were half out of your brains, drugged up. That bloody flat of yours was an opium den for Christ's sake.'

Slightly annoyed, Kev leaned forward. 'That opium den paid for my mother's living expenses. And yeah, I like a puff and a snort here and there, but Luke always brought you at the right times, didn't he? I wasn't drugged up and smoking a spliff while I was cooking in your pub, was I? But I'm a good businessman, Alex. And I've helped make myself and your kids a lot of money. But now we know how word got out, don't we? He knew I was never going to steal Deana's heart, for fuck's sake, Luke knew I was gay. So why the jealousy? That was bollocks. The question is, would she have wanted him? Deana's got plans for her future at university. There's a glint in her eye when she talks about it. They are good kids, Alex. You and Maggie have done a good job and should be proud. Especially of Dan. He's a lot older than his years and is a lot like you.' Kev burst out laughing. 'Oh, don't worry. I don't fancy him. He's not my type and is far too young. I like my men with experience.' He winked.

Alex burst out laughing. 'You said I was your type, once.' Alex smiled jokingly, feeling more at ease with this sensible, grown-up Kev. Not the waster he had met in the past.

'Yeah, probably, in different circumstances, eh, Alex.' He grinned.

Alex warmed to Kev's easy banter, as he carried on. 'I was Deana's first crush, and she will have a million more before she settles down. We've become good mates and I am glad about that. No hard feelings. I should have told her the truth and I'm going to come out now. It's time.' Kev nodded genuinely. 'Whatever else happened, Alex, Dan saved my life and gave me a second chance. A fresh start and I'm going to use it.'

Intrigued, Alex asked, 'What are you going to do Kev? Any plans?'

'I will probably go back into the chef game. I like cooking, I find it therapeutic. Maybe I'll buy a pub across the road from yours and turn it into a restaurant, how about that?' Kev laughed.

'Don't you bloody dare! Maggie will have your guts for garters.' Alex gave Kev a playful punch on the arm.

'Luke wanted the lot, Alex. He was playing the long game, but Dan fucked it up by saving my life.' Kev looked down at himself. 'What's left of it anyway. He must have hated Dan with a passion. Why else would he write a letter and steal a gun with Dan's prints on? Surely, he should have been pleased I was alive.'

Pondering on his words, Alex nodded. 'It seems Luke duped everyone.'

'Well, he got his just desserts. I'm a big believer in karma. And I won't speak any more ill of the dead. The police have released his body. I'll do my bit and cremate him. Job done.' Kev sat back in his wheelchair. 'I hear they aren't prosecuting that poor old bloke that shot him. Is he okay?'

Alex threw his hands up in the air and laughed. 'How the hell could they take him to court! He isn't fit to stand trial, but they have said he has to go into a proper unit, for his own safety. It's properly designed for dementia patients with trained carers. I know Jen feels guilty about it all and wanted to come and see you, but I get the feeling she is silently relieved the decision to put him in a home has been taken out of her hands. It takes the weight off and Larry has no idea about any of it. In fact, when Jen was talking to Maggie about it, she told her he's enjoying it.'

Kev nodded and then pointed to the letter again. 'Burn that, Alex,' Kev said, dealing with the job in hand.

'I think I should read it first, don't you?' Alex ripped it open and read it carefully. 'Yup, there it is. Dante Silva, and the full address of the pub.' Alex looked up at Kev and read the letter aloud. As he did, his blood boiled. 'Dante Silva killed two men in cold blood and has blackmailed me about it ever since. I have feared for my life and his family have kept me under close scrutiny. Always turning up at my home threatening to harm to my mother. I know he will kill me in the end, but I can't die with those poor men's deaths on my conscience. Dante is a drug dealer along with his sister under their father, Alex Silva's guidance. None of them have any scruples when it comes to money. I have the gun he gave me to hide with his prints on.

'The lying bastard!' Alex shouted and banged his fist on the table, fuming. His face was flushed with anger as he cursed Luke over and over again. 'Maggie and the kids had him under scrutiny? She was helping him with the funeral for fuck's sake. How could he, Kev?'

Kev watched an angry Alex pace the kitchen. He looked like he was about to burst. 'Sit down, Alex. What's the point now? It's over. He did that the same way he set me up and was prepared to leave me for dead. He won the battles, Alex, but we've won the war. Calm down for God's sake.'

Flustered and angry, Alex sat down. 'I just can't believe it, Kev. What a rattlesnake.'

'Let it go, or it will eat you up like poison in your veins. He's dead now and can do you no more harm.'

Alex was breathing heavily with anger and frustration. He wondered what would have happened if this letter had fallen into police hands. It not only accused Dante, but his whole family.

Kev waited a moment and let Alex compose himself. 'Have you seen what Dan organised for me? It's brilliant,' he enthused. Seeing the puzzled look on Alex's face, Kev carried on, 'Come and see.'

Numbly, Alex stood up and followed as Kev wheeled his way out of the kitchen. Kev pointed to the door that led to the garage. 'Look, he's lowered the handles so I can open the door, and wait, this is the best bit.' Kev grinned and opened the door. 'A ramp! He bought a bloody ramp off Amazon for my chair. It's great, isn't it!' Kev exclaimed.

Standing on it to test its sturdiness, Alex smiled. 'You say Dan put the door handle on?' Alex asked quizzically.

Kev was pleased he had changed the subject because he could see Alex's once red, angry face turning to a normal colour. 'Yes, he's a really good handyman. And he organised with that carer agency for one to come in and help me get washed and changed and stuff. At a good angle Alex, I can fire my dick towards the toilet basin, but it's bloody hard trying to wipe my own arse. Unless you want to do it.' Kev grinned. 'And Dan lowered the microwave and stuff so I can use it. Your Maggie has done loads of frozen meals for me. Your lot have been great to me. I really appreciate it.'

'Sounds like Dante has been making himself useful, and I'm sure he appreciates you letting him cook that meth in your home.' Alex wondered if he knew his son at all. Dan seemed independent and capable of doing a lot of things he had never witnessed, including carpentry. Deep inside, Alex realised just how out of touch he was with his own children.

'No big deal and a small price to pay to be able to get around the house. Few more weeks and I might be out of plaster. I tried some of that meth. It's good stuff. Your clients won't be disappointed. And I smoke some weed to take the pain away. Better than all of them pills. They were making me sick,' Kev said, making a face.

'You tried it?' Alex asked curiously.

'Bloody good stuff. They won't be disappointed. Think he's got another couple of kilos to do and then he's finished. Worked his balls off, he has.'

'Yes,' Alex answered quietly. 'I know he has and I couldn't help him with it. I know nothing about this stuff.'

'Aw, Dan is the Gordon Ramsey of meth, Alex. And they sent him good stuff to make it with. Nothing like I got on eBay,' Kev said. 'And what about that? What are you planning to do with that?' Kev pointed at Deana's pink car.

'Crush it or sell it for parts. A mechanic I know might be interested. If you don't mind, I will tell him to come and pick it up.'

'Fine by me. I must admit, I'm gay and even I think it's over the top. What was she thinking of, eh?' Elbowing Alex in the thigh, Kev smiled.

Alex stared at the bright pink car in the garage. 'Fuck knows, Kev.'

'Money goes to your head sometimes and you do stupid things. Talking of money, you owe me a hundred grand.'

'What the fuck do you mean? Where did that come from? What, is this more blackmail?' Alex shouted in anger. 'Is that how much that letter is worth to you? For Christ's sake, what is it about your family?' Alex spat out in disgust.

Shaken by his sudden anger, Kev sat back in his chair. 'No, no, you silly bastard. The ISA. The money you need. Jesus Alex, don't you ever speak or ask a question without blowing a fuse? Must be that Spanish blood for fuck's sake.'

'I'm Portuguese. Now what fucking hundred grand?'

'I know the kids have got a lot of money stashed away and Maggie was saying you have no way of banking it, without causing suspicion...' Kev tailed off and looked at Alex's face. 'She hasn't told you, has she?' he queried, and Alex shook his head.

'No Kev. It seems nobody tells me anything! Who are you, the local counselling service?'

Kev shook his head. 'No, I'm nobody, which is why they tell

me things, knowing my Latin blood isn't going to boil over.' He chuckled. 'Well, I've altered my mum's will,' Kev butted in excitedly. 'She has supposedly left fifty grand each for Dan and Deana in an ISA, to thank them for their friendship during her life.' Looking very pleased with himself, Kev sat back and waited for a very dumbfounded Alex to speak.

Alex frowned. 'Why would she do that?'

'Keep up, Alex, she didn't. She's dead, I did it. Now, you give me the cash and I'll launder your money. I can get rid of the cash easily and Mum was minted, believe me. This house alone is worth a fortune. Shit, I can say she had it stashed around the house. Stuffed in her mattress or something. No one would be surprised at me having that cash.'

'Would you really do that?' Alex asked, taken aback by Kev's generosity.

'Consider it already done. And as it's a gift, there is no tax to pay.' Kev grinned.

Humbly, Alex looked at him. 'Thanks Kev. I don't know what to say…'

'Hey Alex, I'm not that generous. You still owe me a hundred grand. But your son saved my life. I bloody owe him. Don't you understand?'

More than once during this conversation Kev had brought Alex down to earth with a bang. Stunned, Alex stood there and nodded. Kev thought Dan was a hero, while he had lectured him and hounded him about murdering someone. But now he was seeing it from the other person's eyes. Outside of the box. Kev would be eternally grateful for what Dan did that night.

## 27

### A BREAK OF DAWN

As he left Kev's, Alex's heart felt lighter. A huge weight had been taken off his shoulders, and as he had ridden home, he had agreed with Kev that this was indeed the fresh start he had wanted all along. It had just taken a bloody long time to get there!

Kev had said that Dante was nearly finished cooking the meth, so as an afterthought, Alex had turned around and headed for Bernie's place.

As he had expected, her welcome wasn't cheery, but scowling and nonchalant. Inwardly he smiled and wondered to himself if her expression ever changed, even with her wife!

Seeing no one was around, Alex cut straight to the point. 'That delivery you wanted. I believe it will be ready in a couple of days. Do you want me to deliver it, or will you arrange pick-up?'

'Both, laddie. We weigh it together, Swifty. That way we both know whether it's right or not, don't we? You come with the delivery I arrange, then there are no misunderstandings.'

'Fair point.' He nodded. 'By all accounts you're looking at another couple of days. Will that do?'

Her eyes lit up and a wry grin crossed her face. 'Better than expected. In fact, take till the end of the week. Have you had that wee laddie of yours chained to the cooker? Put it in the same barrels and my laddies will pick it up, but you come too,' she warned with a wagging finger.

Nodding, Alex agreed. That was hopefully the last box ticked.

Riding home, he felt tempted to ride his motorbike through the open roads without his helmet and let the wind blow through his hair. He felt happier than he had in a long time as he made his way back to the pub. Home.

Hearing the door, Maggie greeted him. 'Is Kev okay? What did he want?'

Cocking his head to the side, Alex indicated he wanted to speak to her alone. 'The letter has been found and destroyed.' Seeing the joy in her face, he explained everything in detail and saw the relief in her eyes. 'Thank God,' she breathed and hugged him. 'Well, if Kev is willing to set up bank accounts for the kids, I think we should launder the rest of it through the pub. But slowly and carefully, Alex. Nothing to cause suspicion. It's the best option. You're right,' she whispered.

'It's your call, love. No pressure, but I think it's the only option we have. We'll pay the builders for the plastering and decorating stuff in cash, but I need to see the money and make sure there is enough to pay Kev as well.'

Alex suddenly worried that maybe there wasn't as much money as he thought…

\* \* \*

At his request, Dante and Deana took Alex to the storage unit they had hired. Once inside they unlocked the wardrobes. Alex nearly fell to his knees when he saw the mountains of money stashed away. 'Jesus,' he exclaimed. 'You've made this in the short time I was in prison?' he asked disbelievingly. Although they both wanted to smile at their achievements, they held it back and just nodded. 'Plus, the money for the pub,' Deana butted in, but Dante dug her in the ribs to shut up and stop boasting.

Composing himself, Alex pushed the empty suitcase he had brought with him forwards. 'Count out Kev's money,' he almost whispered, still mesmerised by it all. 'The rest will have to wait.' Watching Dan and Deana carefully count out the blocks of money and cram them into the case, Alex was amazed at how much there was left. He couldn't believe it. His kids were millionaires. Remembering he had fifty grand or so stashed at the pub of his own through his dealing with Luke, he thought he would start by laundering that first and slowly but surely the rest would dwindle into accountable money. But it would probably take them years…

\* \* \*

Alex had thought the suspension on the car would break when they'd put the suitcase in the boot. He'd dropped the kids off, along with the suitcase, at Kev's house; Dan had decided to stay and finish off the meth, and Deana had volunteered to keep them both company and make tea. So, Alex thought to himself, that was the debt paid, but how long it would take to drip feed that amount of money bewildered him.

'Guess who called me?' Maggie beamed with excitement when he got home. Shaking his head, he waited.

'That solicitor you went to see. It seems the pub is ours, lock stock and barrel. John did do it legally.' Maggie almost did a little dance at the excitement of it all.

'At a price, Maggie. He made sure they paid him for all his hard work. But at least he didn't rob them. And it's your pub, Maggie. This is your little empire, whatever happens.'

Maggie scowled at him. 'Don't piss on my parade, Alex. All my worldly goods I thee endow.' She reminded him of their marriage vows. 'What about all those years I never worked and you kept me and the kids, eh? You never said it was yours, but ours.'

Wrapping his arms around her and feeling the warmth of her body, he felt a stirring within him. 'You know, I can't remember the last time we did this...' he whispered in her ear. 'My body has missed you, Maggie Silva.'

Feeling the swelling at his crotch, she let her tongue trail around his ear. 'Well, it seems like it's your lucky day and you've caught me in a good mood.' Turning her head, she looked towards the staircase. 'How long do you think the kids will be out?'

Alex's eyes filled with desire as he looked at her lovingly. 'Not long enough, with what I have in mind.' Wrapping his arm around her waist, they both climbed the stairs to the bedroom. Their hunger for each other held no bounds, as their heightened passion engulfed them.

\* \* \*

Dante was as good as his word, and when Bernie sent her delivery men to pick up the barrels of meth, this time they puffed and turned red faced as they placed them on the trollies to put in the van. Alex went along too, as requested, to seal the deal. On arriving, Bernie, as cautious as ever, closed the shutter of her unit behind them and produced a set of scales from nowhere. She was obviously prepared.

Making sure that the scales were at zero, she placed each bag from the barrels on the scale, and made a note of the weight. By the twentieth bag, Alex was bored and hardly looked at the scales, but she prompted him to check the weight. Alex watched her face and hoped to God Dan had done his homework and weighed them out properly. After two hours, Bernie held a bag up. 'This one is light, but I see he has put another bag in just to make sure, Swifty. Good thinking.' She nodded. Presumably, the scales he used were just kitchen scales. 'Do you agree? We can go through them again if you don't believe me, Swifty.'

'No, as long as you're satisfied, I'll take your word for it.' The last thing he wanted was to go through all that again.

'There's half a bag left over. It's yours. Do you want it?' She spied him curiously.

Shaking his head profusely, Alex laughed. 'Absolutely not. If you can make good use of it after everything you've done for me, then do so with my blessing.'

Seriously, she looked him up and down and nodded. 'That's very generous, Swifty, but I will give you ten grand for your trouble. It's the tip of the iceberg of what that is worth, but it shows goodwill between us and something to boot for your laddie's hard work.'

Alex squirmed at her offer. Oh no, he thought to himself. Not more money to launder!

'I accept it with good grace, Bernie, but really there is no need. I feel you and your boss have been more than generous. No money or meth is worth as much of my freedom and the freedom of my children.' As an afterthought, he frowned. 'Unless you want to give some of this cash to that Nick bloke that tried helping Deana? He did indeed give her a mobile, but she never saw it. He tried to save her life and we owe him more than he knows.'

Bernie's face lit up, and she slapped him on the back. 'I knew you were a good bloke, Swifty. Let's say five grand, eh? That should get him back on his feet. Nice one. Plus, one for that appeal judge, while you're talking about your freedom.' She winked, and had a glint in her eye while doing so. Satisfied with his own generosity, Bernie walked to the back of her unit and counted out four grand for Alex. 'You'll find that's all in order. Take it, go on holiday. Get some sun on your back, laddie.'

Taking the money, Alex paused for a moment. 'Just one more thing, Bernie, if you don't mind.' She pursed her lips and put her hands on her hips as she waited impatiently. 'Thank your boss, Mrs Diamond, for her kindness and thank you for being so professional about everything.' Holding out his hand to shake hers, Bernie's huge hand squeezed his tightly.

'I will do that, laddie. You've got good manners,' she acknowledged, impressed by his lack of greed. 'I will pass that on.'

Releasing himself from her grip and nodding at her, Alex left the unit. Taking a huge sigh of relief, he realised that all his debts and troubles were over at last. His kids were in the clear, and he hoped they had learnt their lesson. There was no such thing as a free lunch. There was always payback time. Their foolishness had caused turf wars, which had meant their own lives being in danger. But now they could look to the future.

\* \* \*

Mark came into the pub rubbing his hands together and ordering a drink for himself and Alex, who already had one. 'A proper drink, Alex, not orange juice,' he laughed. 'Well, the summer holidays are here. The kids are out of school and I've got my camper van working. Why don't we all go away for a while?' He beamed.

Horrified at the prospect, Alex looked a Maggie, almost

willing her not to agree. That camper van was always breaking down, and it still needed a paint job. The very thought of it chilled him to the bone. Not wanting to offend him after all of his help, Alex held up his drink and looked at him over the top of the glass, trying to think quickly. 'Actually, Mark,' Alex said, while coming up with a better alternative. 'We were thinking of taking a holiday abroad. It shouldn't be too long before our passports arrive. I know you have a passport, but what about Olivia?'

Puzzled, Mark took a gulp of his drink and smacked his lips. 'She does, why?'

'Because I would like us all to go abroad together. Somewhere we're guaranteed sunshine. United friends and family. What do you think? My treat. I don't want your money, just your company while the girls shop and the kids lounge around the pool,' Alex laughed. The more he thought about it, the better he liked the idea. Mark had been a good loyal friend during his troubled times and he wanted to thank him.

Rooted to the spot, Mark put down his drink. 'I couldn't let you foot the bill for all of us, Alex. It would cost a fortune, especially in the height of the season.'

'There are no pockets in shrouds, Mark, and you can't take it with you. And there are no friends like you. Well, not that I've ever come across.'

Blushing to his roots, Mark was stunned. Alex realised that for all of Mark's generosity to everyone else, no one had ever offered him anything in return.

'I don't know what to say Alex, you've taken me off guard. In fact, you've taken the bloody wind out of my sails. I'd have to speak to Olivia about it of course...' he added. 'No long flights though. I can't do long flights.' He half smiled. 'Got a bit of a phobia about flying.'

Frowning, Alex couldn't imagine Mark having a phobia of

anything. 'I'll tell you what, and please don't tell me you've watched the movie *Titanic*,' Alex groaned. 'What about a cruise around the Med? Good weather, plenty of food and different locations. You have a chat with Olivia about it and let me know.'

Mark nodded. 'Mmm, I think Olivia would like the sound of that. It sounds posh, doesn't it? She would need to book the time off her new job,' Mark sighed, 'and have an operation to take that bloody tabard off. I have nightmares that she's got it on under her nightgown!' he laughed.

Alex laughed with him, glad to have a friend as good as Mark to laugh along with.

\* \* \*

In less than a month, the passports had come and the cruise was booked, even though it had taken the travel agent by surprise when Alex had paid in cash.

Sitting side by side on the deck of the cruise liner, with the sun shining down on them, Alex and Mark sipped a cold beer. 'I have to say, Alex, this is definitely what dreams are made of. Thanks, mate.'

'To friendship, Mark.' Suddenly, Alex's mobile burst into life. 'I'll just take this. You soak up some sun.'

Alex answered, and for a moment he was puzzled at the sound of the woman's voice as it drawled down the phone.

'Bernie has given you a good reference and CV, Alex darling. Enjoying your freedom?'

Suddenly, Alex realised who it was. It was Bernie's boss, Patsy Diamond. The woman who had warned him about the kids and paid off the judges for his appeal. 'How would you like to be the king of Portugal, Alex?' she drawled.

Disbelievingly, Alex looked out at the wide blue sea

surrounding him. 'Portugal doesn't have a royal family.' He laughed nervously.

'I might need a front man to help me now John is otherwise occupied. I have someone there temporarily, but I would like to offer you the job first. You pay your dues, and you have morals, and you have witnessed the extent of my generosity to those that deserve it.' Alex was about to butt in when she stopped him. 'Not now, Alex. Wait until you're tired of being a country publican, without adrenalin and excitement. You have criminal blood running through your veins and you will get restless in time, I'm sure of it. You know who to contact when the time comes. In the meantime, enjoy your well-deserved holiday.'

'How did you know I was on holiday?' Alex asked curiously.

'That's my job. To have my finger on the pulse and look after my friends. You must come to France. I have a chateau there that you and your family might enjoy. We could talk properly there.' With that, the call ended and Alex was left looking at his mobile, somewhat bemused by the offer.

Walking back over to Mark, he could see that Maggie and Olivia had joined him. 'Bloody hell, Olivia. You never told me you got seasick. That's the second time you've thrown your guts up in the last couple of days.'

Maggie smiled and looked over at Alex, but he couldn't think what was so funny about Olivia's illness.

'I'm not seasick, Mark. In fact' – she looked over at Maggie for support, and Maggie nodded – 'I'm pregnant! We're going to have a baby.' She beamed.

Mark, wide eyed, dropped his glass on the deck, spilling his drink and looked up at Alex who burst out laughing. There was nothing else to say but, 'Congratulations Mark. You're going to be a father... again.'

\* \* \*

## MORE FROM GILLIAN GODDEN

Another book from Gillian Godden, *Diamond Geezer*, is available to order now here:

https://mybook.to/DiamondBackAd

## ACKNOWLEDGEMENTS

Thank you to my neighbours and friends for giving me the inspiration to write about Alex Silva and his family's journey.

Thank you to my readers for their continuous support.

Many thanks to Emily Ruston for her guidance and support.

## ABOUT THE AUTHOR

**Gillian Godden** is a brilliantly reviewed writer of gangland fiction as well as a full-time NHS Key Worker in Hull. She lived in London for over thirty years, where she sets her thrillers, and during this time worked in various stripper pubs and venues which have inspired her stories.

Sign up to Gillian Godden's mailing list here for news, competitions and updates on future books.

Follow Gillian on social media:

𝕏 x.com/GGodden
📷 instagram.com/goddengillian
f facebook.com/gilliangoddenauthor

# ALSO BY GILLIAN GODDEN

Gold Digger

Fools' Gold

**The Lambrianus**

Dangerous Games

Nasty Business

Francesca

Dirty Dealings

Bad Boy

**The Diamond Series**

Diamond Geezer

Rough Diamonds

Queen of Diamonds

Forever Diamond

**The Silvas**

The Street

Troublemakers

Turf War

# PEAKY READERS

## GANG LOYALTIES. DARK SECRETS. BLOODY REVENGE.

A READER COMMUNITY FOR
GANGLAND CRIME THRILLER FANS!

DISCOVER PAGE-TURNING NOVELS
FROM YOUR FAVOURITE AUTHORS
AND MEET NEW FRIENDS.

### JOIN OUR BOOK CLUB FACEBOOK GROUP

BIT.LY/PEAKYREADERSFB

### SIGN UP TO OUR NEWSLETTER

BIT.LY/PEAKYREADERSNEWS

# Boldwood

Boldwood Books is an award-winning fiction publishing company seeking out the best stories from around the world.

Find out more at www.boldwoodbooks.com

Join our reader community for brilliant books, competitions and offers!

Follow us
@BoldwoodBooks
@TheBoldBookClub

Sign up to our weekly deals newsletter

https://bit.ly/BoldwoodBNewsletter

Printed in Dunstable, United Kingdom